HEAR NO EVIL

HIDDEN NORFOLK - BOOK 5

J M DALGLIESH

First published by Hamilton Press in 2020

ISBN 978-1-80080-483-8

EXCLUSIVE OFFER

HEAR NO EVIL

PROLOGUE

THE SUN BROKE through the hazy cloud cover stinging his eyes. He scanned the area as he walked, cursing the decision to leave his sunglasses back in the vehicle. A woman passed by him, tugging at her chador with one hand and pulling her daughter alongside her with the other. It seemed as if she deliberately avoided eye contact with him as she passed. That was common; at least it seemed so since his arrival. He glanced in her direction, watching her departing form as she increased her pace. The little girl looked over her shoulder, watching him with a curious expression he found hard to read. Her green eyes seemed at odds with the dark hair and olive skin.

Returning his attention to focussing on the task in hand, he surveyed the ground at his feet. It was dry and littered with loose stones. No matter where he went in this country everywhere appeared much the same; arid, dusty… a landscape far removed from that of his home in the central belt of Scotland. He couldn't have found a starker contrast if he'd tried.

Glancing back towards the Viking, he saw his troop doing the same as he was - searching for a needle in a haystack. Next time they should tell the artillery to find their own stupid drone. Here they were, picking over the ground on the outskirts of a village at the centre of a six-point grid reference which was the best the operators had been able to provide them with. What a waste of time.

This wasn't supposed to be happening.

They should be back at the Forward Operating Base getting something to eat. They'd only been back in camp for an hour before receiving the shout to head out on this little goose chase. Taking a deep breath he scanned for the debris. If the drone came down around here then they should be able to find it unless one of the locals had already scooped up whatever was left. That was their worst nightmare, the drone finding its way into the hands of the enemy. Half the troop were presently on the far side of the village while they worked their way around to meet them.

A shout went up and he looked over his shoulder. His sergeant was bellowing at him and frantically gesturing in the direction beyond, trying to draw his attention to something. Realising he'd drifted too far from the rest of the troop, he touched one hand to his ear piece and tapped it a couple of times. There was a crackle, followed by shouts from troopers signalling multiple contacts as small arms fire erupted all around him. The roar of mechanised armour starting their engines sounded and he looked back in the direction indicated, seeing a puff of blue smoke and a black dot racing towards him. Something whistled past and only when it struck the rocks behind did the reality hit home. The detonation of the rocket-propelled grenade sent shards of rock and shrapnel in every direction. It wasn't like in the movies but it was awesome nonetheless. The Taliban often liked to tamper with the warheads, setting them to airburst at four-hundred metres to ensure they took out at least one man, usually a commander, with the resulting shrapnel. How did they miss him? Debris rained down all around as he sprinted back to the Viking. Both his lungs and thighs burned, rounds fizzing past him in opposing directions as both sides engaged and exchanged fire.

This wasn't supposed to be happening.

Reaching the vehicle his sergeant screamed at him.

"Take your bloody time Trooper!"

He clambered into the driver's seat as an almighty clang sounded, audible above the roar of both engine and gunfire. His ears rang. That was another RPG harmlessly striking the Viking's armour. They'd failed to get him with their second attempt. His ears rang as they moved off in the direction of the enemy positions on the edge of the village.

They entered the village and a car appeared in front of them at the next intersection, turning in their direction. It had sheet metal cobbled together across the front with a single slit in front of the driver to enable him to see where he was going. It must be a suicide mission. The car accelerated, bouncing its way along the uneven road surface towards them. The Viking's Browning M2 rotated and opened fire, tearing through the car's makeshift armour as if it was made of paper. The vehicle swerved to the right, out of control, slamming into the mud-brick perimeter wall of the village. The car exploded, a wall of flames engulfing the entire street.

He woke with sweat pouring from him and his heart beating like a hammer in his chest. For a second he was bewildered. The darkness all but encompassed him apart from a narrow shaft of moonlight passing through the rear window. The gentle breeze drifting through the cracked window wafted the net curtain gently back and forth. He shivered. The perspiration on his bare skin and the cold night air combining to remind him he wasn't in Afghanistan anymore. His right shoulder ached. It was a familiar sensation, particularly on colder days.

Sliding out of the bed, he pulled the duvet with him and made his way outside. The hinges of the door creaked as he threw it open. The lightweight door caught on the wind and slammed against the exterior but there was no one around to disturb.

Once outside he crossed to the fire, the embers still visible, glowing red and orange. He stoked them and added several small off-cuts of timber. The wood was already beginning to smoulder as the makings of a flame began to lick at the edges of the fuel and, drawing the duvet around his shoulders, he sank into an antiquated camping chair. Staring into the growing fire he watched as the flames danced before him, listening to the sound of the sea crashing upon the shoreline in the distance.

It wasn't supposed to be like this.

CHAPTER ONE

TOM JANSSEN FELT Alice slip her arm through his and draw herself closer to him. He glanced sideways at her and she looked up, smiling as the repetitive beat of the drums grew louder. She craned her neck to see as the excitement built among the crowds of people lining both sides of the street. Tom didn't have that problem; he towered above those standing around him. The breeze coming in off the North Sea was bitterly cold but it hadn't deterred people from attending the final day of the annual Scira Viking Festival.

The first line of figures came into view holding their torches aloft. The flames danced in the breeze, casting shadows on their faces, some of which were painted. Others wore assorted metal helms with a variety of nasal or face guards depicting an early period of Norse history. Janssen felt small hands tugging on his leg and he looked down, Saffy stared up at him with pleading eyes.

"I can't see," she said.

He smiled at her before scooping the seven-year-old up with both of his massive hands and hoisting her onto his shoulders. She rested both hands on his head and kicked gently with the heels of her feet into his chest with glee. Alice looked up at her daughter, smiling warmly. The wind blew her loose hair across her face and she swept it away from her eyes, tucking it behind her ear.

The drums were getting louder as the re-enactment party drew nearer. The torchlight procession was the culmination of the week-long event at Sheringham on north Norfolk's coast. Already they'd visited the living history village recreated above the promenade. Here they'd seen displays of jewellery making, cooking and, of course, the fighting drills. Saffy had been utterly absorbed in all of the day's events but she found the hand-to-hand combat fascinating. By midday, Tom had realised his feet and hands were already going numb as the February wind chill made its presence known. Not Saffy. She'd been most upset when the fighting demonstration ended and they ventured back into town to find somewhere for lunch, and for some respite from the cold. Only repeated assurances that they wouldn't miss the battle on the beach had held any sway with the little girl. The constant reminders of the time threatened to wear thin with the adults as she picked over her pasta bolognese, polishing off several pieces of garlic bread while she was at it. Tom couldn't see where such a small, waif-like individual could bury so many carbs with such apparent ease but she did.

The mid-afternoon battle didn't disappoint. Two groups, one of Vikings and the other depicting the remnants of the Saxon locals, faced off across a wet and stony beach. To the sound of horns and drums, the battle was joined under the watchful eye of a pagan sorceress with the Vikings ultimately proving victorious. Saffy had squealed repeatedly with delight and Tom joked he'd need to keep a professional eye on such a blood-thirsty individual as she apparently was. The remainder of the afternoon saw them killing time before the grand finale. A visit to the lifeboat museum passed some time, as did an ice cream on the promenade; an interesting experience on a cold, dark and overcast February afternoon, but as Saffy reminded them, they were on the beach and that meant ice cream. It was the rule.

Now, as the sun set and the day passed into evening, they watched the ceremonial approach of the Vikings marching down the high street. They were one hundred strong and pulling a longboat towards the beach. The torches were a magical sight to behold, transporting the watching crowd back over a thousand years. Strategically placed speakers along the route piped out atmospheric music that only enhanced the sense of wonder at seeing such a spectacle. The flickering torches bounced orange and red shadows from polished helms and the occasional battle cry, shouted in old Norse, punctuated the silence of the solemn marchers.

"Mummy, why do they call it Scira?" Saffy asked, leaning down and almost shouting in order to be heard above the noise of the drums as the procession passed. She must have read the name painted on the side of the longboat.

"I don't know, darling," Alice said, looking to him for support.

He angled his head up, so that she could hear him.

"It's the Old Norse name of the Lord Scira," he explained. Saffy looked down at him suspiciously. "It's where we get the town's name from. Scira was the name of the local Viking lord, and it was pronounced Shira. Heim is Old Norse for home and if you put the two together and give it a few hundred years, you end up with Sheringham."

"Really?"

"Yes, really."

"That's just stupid."

"Why?" Alice asked.

"Because they can't even spell it right!"

Both Tom and Alice laughed. Saffy was nonplussed, seeing their laughter as a slight on her but she shrugged it off as they set off with the crowd, moving in unison towards the seafront for the climax of the day, the ceremonial burning of the longboat. People were crammed in on the beach by the time they reached it. Tom scanned the surrounding promenade and streets overlooking them to see people packed in in every direction. There must be thousands of people in attendance. Every year the number of people visiting the town for the festival was growing. The week-long Viking experience was proving to be something of a draw on the town's events calendar. It could only be good for the area, pulling in tourists and locals alike during the off season and boosting the local economy no end.

From their vantage point, they were able to see the longboat being manhandled down onto the shoreline. Saffy had taken to her new perch and was keen to remain where she was, so he felt no need to try and get any closer, choosing to remain on the promenade overlooking the goings-on below. Keeping the spectators entertained in the meantime was a fire juggler. Turning his attention to the lone man, Tom was impressed. Twirling a baton, easily five-feet long and lit with flames at either end, he formed glowing rings of red and yellow in and around himself, marking the baton's path. He launched it into the air before deftly catching it with one hand as it fell to earth drawing a gasp from many of the children standing nearby. Saffy applauded enthusiastically.

The juggler concluded as the longboat was placed in position. The torchbearers lined up facing one another and raised their flaming torches to form a tunnel of fire as the leader of the group marched between them. Another line of Vikings appeared, walking past the others in single file. These men and women carried bows. They formed up in one long line facing the sea. In unison, they drew arrows from their quivers and nocked them onto their bowstrings. Another person walked along the line with a flaming torch. Each of the archers touched the head of their arrow to the flame as it passed and they ignited. Before long, the entire line of archers had their flaming arrows ready. The assembled Vikings formed circles and on a given signal raised their swords in the air, reaching forward to touch the points together as one. A horn sounded and the archers loosed their charges.

An arc of flaming arrows passed through the darkening sky to be followed by the bearers stepping forward and hurling their burning torches into the longboat. The boat erupted in flame, fanned by the wind whipping in from the sea behind it. The fire spread rapidly, the boat having been filled with sacks of dry timber and old wooden pallets, and the hissing and crackling of the timber carried to them on the breeze.

Tom looked at Alice who met his eye. He could tell by her expression the day had been worth it. This was the first quality day they'd managed all together in weeks due to their conflicting shift patterns. Alice found that with her job at the hospital, some periods in her schedule would be quite agreeable but when the crossover came it required some readjustment. If that coincided with an unfavourable pattern in Tom's schedule, then they didn't see much of one another.

The boat was well ablaze now, casting dancing shadows on the surrounding sand with the approaching tide lapping at the base of the hull. The boat would most likely burn down in its entirety before the sea reclaimed what was left. Saffy patted the top of his head and he smiled. She must be enjoying the spectacle. He didn't comment and she continued, hitting him harder. At the same time, he felt her body tense, her legs clamping more firmly around his head and neck. Only then did he notice other people around him looking away from what should have been their obvious focal point; the burning longboat.

It was a handful at first but then these people began nudging those next to them and a few pointed. He turned, along with Alice, and the two of them looked in the direction of the pointed fingers. A scream went up, followed by a few shouts as he caught sight of what they were all seeing.

Further along the promenade, above them on the cliffs overlooking Sheringham town, barely a hundred metres from where he stood with Saffy on his shoulders, a bonfire raged, framed beautifully by the inky backdrop of the night sky. Only, as the flames danced, he realised it wasn't a bonfire at all. It was a person lit up inside a ball of flame. The figure thrashed around at the cliff edge, throwing their arms around in wanton abandon in a desperate attempt to free themselves from the all-encompassing fire but to no avail. The moment seemed never ending, the crowd below looking on in abject horror. Several people shrieked in pity and Tom heard a woman nearby cry out as the scene unfolded.

Realising Saffy was watching this develop, he quickly lifted her from his shoulders and passed her across to her mum. Saffy buried her head into Alice's shoulder, turning her gaze away from the horrifying sight. Alice placed a gentle hand on the back of the little girl's head, issuing soothing sounds into her ear but she, too, couldn't draw her eyes from the cliff top.

Seconds later, the figure appeared to give up on the futile battle with the flames and staggered forward, only to pitch headlong over the precipice. The fireball plummeted to the shoreline below leaving a dissipating tail of flame behind it as the body fell from view. The frenetic activity of the burning figure now replaced by an orange glow softly illuminating the cliff face immediately above.

An eerie silence descended over the onlookers. It was as if thousands of people had been frozen in place, having watched the events unfold. The stunned silence of the crowd was punctuated by the occasional murmur or sob. No one knew what to say, never mind what to do. A few in the crowd began to move along the promenade, either seeking to help or investigate through a sense of morbid curiosity. Tom turned to Alice, reading her fearful expression.

"Go," she said softly.

He nodded, placed a reassuring hand on Saffy's back and leaned in to kiss Alice. He could read the shock in her eyes, the terror at what she'd just witnessed and knew it would be reflected in his own. It was evident on the faces of everyone around them.

Without another word, he pressed himself into the throng of people. The promenade was wide enough to handle the influx of tourists at peak season but, right now, the spectators were crammed in like sardines. He needed to make maximum use of his imposing stature in order to force a path through, unsure of what he was set to find waiting for him at the foot of the cliffs.

CHAPTER TWO

THE FLASH of a camera bulb broke his concentration. Tom Janssen remained on his haunches as close to the body as he dared get without getting in the way of the scenes of crime officers. Having fought his way through the crowd along with a handful of others, he reached the stricken man only to realise that any hope was lost. Although the body was still on fire when he reached it, it was evident that the victim suffered a severe head injury from the fall. He had removed his coat and began beating down the flames as best he could, joined in his efforts by several others, but it was a futile attempt. Even if they'd managed to put the flames out quickly, which turned out to be very difficult, it was clear that if the victim hadn't succumbed to the flames then the fall would certainly have done for him. He was dead.

Janssen swiftly slipped into professional mode and pushed back those in attendance. Joined in quick time by uniformed officers and emergency services, all present for the festival, they were able to keep the crowd at a distance and secure the area. Not that many of the public wanted to come closer. The scene was sickeningly gruesome.

The fire burned with such heat and intensity that any externally exposed hair or skin had suffered extreme degradation.

Inspecting the body, Tom could see it was clearly a man although the hair was gone and the exposed skin was blackened and charred to such an extent that a visual identification would be impossible.

"I imagine an accelerant was in play."

Tom looked up to meet the eye of Dr Williams, the on-call forensic medical examiner. She read his questioning expression.

"That's why there is so much damage to the extremities and the skin of the face and head," she said. "And explains why you found it so hard to put him out. The accelerant soaking into the clothing which itself then becomes a magnifier. The fire burns hotter and more intense."

"That figures with what I saw," he said, exhaling heavily. Dr Williams leaned in towards the body having been given the confirmatory nod of approval by the CSI technician. "You can still get a faint whiff of fuel from the foot of his coat."

Tom leaned in, the pungent aroma of a burnt cadaver was strong despite the breeze coming at them off the sea. He smelled the telltale aroma.

"Petrol?"

She nodded. "I would say so. The lab will confirm it. It's lucky he landed in the sand as he did."

"I don't think he feels particularly lucky," Tom replied.

"No, of course," she said glumly. "I meant from a forensic point of view. The fire continued to consume both clothing and organic matter but heat rises and the flames follow that path, hence why you'll get the trace evidence from the back of his coat."

"Yeah," he said quietly, still examining the body. "Use of an accelerant indicates a murder, unless we find a spent jerry can and a windproof lighter up there." He cast his eyes upwards in the direction of the top of the cliffs. Self-immolation couldn't be ruled out just yet but it would be something he'd never seen before. Dr Williams appeared to read his mind.

"I doubt he did this to himself."

He met her eye. She appeared focussed, confident in the opinion.

"I imagine you're right but why are you so sure?"

"Look here," she said, taking the tip of her pen and drawing it level with the victim's mouth. "Do you see this gooey residue here."

He could see what she was indicating but he had no idea what it meant. He encouraged her with a flick of the eyebrows.

"When a body burns, particularly as extensively as this, there is an automatic response. The body pushes fluids to the affected area as quickly as possible," she said, withdrawing the pen. "Now, our skin usually keeps those fluids, blood for example, within the body but once the skin has been consumed by the fire those fluids ooze out."

"Is that what this is?" he asked, aware of his lack of knowledge on this subject. She shook her head.

"No. One might think so but my guess is this is leftover residue around the lower face," she said, returning the pen tip to the area and moving it in a controlled circular motion. "I saw something similar on a case last year. That was an industrial accident in a power station. Someone had bodged a repair with a large amount of gaffer tape…" She waved her hand in the air to dismiss the remainder of the anecdote. "Anyway, that's what I think this is, gaffer tape or something similar. The adhesive doesn't burn as fast as the fabric, or indeed the skin for that matter. The tape is also plastic and designed to operate in extreme conditions. At least, up to a point."

"You think he was gagged?"

She looked thoughtful. "You'll have to run some tests to be sure but I wouldn't be surprised. Did you hear him scream when he fell?"

Tom shook his head. "No, I can't say I did but we were all some distance away."

"Well, until the heat burns down and destroys the nerve

endings, this man would have been in excruciating agony," she said quietly. "Poor soul."

"Could he still be moving at that point?"

"Oh, I would say so, yes. The body is a remarkable vessel. He would have been flooded with adrenalin in order to combat the rising pain which would give the impression of an almost superhuman ability to move but following that the body goes into shock and shuts down… on all levels."

"Probably when he fell."

"I dare say," she replied.

"Tom?"

He looked back over his shoulder towards the police cordon to see DS Cassie Knight approaching. Thanking Dr Williams, he rose and crossed to meet her.

"There's someone wanting to speak with you," Cassie said, dispensing with a greeting and looking past him at the remains of the deceased. "Bloody hell. That looks nasty."

"Yeah, it is," he said. "Who wants me? If it's the press—"

"No, not the press. I'd have told them where to go already," she said with a half-smile. Cassie was still new to the team and he loved the level of honesty she brought with her speech. "It's some woman. Got a kid with her. Cute."

"Who? The woman or the kid?" he asked, looking over and catching a glimpse of Alice among the crowd. He didn't realise she was still here, thinking she would have gone home by now. Then he realised, he had the car keys and had driven them all here. With the amount of people in the town for the festival there was no chance she'd have been able to get a cab.

Cassie glanced back to where he was looking. "Both. Only in different ways, obviously." She moved towards the body and headed in the opposite direction to the cordon's edge. Alice came to meet him. Saffy was in her arms, head resting on her mother's shoulder. At first he thought she was asleep but then he saw her eyes were open staring at the waves breaking on the shore. Or at least, that's where she was looking but how much attention she was paying them was anyone's guess.

"I'm sorry. I should have thought," he said, grimacing to accentuate the apology.

"It's okay," Alice said and he was relieved at her sincerity. "We went into the town and I got Saffy a little bottle of coke."

"A proper glass one?" he asked with a smile, leaning around so that the seven-year-old could see him. Her eyes flitted to his and she nodded slowly but didn't speak. It was after nine o'clock. She would usually be sound asleep by now. "Would you be all right driving yourself home?" he asked, turning to Alice and glancing back over his shoulder to see Cassie kneeling beside the body. "It's just I don't think I'll be done here for a while yet."

"Of course," she said. He rooted around in his coat pocket for the key fob, producing it and placing it in her palm. She met his eye and smiled weakly. "Quite an eventful day."

"Not quite what we planned," he said. "Are you sure you'll be okay?"

"Yes, don't worry. Will you come over to ours when you're through?"

He looked between her and the crime scene. "I've no idea when that will be."

"I don't mind. I want to see you," Alice said, her fingers curling around his and squeezing his hand. He nodded. "Wake me when you come in if I'm asleep, okay?"

"Okay."

She squeezed his hand once more and took the fob from him, accompanied by a smile. He ran a gentle hand through Saffy's hair and she smiled in response as her mother turned and walked away. Saffy raised a hand and offered him a little wave. He returned the gesture with one of his own. As they mingled with the crowd of onlookers and disappeared from view, he made to turn and join Cassie. DC Eric Collet appeared at his side. He wasn't surprised to see him despite the constable having the weekend off. Tom had spoken with him and his girlfriend, Becca, earlier in the day. Like much of north Norfolk, they had also turned out for the first festival of the year.

"Is Becca all right?" he asked.

Eric nodded. "Yes. We missed the…" He struggled to find the words and gave up after hesitating for a few moments. "The thing, you know. We were round past the lifeboat museum and only heard about it on the grapevine. Sounds bad."

Tom nodded, indicating with his head for them to join Cassie. If Eric was thrown by the image of the deceased, he didn't show it. Cassie stood up as they approached, holding up a transparent evidence bag for them to see. It contained a wallet.

"Survived the cremation," Cassie said triumphantly. She must have read the disapproval in his expression because she corrected herself. "Sorry. I mean, his wallet didn't get a chance to be destroyed."

Tom donned a set of nitrile gloves and Cassie took the wallet out, carefully searching through the contents for some photographic identification. Eric focussed on the body, recoiling as he got too close for comfort. He'd seen death before but this was different.

"Here we are," Cassie said, producing a driving licence and flipping it between her fingers for Tom to see.

"Who is he?" Tom asked.

"Fred Alexander Mayes," she said, reading aloud.

"Freddie Mayes?" Eric asked. Both of them turned to look at the DC. He was kneeling beside the body but his expression was expectant as he flicked between it and them.

"You know him?" Tom asked.

"Yeah, can't be too many Freddie Mayes around." He looked back at the deceased. The features were unrecognisable but Eric's eye swept the length of the body, clearly weighing up height and build. "I reckon it could be, you know. What is he, in his forties?"

Cassie glanced at the date of birth on the licence, doing a quick mental calculation. She nodded. "Yeah, forty-five it says here."

"That'll be Freddie all right," Eric said, eliciting no joy from the confirmation.

"You know him?" Tom asked.

Eric shook his head. "Not really. He's a local builder. He put up my uncle's extension a couple of years back. Did a decent job of it too. Bloody shame."

"What else do we know about him?" Cassie asked.

Eric's expression went blank and he shrugged. Tom looked between them.

"Right, Eric, get up on that cliff above and make sure uniform have secured the area properly. Come first light, I want a fingertip search of the ground to see if there's anything useful that's been left behind." Eric nodded and Tom turned to Cassie. "In the meantime, I want you to find out everything you can on Freddie Mayes."

Both of them set off and Tom turned his attention back to the body. The nature of the man's death indicated this was a case very different to anything he'd worked before. If Dr Williams was right, then a dark sadistic mind was at work and that left him with a deeply unsettled feeling.

It was a little after two in the morning when Tom reached Alice's house, Cassie dropping him off on her way home. His car was parked in the driveway and a light had been left on for him above the porch. He made his way upstairs, poked his head in on Saffy and found her sleeping soundly, one arm draped across a stuffed polar bear that was once the equal of her in size but now seemed to have shrunk. Coming to stand beside her bed, he leaned over and lightly kissed her forehead. She stirred, murmuring something unintelligible before rolling onto her back and for a second he worried he'd woken her but her breathing remained settled. He smiled. She was growing up fast.

Backing out of the room, he made his way across the landing

to the bedroom he frequently shared with Alice. She was also sound asleep and he got undressed as quietly as he could. Alice said to wake her but there was nothing to say now that couldn't be said in the morning. Lifting the duvet, he slid into the bed. Gently placing an arm across her. Instinctively, she backed into him and he kissed her shoulder before laying his head on the pillow. It had been a long day and he was dog-tired but sleep wouldn't come. The image of a flaming man, arms flailing as he fell to his death, remained at the forefront of his mind.

First thing tomorrow, he and Cassie planned to visit the home of Freddie Mayes armed with as many identifying features as they could establish. The body was so damaged that they were hopeful of finding some revealing marks, scars or tattoos that would aid identification. None of this was available to them until the body reached the pathologist and could be stripped of clothing in the hope that beneath them the damage was not as severe.

Alice stirred.

"Tom. Are you okay?" she mumbled.

"I'm fine. Go back to sleep." He was unsure of whether she heard him but she drifted off quickly. For him, the sanctuary of sleep didn't follow.

CHAPTER THREE

Cassie was waiting for him at the end of the drive as Tom Janssen stepped out of the house, kissing Alice goodbye before closing the door behind him. She was rostered off and they'd planned another day out but that wasn't happening. He was grateful for her understanding. She never once complained about the odd hours he was often forced to work. He wasn't sure many others would be as forgiving. He glanced back towards the house as he reached the car, catching sight of Saffy at the front window, still in her pyjamas, and waving him off with the same hand holding half a slice of jam on toast. He prayed that she had a strong hold on the toast seeing as it would most likely stick to the carpet as well as it had stuck to the corners of her mouth.

He returned the wave before getting into the car alongside Cassie. She passed him a takeaway cup of coffee which he gratefully accepted.

"It should be cool enough to drink by now," she said, flicking her eyes towards his car parked in front of the house. "I thought you'd use your own car today."

"No, Alice's car is in the garage," he said, sipping at the lip of his cup. It was black, bitter but just as he liked it. He placed the cup down and drew his seatbelt across his chest. "What did you turn up on Freddie Mayes?"

"Interesting," Cassie said, reaching behind them into the rear and producing a manilla folder which she passed to him once he was ready. She engaged first gear and pulled away. "Eric was right. He runs a local building firm. It's been trading for the last ten years and seems to have a decent reputation from what I can tell. The firm is accredited with various trade associations and I checked their registers and it's all legit."

"It would be a bit of an overreaction for a bit of shoddy brickwork to lead to what we saw last night."

"Right enough," Cassie said, looking in both directions before pulling out onto the main road and away from Alice's housing estate. "What's really interesting though is Freddie Mayes was reported missing."

Tom glanced up from the folder in his lap. "When?"

"Three days ago. His wife called it in the day after he failed to return home from a night out."

"That's not unusual, why raise the alarm so early."

"Apparently, it is unusual for him," she said, not taking her eyes from the road.

"I wonder where he could have been for the better part of three days?"

"His wife was quite agitated by all accounts. She reckoned it might be related to an incident from a little while back. Seemingly, Mayes was involved in an altercation which saw him arrested along with one other in the town one afternoon."

"The nature of which was?" Tom asked.

"A bit of a fracas," Cassie replied. "Nothing too serious from what I read. Both men were released later in the afternoon once they'd calmed down a bit."

Tom thought on it.

"With what happened yesterday, it's not a bad shout."

"If it's him," Cassie said.

"If it's him," he echoed, returning his attention to a clutch of photographs in the folder.

Taking them out, he sifted through them. They were images of areas of the deceased's body untouched by the heat and flames. There was a distinctive scar located on the upper chest to the left side, perhaps four inches long, and most notably a tattoo on the upper right arm. The tattoo was distinctive, a skull and crossbones above a banner stretching between the bones that read 'or glory'. If he had to guess, he'd reckon on it being a regimental badge of some sort but not one he recognised. Beneath this was a name – Tilly.

"Did Mayes have a military background?" he asked.

"Yeah, he did," Cassie said, glancing across at him. "Light cavalry. How did you know?"

"Lucky guess," he said absently. "What did we do regarding his disappearance?"

"The usual. Uniform called round and took down some details, circulated his description but you know the drill. He hadn't even been missing for twenty-four hours at the time. And he's a big boy."

"Hmmm," Tom replied. "Looks like there may have been more to it after all. Who are we expecting to see this morning?"

"The wife. She called it in. They have a teenage daughter but she's not living with them as far as I can tell."

"What's her name, the daughter?"

"Annabeth. Why?"

"Just curious."

THE MAYES house sat on a large plot, detached and set back from the road, encompassed by mature trees on every boundary, shielding it from view. Approaching the front of the house via an extensive approach road, Tom found himself impressed. He'd never coveted property but if he were asked to describe his forever home, then this came pretty close to it.

The house was named *The Old Rectory* and was representative of the Victorian period, very grand, although by the look of it, it had been extended in recent years. This was unsurprising considering it was now owned by a builder. To the right of the frontage was a three-bay garage with a covered area that could easily accommodate a further two vehicles. Cassie parked the car and they both got out. Tom noted a BMW Tourer car parked alongside a two-seater Mercedes. They liked their marques. There was no evidence of a slump in the construction sector around here.

They walked to the front door but before they were able to ring the bell, it swung open and a woman greeted them. Her body language oozed nervous anxiety.

"Is there any news? Have you found him?" she said, her eyes darting between the two of them. "You are police, right?"

Tom smiled and nodded. "Mrs Mayes?"

"Katrina, yes. Have you found him?"

"I'm Detective Inspector Tom Janssen. Could we please come inside?"

She appeared ready to argue, to press him further for an immediate answer but then her eyes drifted down to the folder in his hand and she pursed her lips. Silently bobbing her head, she gestured for them to enter. They passed from an entrance hallway into an impressive atrium with a wraparound staircase leading to a landing on the next floor that ringed the building. A roof lantern, set directly above them, bathed the interior in natural light. Tom glanced up at it and deduced it was original, knowing you were unlikely to ever see the likes of it in a modern house of a similar size.

Katrina Mayes led them into a sitting room. It was furnished in stark contrast to what one might expect from such a grand house, bright and modern with contemporary sofas, chrome switches and a television that Tom was certain he wouldn't be able to get below deck on his boat, let alone be able to watch something on it. Katrina offered them both a seat and they took it.

Tom took in her measure. He guessed she was in her early forties but it was hard to tell. She looked tired, possibly overwhelmed. There were dark rings around her eyes which were also sunken. It didn't look like she'd been sleeping well. She wore her hair up. She was blonde but her natural colour was much darker and, at the roots, shoots of grey were visible. Tom had the impression she would usually be fastidious about her presentation but he also noted two of her fingernails had lost their coverings, failing to match the deep red of the other eight.

"You've found my husband," Katrina said. It was a statement, no longer a question. Tom and Cassie exchanged glances. "I'm not green," she said. "You wouldn't be here if it wasn't serious."

"We have found a body," Tom said. Katrina took a sharp intake of breath. "And we believe it is possibly your husband. He was in possession of your husband's wallet."

"Then you will have his driver's licence. He always carried it."

"Yes. We found it inside, along with credit cards and a significant amount of cash."

Katrina laughed but it was without genuine humour. "He always carried what he called *flash money*. He got a thrill out of it. Is it him?"

The question was asked pointedly. Katrina steeled herself for the confirmation.

"I'm afraid we aren't sure."

The reality of that comment sunk in and Katrina's lower lip trembled and she looked to the floor, clasping her hands before her so tightly that her fingers turned white and the extremities red as the blood pooled at the tips.

"We have some photographs here," Tom said, slowly opening the folder in his lap, "that detail some distinguishing marks. Would you be willing to take a look at them for me?"

Katrina looked up at him, then to the pictures he held before once again meeting his eye. She took a deep breath and nodded.

He admired her courage. The first photograph he took out was the most easily identifiable, the one depicting the tattoo. He passed it across to her and she held it in her left hand, the right moved up and clamped across her mouth. Her head dropped and her shoulders sagged forward. Tom glanced at Cassie and she pursed her lips. They had their identification. Katrina screwed her eyes shut. When they opened, they were moist and as she looked at him, all she could do was confirm what they thought with a brief nod.

"You're certain this is your husband?" he asked softly.

Again, she nodded briefly. "I'm sure. Tilly is our daughter... was our daughter," she said, removing her hand from her face. "She passed away while Freddie was overseas. He had that done, her name, to honour her."

"Was that while he was serving?" Cassie asked.

"Yes. I don't think he ever forgave himself for not having been here for her... for me."

"What happened?" Tom asked.

"Car accident," Katrina said. "Fifteen years ago next month. Three weeks tomorrow."

Tom was momentarily surprised at her accuracy but then he figured a parent would never forget the day they lost a child, no matter how many years passed.

"I'm sorry for your loss," he said, although the words sounded hollow in his head.

"Thank you," Katrina replied, looking around in search of something. Tom figured she was looking for a tissue as her eyes were threatening to overspill. He eyed a box of tissues on a nearby table and he got up to retrieve them, returning and passing the box to her. She accepted gratefully.

"Can you tell us about the other night? The night of your husband's disappearance."

She could have been forgiven for pointing out she'd already given the police the details but she didn't, merely steadied herself and appeared to focus hard on arranging her thoughts.

"He came home on the Thursday evening as normal, albeit a little earlier than usual," Katrina said, raising her eyes to the ceiling. She was struggling to keep it together, Tom could tell. "We had dinner reservations for later and I didn't want it to be in all of a rush to get there. As it turned out, the restaurant had double booked and they called to ask us to rearrange the booking. I was furious but Freddie, which was his way, was pretty calm about it." She smiled weakly.

"What happened then?"

"We were going to do something at home instead, you know, still try to make an evening of it. So I went out to the shops to get the food, we hadn't had our weekly delivery yet and nothing we had was suitable."

"And what did your husband do?"

"He called me while I was in the supermarket," she said, glancing at him, her eyes narrowing. "He said he'd had a call about a job, not one he was working on but something new. He was excited, said it was a great opportunity but the client was heading out of town and had been let down by another contractor. Freddie had to go and walk around the job that evening."

"Where was it? Did he say?"

Katrina shook her head. "No, he didn't say but it was local. Freddie said he could be there and back before nine. We could still manage dinner. I was a bit annoyed, I had my hands full at the time but I said okay and hung up."

"And then?"

"Then nothing," she said flatly. "I came home, made dinner. I was showered and dressed... but Freddie didn't come home."

"You called him?"

"Yes, of course I bloody called him," she said, checking her rising anger and holding up the palm of her hand by way of an apology. Tom waved it away. There was no need. "I called him repeatedly that night and again the following morning. I went to bed at two, hoping he would wake me up when he came in having gone for a few beers with the lads or something. I... hoped for anything… but I knew, somehow I knew it wasn't right. That's why I called you. Not that you did anything about it."

The last comment was spoken with venom but Tom didn't take offence. It was to be expected.

"Where did you find him? Where was Freddie?"

"Your husband was found in Sheringham, yesterday evening."

Katrina gasped, her mouth falling open as her eyes widened. She shook her head slowly, staring at Tom, her eyes imploring it not to be true.

"Not that man… the one on the news, at the festival? Not him."

Tom nodded slowly. "Yes. I'm sorry."

Katrina's head dropped forward into her hands and she wept openly.

CHAPTER FOUR

CASSIE BACKED into the room with a tray of mugs held in both hands. They decided to give Katrina Mayes a bit of time to collect herself and Cassie went through to the kitchen and made them all a cup of tea. Normally, she wouldn't do so unless asked, but on this occasion it seemed fitting. Katrina was sitting where she had been fifteen minutes earlier, her hands clasped together in her lap clutching a scrunched up tissue. She afforded Cassie a weak smile as she set the tray down on the coffee table. The detective sergeant passed her a cup of sweet tea. Her mother had always said sugary tea was good to have in response to a shock. She had no idea whether that was true or not.

Tom Janssen was standing before the fireplace looking over a collection of framed photographs on the mantelpiece. He looked at Katrina, catching her eye.

"May I?" he asked, indicating one of the pictures. She confirmed he could with a brief nod and he picked it up, returning to where they were sitting and sat down next to Cassie. "Is this your husband and his team?"

He angled the frame towards Cassie and she scanned it before he passed it to Katrina. She smiled, stroking the rightmost figure in the picture. There were six men in the shot, all posing in their military fatigues with an assortment of weapons in their hands. Cassie had seen many of these before at friends' homes, it was pretty standard practice for anyone who served on combat operations.

"Yes. This was Freddie's troop," she said, leaning forward and holding the frame in such a way as they could all see the men. "This is Freddie on the right."

The man she pointed to was unrecognisable from the body lying in the mortuary. Cassie felt immense sadness for the woman sitting opposite her.

"Was that taken in Afghanistan or Iraq?" Cassie asked, drawing Katrina's attention away from the picture.

"Helmand, Afghanistan, on his first tour, I think."

"How many did he do?" Tom asked.

"Three in Helmand," Katrina said proudly. "Another two in Iraq before that. To think... he made it through all of that... only to..."

Katrina fell quiet and an awkward silence followed. There was no easy way to ask the questions that needed to be asked, but Tom did so in a calm and assured manner.

"Do you know of anyone who would wish your husband any harm, Mrs Mayes?"

Katrina fixed him with a stare. "No, not at all. Freddie was a great guy. Everyone loved him. I can't see any reason why someone would... would do something so awful to him."

"Has he fallen out with anyone recently, over work or in the pub maybe?" Cassie asked.

Again, Katrina shook her head. "No, not that I know of anyway. I'm sure Freddie would have said so if he had."

"How about Freddie himself?" Tom asked. "Have you seen a change in him at all, his habits perhaps? How is his business?"

She thought about it, taking some time to consider the question.

"Business has been good. No, better than that, it's been great. He works... worked so hard at it."

"What about in himself?" Cassie asked.

"He's been drinking more recently, that's true. I mean, he's always been a big drinker. Many of the guys are but recently, yeah, I'd say that was all. My Freddie has never been the chattiest of blokes, not until he's with his mates, then it's all a bit different. He seems to grow, becoming larger than life. It was all an act, though. With me, he's always been quite a quiet guy."

"Any idea why he might have been drinking more?" Cassie asked. Katrina shook her head. "Is there anyone else he was close to who might know?"

"Anyone else?" Katrina asked. "Is that your polite way of asking if he was having an affair or something?"

"No. Not at—"

"Well, he wasn't okay!" Katrina shot back. Tom wondered if they'd inadvertently struck a nerve. "Not my Freddie. He wasn't like that at all."

"I was thinking more about friends," Cassie said, indicating the photograph. "Former comrades perhaps? Is he still close with them?"

Katrina's stance softened and, again, she apologised with the flick of a hand and a brief shake of the head.

"They are still tight," she replied. "Or he is with some of them anyway."

"Anyone local?" Tom asked.

Katrina sat forward, pointing to two men in the picture.

"The guy on the far left is Eddie, Edward Drew. He was Freddie's corporal on two tours, and in the middle there, kneeling…" she jabbed at the centre, "that's Harry Oakes. Freddie still sees the two of them quite a bit. I think some of the others are still knocking around but you'd be best talking to Harry and Eddie about them."

"Thank you, we will," Tom said, glancing at Cassie. She was already making notes and realised he was just making certain she'd got the information. She turned to Katrina.

"Do you know where we can find them?" she asked.

"Harry owns that large nursery over Burnham Market way. I haven't seen him much recently, not since he and Tina had the kids. What with them and trying to build the business, I think he's been pretty tied up."

Tom nodded that he knew where she was talking about. "Is Eddie Drew the same man who has the car dealership in Sheringham?"

Katrina nodded enthusiastically. "Yes. Freddie said he's been doing well for himself."

Cassie didn't know either of the two businesses but made a note all the same. She was still new to the area and that level of local knowledge would come with time.

"I think we have all we need for now, Mrs Mayes," Tom said. "I am afraid as Freddie's next of kin, we will need you to carry out an official identification. If we could arrange that for later today would you be willing to come in for it?" She nodded solemnly, although it was clear the thought distressed her enormously. "We will set it up. In the meantime, is there anyone we can call for you, a friend or relative who could come over perhaps?"

She shook her head. "No, thank you, Inspector. I can take care of it myself."

"If you're sure?" Tom said.

"I am but thank you. That's the thing about military wives, Inspector. We get to spend so much time with our other halves away on operations that we form our own support network. I know who I can call on if I need to."

Tom nodded and looked at Cassie. She smiled at Katrina and stood up, leading the way out.

"I'm deeply sorry for your loss, Mrs Mayes. We'll see ourselves out," she said.

———————

"I'VE GOT his service record, Tom," Cassie said, poking her head into Tom Janssen's office. He looked up.

"Get Eric to stop what he's doing and you can fill us in," he said, rising from behind his desk.

She nodded and turned back into the ops room. Eric was at his desk, hunched over his keyboard paying her no attention. She picked up a piece of paper, scrunched it into a ball and launched it in his direction. It arced through the air and struck the constable square on the back of the head.

"Oi!" he said, spinning round with an expression of indignation that swiftly morphed into a smile. "What was that for?"

"Come on, Eric," Tom said leaving his office. "Stop messing around."

Eric glared at Cassie and it was all she could do not to laugh as he made ready to protest. Eric thought better of it and knelt to pick up the offending ball of paper.

"Right," Cassie said, pointing at the white board on the wall. "Freddie Mayes, forty-five years old, director of FM Design and Build." She stuck a photograph of him in one corner. "He's been running this business since he left the military just over ten years ago."

"Who did he serve with?" Tom asked, folding his arms across his chest.

"Queen's Royal Lancers. They were an armoured regiment but towards the end of their time they evolved into an armoured reconnaissance unit. That evolution took place during the early years of the war in Afghanistan where Freddie Mayes saw active service completing three tours. By all accounts he served with distinction and was decorated twice for valour."

"You said *towards the end*."

"Yes. Under the last strategic review the regiment was amalgamated with another cavalry regiment to form one, the Royal Lancers. That took place after the deployment in Afghanistan ended."

"What do we know about his friends, who was it... Eddie Drew and?"

"Harry Oakes," she said.

Eric appeared to catch up at that point. "Eddie the car man?" he asked. She nodded. "Becca bought her car from him. Well, probably not from him directly. I mean his place. He'd be far too busy to do it himself—"

"Don't worry, Eric. We get it. And I can't see any conflict there for you to worry about," Cassie said with a wink.

"No. That's not what I meant," Eric said before realising she was only making fun of him. He frowned.

"How was his business doing?" Tom asked.

"All above board and doing well," she said. "I've been on the government portal this morning and he's not missed a beat with his filings. The company position appears financially secure and I couldn't find any indication of litigation or problems related to the firm in the media. By any measure, Freddie Mayes was doing well."

"Well, somebody had an issue with him," Tom said.

"What about this arrest last month?" Eric asked. "Didn't you say earlier he had a ruck with someone?"

"Yes, that's right," Cassie said, turning back to the board and placing another picture in the opposing corner. "Joe Woodly. He was arrested along with Freddie after the two came to blows in Sheringham centre on the fourteenth of January."

"What do we know about Joe Woodly?" Tom asked.

"Local lad," she said, glancing back at Tom. "Twenty-four, been in a bit of trouble as a teenager. Nothing too serious back then: vandalism, a caution for possession. However, he's stepped it up a bit in his twenties. To date, his greatest offence is an attempted burglary. Apparently he's not very good at it. His file suggests he's a habitual drug user which might explain a lot."

"Any idea what the fight was about?"

She shook her head. "Neither of them seemed keen to talk about it. It wasn't clear to the arresting officers who was in the wrong and there were no witnesses present or a traceable complainant, so they released both and cautioned them regarding their future behaviour."

Tom took his hands from his hips and perched himself on the edge of a desk, putting his hands together in his lap.

"Anything more?"

"Yes, regarding the fight between the two of them," she said. "We were notified by a member of the public who didn't wish to leave their name. She stated that there were three men involved in the incident. However, only Freddie and this lad, Joe, were present when uniform arrived."

"Any idea who the third man was?"

She shook her head.

"Well, seeing as Freddie is such a stand-up guy, the two of you better go and have a word with Joe Woodly and see what he has to say for himself," Tom said.

"Will do," Cassie replied, looking at Eric and indicating towards the door with her head. "And this time, we won't take silence for an answer."

"I'll go and have a word with one of Freddie's friends and start building a picture of what was going on in Freddie's life. If they are as close as his wife says, then his friends should know. Military veterans may well confide in their old comrades more than they would their other halves."

Tom Janssen stood up and crossed to the board, concentrating as he read over the information afresh. Cassie picked up her coat, a ball of paper bounced off her forehead. She glanced over her shoulder to see Eric slipping his arm through his coat, his expression a picture of innocence.

CHAPTER FIVE

"HAVE you come across Joe Woodly before this?" Cassie asked, glancing at Eric before turning her gaze to the outside. They were passing through countryside on the main coast road. In many ways it was similar to her native north east but somehow different. The greens of the trees and the fields seemed brighter somehow than they did in Northumberland. Maybe it was perception, maybe not. She couldn't think of a reason why this might be the case, aside from the fact Norfolk garnered more sunshine per days of the year than anywhere else in the country. At least, that's what Eric told her and she had no reason to doubt him.

"Can't say I have, no," Eric replied, not taking his eyes from the road as it swept down and cut through a small village by way of a series of tight bends.

"You mean to say we're going to meet someone new to you?"

Eric glanced across. "It does happen occasionally."

Cassie laughed. She'd quickly realised how extensive Eric's knowledge of the locality and its residents was. He was better than a police database when it came to understanding how things worked around here; who was integrated with whom and how past goings-on shaped the present. These were often details you couldn't get through reading reports or statistics, no matter how well prepared they were. Eric was very much the eyes and ears of the team. If he didn't know, then he would more often than not know someone who did.

Eric slowed the car and purposefully switched on the indicator. He always did so by removing one hand from the wheel and using three fingers to move the stalk. Taking the turn, he fed the wheel through his hands, always keeping them located in the ten-to-two position.

They were in a small housing development of modest size, well established and popular with young families. The housing stock was brick built, post war, and largely uninspiring in detail. Seemingly, the benefit of living here came from the size of the plots each property was built on. They were set out in one long line with each house, even the semi-detached ones, offering a generous front garden and they all backed onto farmland as far as Cassie could see.

They approached number fourteen, the registered address of Joe Woodly. A woman was in the front garden tending to the flower beds that fronted to the roadside. Eric pulled the car into the kerb taking great care to park the car as close as possible, craning his neck to see the ground using the nearside mirror. Once he was satisfied, he switched off the engine to find Cassie eyeing him with a raised eyebrow.

"What?" he asked.

"How long have you been driving, Eric?"

He thought about it, doing a mental calculation. "Coming up for eight years. Why?"

Cassie inclined her head slightly and smiled. "No reason. Come on."

They both got out and approached the driveway. It was gravel lined, as were most in the row, and the woman tending to the garden looked up as they approached. Her forehead bore a sheen of perspiration despite the February weather being far from warm. She must have been at it for some time today, at least three metres of flower bed had been cleared of winter weed growth and turned over in preparation for planting. She lifted the fork out of the ground, bringing herself upright before driving the tines back into the soil and resting one foot where the socket met them. She crossed her palms on the handle grip and pursed her lips.

"What's he done now?" she asked.

Cassie and Eric exchanged glances.

"You are police, aren't you?"

"Yes. DS Knight and DC Collet," Cassie said, opening her wallet and offering her warrant card. The woman dismissed it with a casual sweep of the hand.

"It's been a while since he's been in trouble. Must be almost a month since one of you came calling. It's not usually plain clothes though."

"Who do you think we're here to see?" Cassie asked.

"My son, Joe. Who else would it be?"

"Yes, but he's not in trouble. At least, it's nothing new to worry about. You're Mrs Woodly?"

"Sheila, yes. I think that my son will always be a worry to me, Detective Sergeant. No matter how many times he brings the police to my door," she said, regret edging her tone. "Joe's in the house. He's most likely still in bed. Come in and I'll rouse him for you."

Cassie checked the time on her watch. It had been many years since she'd slept in until this time. Sheila removed her gardening gloves, putting them together and setting them down on a wheelbarrow next to her and gestured for them to come up to the house with her.

"You'll not be long, will you?" Sheila asked.

"No, not really. Why do you ask?" Cassie said.

"Oh, it's just Joe's dad. Our son is far from perfect, which you obviously know or you wouldn't be here," she said, mock frowning as she spoke. "But he clashes with his dad and if he comes home to find the police here again... well, I dread to think what he'll say."

"I understand," Cassie said, smiling. "We'll try not to be too long and besides, it's just a quick couple of questions."

"It always is, dear," Sheila said but it sounded insincere.

The garage door was open, the interior appeared full of equipment: gardening and assorted power tools. The garage was separated from the house by an alleyway running between them. There was no barrier here and Cassie caught a glimpse of rolling fields to the rear, as she had suspected. The front door to the house opened and a young man appeared. He was startled by the three of them and took a step back across the threshold of the door, eyeing Cassie and Eric warily.

"The police are here to see you, Joe," Sheila said. Joe looked between his mother and the two of them, then cast a glance sideways and away from them, shaking his head as he made the movement.

"Seriously, I've not done anything. I've been home for days."

Sheila rolled her top lip over the bottom, looking at Cassie. "It's true. He's barely left the house apart from Saturday."

Cassie found that snippet intriguing. "Where did you go on Saturday, Joe?" She kept the tone casual. Joe met her eye.

"To the town. To watch the boat burning, same as everyone else I reckon."

"Isn't it awful what happened to that poor man," Sheila said, frowning. "That was terrible."

"Yes, it was, Mrs Woodly," Cassie said. "Joe, could we have a word. It'll not take long."

Whether it was the gentle nature of how she asked or Cassie's warm smile, Joe visibly appeared to relax. He nodded and stepped out of the house.

"If you were just heading out, we can take a little walk along the street," Cassie said, aiming the comment more at Sheila than her son. Joe nodded.

They headed back down the drive and into the street. It wasn't a thoroughfare and Cassie scanned the surrounding farmland as they walked, Joe thrusting his hands into his pockets and barely raising his gaze from the ground in front of them. Cassie looked to their right as the trees opened up and she could see down the hill across open fields to the sea in the background.

"Were these houses originally built for farm workers?" she asked.

Joe glanced up at her and shrugged.

"We need to speak with you about the incident you were involved in a few weeks ago in Sheringham town centre."

"Ah... what, really? That again," Joe said, shaking his head forcefully.

Cassie eyed him. He was in his early twenties, slim and didn't seem to take a great deal of pride in his appearance. His hair was unkempt and he couldn't have shaved for the last couple of days. It was more than that though. His eyes looked hollow, red-rimmed, and the more they walked, the more fidgety he became. Joe repeatedly touched his nose with the tips of his fingers and the movements of his head each time he spoke were jerky. If she didn't know better, she'd say he had some kind of a disorder. In reality, her experience suggested he was suffering the onset of withdrawal.

"We need to know what was going on between you and Freddie Mayes that day. What did you fall out about?"

"We didn't. It was just a misunderstanding."

Cassie placed a gentle restraining hand on his forearm, stopping their little walk. They'd just passed the last house in the row.

"Come on, Joe."

"It was nothing!"

"Joe, people don't get arrested over nothing," Cassie said. She stepped in front of him, looking him square in the face. "Now, I know you have somewhere else you'd rather be right now but we don't. Do you understand what I'm saying?" Joe met her eye but didn't speak. "We have *all day* if that's what it takes," she said as he averted his eyes from her gaze. She angled her head down so that she could look up into his eyes, forcing contact. "And I know you don't want that, do you?"

Joe exhaled, shaking his head. "Look, it really was nothing. Freddie thinks he's some kind of a big shot, likes to push around the little guy. That's all."

"He was threatening you? Is that what the fight was about, you pushed back?"

"Nah, it wasn't like that," Joe said. "He wasn't pushing me around. I just got involved you know."

"So, he was pushing someone else around," Cassie said, glancing at Eric who nodded.

"Yeah, the other guy," Eric said. "Freddie was pushing him around and you got in the way?"

Joe looked at Eric. "Yeah, it was the other guy, not me."

"So who was he?" Cassie pressed. "This other guy. What's his name?"

Joe looked back at her, his lips parting as his eyes widened. "Ahh... yeah, I don't really know him."

"And yet you stepped in to protect him?" Cassie argued.

"Not to protect him, like, you know. It was... it all happened so fast," he said with a broad smile. "You know how it is."

Cassie screwed up her face in mock concentration before shaking her head. "No, not really, Joe."

"Well... that's the way it happened."

"I have to say you're not very convincing, Joe," she said, keeping her eyes trained on him but addressing Eric. "Do you find him convincing, DC Collet?"

"No. Not really," Eric said with a shake of the head.

Joe laughed but it was borne out of nervous tension rather than humour.

"Look... I... d-don't know." His stammered response only encouraged the idea he was lying.

"You've got a bit of a sweat coming on, Joe," Cassie said, making a show of examining his face and shaking her head. "You look a little peaky. Are you sure we shouldn't take you down the station and discuss this somewhere more comfortable?"

Joe Woodly became agitated, shifting his weight between his feet and rubbing the underside of his nose with his forefinger.

"No, seriously... please, don't do that."

"Then tell me something useful, Joe. Then we won't have to waste any more of each other's day and you can crack on with your busy plans."

Joe stared at her intently. She held his gaze. He was testing her resolve as much as she was his.

"Okay, okay," Joe said.

Cassie smiled. "Good lad."

"Freddie was roughing up a homeless guy, okay? That's what it was about. I thought he was out of order, as usual, and I said so."

"Then what?"

Joe shook his head, his eyes flicked heavenward. "How should I know? Freddie turned on me. He doesn't like me much either. Those ex-army lot don't like people like me."

"You knew each other, you and Freddie?"

Joe nodded. "Yeah. It's a small town. I used to do some work with Freddie... labouring and that sometimes. He could be a bit of an arse but he paid well."

"And the fight?"

It wasn't a fight! How many times do I have to say it? We just had a bit of handbags, you know. I told the police that, so did Freddie. No harm done."

Cassie looked at Eric who flicked his eyebrows up to suggest he had no further questions in mind. Cassie turned back to Joe.

"What was the homeless man's name and where can we find him?"

"I've no idea," Joe said flatly. "I really don't."

"Okay, that'll do for now," Cassie said. "Tell us again where you were Saturday between four and seven?"

"At the festival, watching the procession and stuff."

Cassie smiled, bobbing her head. "That's right, you said so before. And the ending, did you see what happened?"

"What? That bloke burning and falling from the cliff? Yeah, I saw it. Didn't everyone?"

"Did you know that was Freddie Mayes?"

Joe's jaw almost hit the floor, his lips moved but no words were forthcoming. He looked completely blindsided by the information.

"I'll take that as a no, should I?"

"Yes… I mean, no. I had no idea," Joe said. Cassie saw his pupils dilate, a classic response by the autonomic nervous system when under intense stress, more commonly referred to as fight or flight. It could just as easily be related to the rapidly increasing withdrawal symptoms he was experiencing though. Cassie hadn't been exaggerating, Joe Woodly really did look unwell. "Can I go now?"

Cassie smiled. "Yes, of course. Do you need a lift anywhere?"

"No. I'm good."

Joe stepped to one side and walked past her, continuing on down the lane towards the open fields. The tarmac ended where they were standing and only farm vehicles went past them judging from how much the ground had been churned over.

"Where do you think he's going in such a hurry?" Eric asked, watching the back of Joe Woodly's retreating form. "Other than to see his dealer, obviously."

"He seemed broadly on the level," Cassie said softly. "Although, you can never take the word of a junkie, can you?"

Eric shook his head.

"How much of a homeless problem is there in Sheringham, Eric?"

"There are always a few wherever you go."

"True enough. Looks like we'll have to find this guy."

"Maybe we can revisit the area where he had the altercation with Freddie. You never know, one of the shops might have some CCTV that could be useful," Eric said. Cassie agreed and the two of them set off on the short walk back to the car.

CHAPTER SIX

JOE WOODLY COULD FEEL their eyes on his back as he walked. His face flushed, his cheeks burning under a winter sun that emitted very little warmth. He tried to straighten up, to take each stride with confidence but all it did was put him off balance and he repeatedly caught his feet on the lumps and bumps in the track. He must have looked guilty. He felt guilty. But then again, that was normal for him. Every time he looked into his mother's eyes, reading the hollow expression of despair staring back at him, he felt the wave of anxiety manifesting. He knew he disappointed her, disappointed anyone who cared about him.

The path dipped and when he walked up the next incline, he chanced a glance back the way he'd come. There was no sign of the police. He could still see the houses, his parents' house, the fourth from the right. *What would Mum tell Dad when he came home?* Probably nothing. She would cover for him. She usually did if given the chance. Turning he set off once more, only this time he increased his pace. Reaching the crest of the slope, he saw the barns ahead of him. Two giant, sheet-metal agricultural barns, standing side by side in what appeared to be the middle of nowhere. Following the path, it led right past them. It was Sunday and the area was closed up. When gathering in the harvests this place would be a hive of activity seven days a week. Migrant workers were bussed in from all over and the tractors and combines operated day and night if required. Today, the barns were secured and the area was quiet.

He paid them little attention as he passed by, turning right onto an adjacent track between two fields that headed directly towards the sea rather than going straight on and joining the metalled road down towards Thornham. Standing here, he was at one of the highest points in the local area, able to see for miles in every direction. What was expected to be an overcast day turned out far brighter, with the clouds breaking overhead to allow light from the low winter sun. The track he walked down was lined on either side with a mixture of mature trees and hedgerows, delineating the respective field boundaries. These provided shade from the sun and he felt the cold. The wind was coming in straight off the sea and was funnelling the breeze up the track directly towards him. He shivered, drawing his arms across his chest and hugging himself as he walked. It probably wasn't only the cold.

Rounding the next turn he saw his destination up ahead. The track opened up a little at this point and it was here, before the route began to incline steeply down towards the village, that the vehicles were parked. Not that the description held much water. They hadn't moved in years. The only way they'd be moving is if they were dragged clear. Approaching the makeshift settlement, he saw no sign of movement. He knew only one person lived here, there used to be more, but now it was just him and he lived alone.

He made straight for the caravan. The windows were obscured with heavy net curtains blocking any view of the interior to prying eyes. The roof of the old caravan was covered in moss and the exterior panels had some weird green algae growing across them. The caravan sat at an awkward angle, propped up on concrete blocks.

He hammered on the door, it flexed under the pressure.

Glancing to his right, he spied the old ruins of the brick and flint barns further along the track. He knew someone lived in a static home on that site but he didn't venture up this way. Everyone had always steered clear of this little encampment, it had a reputation that it no longer deserved.

Turning back to the door, he raised his hand again only for it to open. He stepped back. A bleary-eyed individual stared at him warily.

"What are you doing here, Joe?" he asked, looking both left and right.

"It's just me, Johnny."

A dog barked from within the caravan. A little terrier appeared in the doorway showing an excited interest in him.

"Aye, but I told you after last time—"

"I know, I know," Joe protested, holding up both hands in supplication. "I... I... I'm just not doing too good at the moment."

"You're not looking great, that's true."

"Can you help me out? Please. I'll not be any trouble."

Johnny clicked his tongue against the roof of his mouth, then exhaled while slowly shaking his head.

"Have you heard?" Joe asked.

"Heard what?"

"About Freddie? About what happened last night at the festival."

Johnny's eyes narrowed, his body stiffening. Joe felt awkward, feeling his confidence draining away.

"No but I reckon you're gonna tell me."

"He's dead," Joe said. Johnny seemed unfazed by the revelation. Joe wondered if he'd heard him. "You'll not believe it, someone set him on fire... right in front of everyone watching."

The man sniffed, rubbing his thumb and forefinger against his chin. He flicked his head towards the interior.

"Come in. I'll see what I can do."

Joe grinned, feeling a flash of expectation. He nervously

looked back the way he'd come, worried someone would see him and then followed Johnny into the caravan, pulling the door closed behind him.

CHAPTER SEVEN

THE OAKES NURSERY was situated a quarter of a mile outside Burnham Market. Tom Janssen must have driven past it numerous times without ever paying it much attention. Pulling into the public car park he found it barely half full, which shouldn't come as a surprise seeing as it was only February. Once the weather picked up, you probably wouldn't be able to move in a place like this. Parking the car, he looked around. There didn't appear to be a specific entrance. There were several access points to enter the beds with a wider paved path leading to the rear of the main building which looked like it doubled as a residence.

He set off in that direction and he hadn't gone far when he caught sight of a man advising a couple off to his left. In the absence of anyone else to speak to, he walked over. As he drew nearer, he could hear they were receiving some care guidance for purchases they'd already made. Tom lingered in the background, making a show of examining what was on offer but he knew nothing about foliage. Soon enough, the couple conveyed their thanks and moved off. He had already been spotted and the member of staff approached him. He was in his late thirties, very tall and athletically built and moved with considerable poise for one of such height. Tom would know and this man was easily his match which didn't happen to him very often.

"Can I help you?" he asked.

Tom took out his identification and opened the wallet. "DI Tom Janssen from Norfolk Police. I'm looking for Harry Oakes. I believe he runs this place," he said, casting an eye around them.

"Yes, I do," Harry Oakes said with a smile. "I also own the place. How can I help the police?"

"Katrina Mayes pointed me in your direction. I understand you're good friends with her husband, Fred Mayes."

"Absolutely," Oakes beamed. "Freddie and I go way back, served together."

"In the Lancers?"

"That's right, yes. Three tours, side by side. What's this about?"

Tom drew himself upright. There was no easy way to sugarcoat such a message, the best course he'd found over the years was to be direct.

"I'm sorry but I have some bad news for you. Freddie passed away yesterday."

Oakes was aghast. For a moment, he didn't know what to say. "What? How did it happen," he asked after taking a moment to compose himself.

"It is most likely that he was murdered."

"Murdered? I don't believe it."

"Last night, at the end of the Viking festival—"

"My God! That was Freddie?" Oakes asked, leaning back against the table the plants were sitting on. Tom confirmed it with a nod. "My God," Oakes repeated.

"You were there?"

Oakes shook his head. "No. It's a shame. I mean, we considered it and everything, but the kids are still quite young and it's a long day."

Tell me about it, Tom thought to himself.

"We went earlier in the day, walked the encampment with the girls but we left before it got dark."

The sound of voices. From the other end of the section they were standing in two girls appeared. They were the spit of one another, both with shoulder length blonde hair, blue eyes and wide smiles. They ran down and launched themselves at Harry Oakes.

"Excuse me," he said to Tom, kneeling down and giving them both a hug. "Hi girls. Did you have a good time with Grandma?"

Both of them shrieked with delight and tried to tell him what they'd been up to, obviously choosing to recount different parts of the day at the same time. "Whoa, whoa," he said, placing one hand on each of their shoulders. Another person appeared, this time it was a woman. Judging by how much the girls resembled her, Tom figured she was their mother.

She came to join them, slipping an arm around Harry's waist and smiling at Tom. "This is my wife, Tina," Oakes said. Tina offered her hand and Tom shook it. "He's with the police, honey."

"The police? Whatever's the matter?"

Harry Oakes looked down at the kids who were now standing to either side of him, hugging a leg each. "Girls, why don't you go and play in the garden and I'll be along in a bit, when I've finished up here."

Both girls looked to their mother for confirmation and she nodded. They smiled in unison and took off at speed.

"Lovely girls," Tom said. Harry Oakes smiled awkwardly but Tina grinned.

"Thank you," she said. "Now, what's so important that the girls couldn't hear it?"

Harry tightened his grip on her waist. "It's Freddie. He's dead."

"Oh no!" Tina replied. "How?"

"Apparently, someone killed him."

"Why would anyone do such a thing? Do you know who it was?" Tina asked, looking to Tom.

"The investigation is underway, Mrs Oakes. That's why I'm here, trying to get some background on Freddie."

"I didn't really know him that well myself," Tina said. "Don't get me wrong, we spend some time with Harry's old friends from the service but that's the link, their army time together. I'm not really in the loop. I'm sure Harry can help though."

"That would be great, Mrs Oakes."

She smiled, turning to her husband who nodded, releasing his grip on her. She said goodbye to Tom, offered her husband a supportive kiss on the cheek that he appreciated, and went in search of the children. Once she was out of earshot, Harry Oakes inclined his head to one side.

"Don't think ill of her, Inspector. She doesn't mean anything by it but, like she said, Freddie was more my friend than hers. Tina is from… how can I put this, a different background to me and the other boys in the troop. I reckon she puts up with them a handful of times a year for my benefit but, to be fair, they don't have a lot in common."

"I had the impression you spent more time than that with Freddie."

"Oh, yes. I did. I saw him frequently, just not with the family. You know, a few drinks, game of pool or whatever."

"When did you last see him?"

Oakes thought about it. "Probably early last week, Monday or Tuesday night maybe."

"How was he? Anything bothering him at all, did he seem out of sorts?"

Oakes shook his head, turning the corners of his mouth down. "Can't say anything struck me as unusual. He seemed larger than life. He always was when he was out and about."

"What about behind closed doors?" Tom asked, sensing a hidden meaning in his statement.

"Prone to melancholy," Oakes said. "On occasion. Don't go away thinking he was depressed or anything." He folded his arms across his chest, turning his gaze towards the outside. "Damn. I can't believe he's gone. And it's murder you say?"

"I'm afraid so, yes."

"Damn. That's... geez."

"Is there anyone you can think of who might hold a grudge against Freddie?" Tom asked.

"Plenty," Oakes said, meeting his eye. "He liked to be the centre of attention, particularly when away from his other half, you know? He liked to put himself around a bit. Making up for personal insecurities I always said – not to his face though. Don't get me wrong, Freddie was one hell of a bloke, but if you got on the wrong side of him he'd let you know about it."

"Anyone who'd be angry enough to set him on fire?"

Harry Oakes brought himself upright, dropping his hands to his sides. "No. Certainly not. Freddie may have given a few boys a bit of a hiding, got in people's faces occasionally, but nothing that'd spark something like that. No way!"

"What about his business? How was that doing?"

"Fantastic. His order book was full."

"Katrina said he went out on Thursday to price a job and hadn't been seen since."

"Yeah, she called on Friday and I spoke to her," Oakes said, pursing his lips as he recalled the conversation. "I have to admit, I told her he'd probably gone off on a session with one of the boys and would be back once he'd slept it off. It sounded lame and I thought maybe..." he stopped, checking to left and right to make sure they were alone; they still were, "...maybe he'd hooked up with someone, you know?"

"Was he known to do so?"

Oakes raised his eyebrows and slowly nodded. "Yeah. It was arguably his one weakness... or vice, if you prefer. Women."

"Anyone special?"

Oakes shook his head. "No, not that I'm aware of. He just used one of those hook up apps. Tinder, is it?" Tom nodded although he had no experience of it personally. Oakes sought to stress that was the same for him. "I'm not familiar with it myself but Freddie was.

He'd often boast about what he got up to. Not that I was ever sure if much of it ever happened. Freddie loved a good story."

"I see. Was Katrina aware?"

Oakes's brow furrowed. "Not sure. He never mentioned it and I wasn't likely to ask was I?"

"Guess not," Tom said, making a note. That revelation left the door open for any number of disgruntled husbands or partners to take issue with Freddie Mayes. "Is he likely to have discussed it with any of the others, do you think?"

Oakes put his hands in his pockets, exhaling deeply as he considered the question. "You'll have to ask them yourself. I can't say it came up much beyond Freddie banging on about his latest conquest. Ed would be the best person to ask."

"Edward Drew?"

"Yeah, Eddie. Or Greg." Tom raised an eyebrow, asking for more. Oakes obliged. "Greg Ellis. He runs the golf club on the coast road heading towards Cromer. Do you know it?"

Tom shook his head. "I don't play."

"Never mind. Greg was another member of our troop. Both he and Eddie were closest to Freddie."

"Katrina didn't mention Greg to us."

Oakes cut a wry smile. "Unsurprising. Katrina and Greg used to be an item. Long before she married Freddie, I should add. They sort of tolerated one another for Freddie's sake."

"I see," Tom said with a nod of appreciation, noting down the information. "Okay, I guess we can leave it there for now."

"I'll walk you out," Oakes said, falling into step alongside him.

They came out from under cover and walked to the car park. Tom was about to say goodbye when a thought occurred to him.

"Would you say Freddie's behaviour with women was related to his time in the service?"

Oakes thought on it. "I dare say it might, yeah. I mean, we all found our own coping mechanisms. Have you served?" Tom shook his head to say he hadn't. "Well, we were tight over there, particularly after Helmand. It was a stressful time back then. It definitely affected everyone. It certainly did me."

Tom felt a few spots of rain and glanced skyward. The clouds had been bubbling throughout the day and the threatened rain now appeared likely after all. He thought of one last question.

"How did you cope?"

"Me?" Oakes looked around, ignoring the increasing patter of the coming shower. "I've got this place, Tina and the girls. After I got out, I was in a bit of a state. A few of us were, looking back." His expression took on a faraway gaze. "Then I met Tina, we got together, against the odds, bearing in mind what I said earlier about her family and stuff. This place was her grandfather's, not that he ran it as a going concern. It'd largely been left to go to rack and ruin."

He pointed behind them, past the beds where they'd been previously towards three hothouses, one larger than the others, probably three times the width of the residential building that stretched backwards ending well beyond their view.

"There's so much scope for improvement here. Business is good and we've got some big plans for the place, for us. It's a massive commitment, and I must admit to a few sleepless nights with the level of borrowing we've undertaken." Oakes frowned, looking at Tom. "But it's worth it. I've developed a hankering for a quieter life. The idea of growing things appeals to me these days... as opposed to being surrounded by death. That might sound odd to you but, believe me, I've seen enough of that to last me a lifetime."

There was something contained within those words, something darker that he was only alluding to but didn't want to speak about directly and Tom didn't press him. The moment passed and Harry Oakes broke into a smile. It was forced and came from a desire to be polite rather than anything else. He offered Tom his hand and he accepted it.

"If there's anything else you need from me, Inspector. You only have to ask."

"I'll bear that in mind, Mr Oakes. Thank you for your time."

Tom walked to the car, increasing his pace as the rainfall steadily built. Getting in, he looked back towards the nursery but Harry Oakes was nowhere to be seen.

CHAPTER EIGHT

THE RAIN WAS STEADILY FALLING NOW, GROWING in intensity by the minute, so much so that he'd had to lengthen the gap between himself and the car in front. The surface was now greasy and liable to flood for a time until the water managed to drain away. Keeping his eye on the car in front was easy. The red taillights were blurry up ahead; his wipers, set to maximum, swept across the windscreen clearing his view for barely a second. He eased his foot off the accelerator.

It wouldn't be long now.

It was dark and the passing rainstorm shrouded the local landmarks to such an extent that only what fell into the beam of the headlights was visible. Not that it mattered. He knew this area. He could navigate it almost blindfolded. There was nothing between them for the next two miles aside from some isolated farmhouses and even they were set way back from the road. Too far away to be a concern.

The brake lights lit up on the car in front as it pulled off the road into the lay-by as he anticipated. Slowing his own car as he approached, he glanced sideways as he passed. The driver's head was down, looking into his lap. He turned his attention back to the road ahead, eyeing the next junction. He switched off his lights and turned right at the intersection, pulling his car onto the grass verge. The rain thundered on the roof of the car and he didn't hear the mobile phone beep but the screen lit up. He opened the text message. *I'm here. Where are you?*

Typing out a reply, he didn't press send. Instead, he reached around into the rear of the car with his right hand and picked up the shotgun. Pulling it through to hold it in his lap, he ran a thumb over the barrel ends. They were smooth to the touch. The weapon was much more manageable now. Breaking the barrels, he checked the cartridges were present. He'd already done this twice before setting off but preparation was habitual. A mistake now would be costly.

Pulling the hood of his coat over his head, he zipped up the front to just below his chin and cracked the door open. The verge was soft underfoot, turning to mud as he reached the field boundary. Here, there was a break in the hedgerow to allow farm vehicle access and he entered the field, turning to his right and jogging towards where he could see the car parked, its headlights still on. Forced to slow his approach by the uneven ground, he came to the field boundary and stood behind a sprawling thicket through which he viewed the car and its incumbent. The driver had switched on the interior light and appeared to be scrolling through the screen on his mobile phone, probably killing time. There was no chance he would be seen from his vantage point.

Moving to his left, he kept low. Again, this was due to force of habit rather than necessity. There was a break in the undergrowth and he eased aside the branches and slipped through, emerging in the lay-by some twenty feet to the rear of the car. With the shotgun in his right hand, he took the mobile from his pocket with his left and pressed send. Tucking the mobile back into his pocket he approached the car, the rain relentlessly drumming on the hood of his coat.

Staring straight ahead, he saw the driver look to both his left and right before glancing over his shoulder and out of the rear window. Even now, he knew he wouldn't be visible from anyone inside the car. He waited in the darkness. The driver's door opened and a man got out, drawing his coat about him. He looked directly at him, walking to the rear of the car.

"Why on earth did you want to meet out here?" the driver called, turning his collar up and leaning forward in an attempt to shield himself from the driving rain.

He didn't reply, remaining focussed on his goal. He walked on, hearing his boots crunch on the loose stone of the lay-by. There was no going back now, not that the thought had occurred to him. His target screwed up his face, peering vainly into the darkness as he approached.

"What the hell?" The driver exclaimed as his eyes caught sight of the shotgun in the reflected glow of the car's rear lights. He raised both hands before him in supplication. "No! Don't—"

The appeal fell on deaf ears as the first barrel discharged. The blast struck home in the centre of the chest and the victim was punched from his feet, landing on his back beside the driver's door. There was no cry of pain, no further protestations.

Walking forward, he shifted his finger to the next trigger and came to stand over the stricken figure whose left arm was splayed wide at his side whereas the right was draped over his chest, across the gaping wound left by the shotgun. His head lolled from the right back to the centre, eyes drifting up to meet those of his would-be assassin. Shock and fear turned to recognition and his eyes widened… before the second barrel discharged.

CHAPTER NINE

THE DELUGE that came down overnight had passed to leave a freshness in the air and the promise of a brighter day ahead. Tom Janssen pulled up behind the line of police cars and switched off the engine. The vehicles were blocking the carriageway but it didn't matter, the road had been closed at both ends, with traffic, as much as passed this way on a Monday morning, diverted along other routes. He got out of the car and approached the second cordon, the one marking out the outer limit of the crime scene at the mouth of the lay-by. DS Cassie Knight saw him arrive and came to meet him as he ducked under the blue and white police tape hanging between two trees either side of the entrance.

"Morning, Tom," she said as he donned a set of nitrile gloves.

He nodded a greeting but dispensed with any further pleasantries. His mind was already focussed on the scene. Only one vehicle was present in the lay-by. It was a white Audi saloon. The passenger door was open and the interior of the car was already being processed by the team from forensics. On the other side, the driver's door was cracked open and a body lay on the ground alongside it. A crime scene technician was already photographing the victim. Tom came to stand alongside the deceased, Cassie next to him.

The victim's upper body was drenched in blood. That which had soaked into the surrounding clothing was starting to dry, probably doing so when the rain eased off overnight. The blood that must have formed underneath the body had run off to the victim's left, following the slight incline of the lay-by, pooling where the gravel met the verge before draining into a shallow ditch this side of the bracken at the edge of the field. It was clear there had been a second shot. The victim took this one straight to the face. The sight was brutal, gut wrenching.

"I'd say a shotgun. Both at close quarters," Cassie said. He was inclined to agree. They'd made a real mess of the victim. He indicated the man.

"What do we know about him?"

Cassie produced her pocketbook and read from it.

"The car is registered to Andrew Lewis. Thirty-eight years old and is listed as a resident of Hunstanton." She glanced at Tom. "I've got the description from the police national computer... but your guess is as good as mine as to whether this is him."

Tom nodded slowly, grimacing. "Messy." He scanned the dead man, noting that his legs were crossed at the ankle. "Dead man's drop," he said, pointing to them.

"Excuse me?" Cassie asked.

"When a person dies, or is incapacitated, from a standing position, when they fall their feet cross like that. It's one of those strange quirks of nature that always seems to happen."

"I never knew," she said. "If I had to say, I reckon this was personal. Wouldn't you?"

"What makes you think so?" he asked. The same occurred to him but he was keen to hear her thought process.

"Several reasons. The guy got out of the car to address the killer. He'd closed the door, done his coat up. That doesn't imply he was hurried or seeking a confrontation. It's measured, taking into account the weather as well as the surroundings." Cassie indicated the car. "This car is worth a fortune, the victim's wallet and mobile are still inside. The wallet has a wedge of cash in it.

None of it was taken. By the look of the damage to the chest, I would say that was the first shot."

"Agreed."

"Close range. Probably from two metres, not much more. The second… was point blank." She knelt alongside the victim, examining what was left of the face and head, which wasn't much, before looking back up at Tom. "This second shot was up close, which suggests rage… and that's personal. Very personal."

Tom turned his attention to a plastic crate nearby housing a number of transparent evidence bags.

"The wallet. Does it belong to Andrew Lewis?"

Cassie nodded. "Yep," she said, rising and coming alongside him as they crossed to the crate.

She lifted out the bag containing the wallet and passed it to him. Tom carefully opened it and took out a small black leather wallet. The clasp that usually kept the wallet closed was broken and it fell open in his hands. There were the usual bank and credit cards, a supermarket loyalty card and two membership IDs. One was to a golf club and the other a local gym. Tom knew of the latter but he didn't attend it. All of the names on the cards were variations of Andrew Lewis. Roughly thumbing through the clutch of notes within the wallet, he estimated there must be at least two hundred pounds there. He was already confident they could rule out robbery as a motive.

"Any sign of another vehicle?" Tom asked, looking around. "If the driver got out then it stands to reason it was to speak with someone else. You wouldn't get out of the car, not in last night's weather, if you'd driven here together."

"I've set up a group to carry out a fingertip search of the area," Cassie said. "Just waiting on more bodies turning up."

Tom nodded. "Good. The ground will be pretty wet after last night. Tracks should be visible."

"It's a well-used lay-by, though," Cassie said, pointing to the churned-up ground. The lay-by was gravel lined but even so, the close proximity to the working agricultural land meant the stretch seemed to be traversed by tractors and other plant on a regular basis. Differentiating between what was freshly put down the previous night and what went before would be tricky. "It's been cold of late. The ground will be pretty solid. I'm not sure there was enough coming down last night to break it up."

Tom saw her logic. "Well, we can but try. You said he had a mobile."

"Yes, he did."

Cassie rooted through the evidence bags and produced one containing the mobile. She passed it to him and he held the bag aloft. It looked brand new. There were no scuffs or scrapes to the casing or the screen that he could see. Opening the bag, he reached in and took it out.

"It's switched on and still has power but it's locked. I kinda hoped he'd have his password written on a slip of paper in his wallet but I couldn't find one," Cassie said.

"Do people still do that?"

She shrugged. "My mam does. And her PIN for her cash card." He frowned disapprovingly. "I know. I badger her about that kind of thing all the time but she won't have it."

Tom shook his head, turning the handset over in his palm to inspect the reverse. He walked back to the car. Cassie followed, coming alongside the body. The CSI technician indicated he was done with his photographs and Tom dropped to his haunches.

"Right or left handed do you reckon?" he asked.

"Right, I'd say. Statistically, most people are," she said and Tom pointed to the deceased man's right hand.

"Forefinger," he said. Cassie dropped down herself and reached over, lifting the man's hand and extending the forefinger. Tom placed the handset underneath and pressed the fingerprint scanner against the flat of the fingertip. Righting the mobile, the screen flashed into life.

"Good thinking," Cassie said, gently lowering the dead man's hand back to his chest.

They stood up and Tom gave the unit a cursory examination.

Accessing the call records he found the list detailing the most recent calls made or received. The owner hadn't made a call himself since the previous morning and that was made to someone named Charlie. That call had lasted a little over five minutes, so he guessed they were probably friends. Work-related calls would most likely either be longer or far shorter and the entry of only the first name in the contact list was suggestive of a closer association.

"Now this is interesting," Tom said, having switched to the text messaging records. "There's an exchange last night. The first message asks him to meet here, at ten o'clock, states it's urgent but doesn't say what they need to discuss. He agrees without much argument."

"That's weird," Cassie said, looking around. "Why here?"

Tom shrugged. "Doesn't say. The next message was sent by…" He looked at the body. "Let's consider this is Andrew Lewis for the time being until we know otherwise. It was sent by him to say he'd arrived and is asking where the other guy is. The reply comes a few minutes later."

"Saying what?"

"Saying *I'm right here*," Tom said, exhaling and looking to where he envisaged the attacker was standing when he most likely fired the initial shot. "If the victim got out and approached the killer, that would put the time of death at around 10 pm, last night."

"Yeah, that figures," Cassie agreed. "So, who sent the message? Who had he agreed to meet?"

"That's the really interesting part," Tom said, turning the mobile in his hand so Cassie could see the screen. "It was sent by Freddie Mayes."

"Get out!" Cassie said, leaning in closer to see. "Damn."

"Yeah, that leaves us with a couple more questions. Is it Freddie we have in the mortuary? The pathologist will have to confirm that for us and secondly, if not, then who fell from the cliff in a fireball?"

"Either way, the two murders are related. Katrina Mayes was pretty sure that tattoo was Freddie's, what with the name of their daughter beneath the regimental badge and all. To agree to come out here last night suggests Freddie and this guy are close. Freddie Mayes hung out with his old military friends... I'd be interested to know if they served together. That would either imply or rule out a link to Freddie's military past."

Tom nodded, slipping the mobile back into the evidence bag and sealing it. He returned the bag to the crate alongside the other pieces that had been catalogued. Glancing back at the car, he spied a sticker at the foot of the rear window.

"Did you notice that?" he asked, pointing to it.

Cassie looked. It was a sticker sold to raise funds for the armed forces charity *Help for Heroes*. It was far from conclusive but was certainly suggestive of a military link with the deceased.

"We should head over to Hunstanton, notify the next of kin and make certain," Cassie said. Tom nodded solemnly. "If they served together, then we'd better start tracking down everyone in Freddie's unit locally. Whatever the motivation, it looks like someone has it in for Freddie and his mates."

"Yes, but let's keep that possibility to ourselves for the time being," he said. "I don't want to start scaring people unnecessarily that there might be a serial killer floating around."

CHAPTER TEN

Tom Janssen and Cassie Knight stood back as Sophie Lewis offered a brief nod to the technician. The movement appeared reticent and, as the sheet was pulled across to cover both the left arm and hand, Tom knew it was indeed Andrew Lewis who had been shot and killed the previous night. Sophie remained where she was for a moment longer, staring at the body now fully obscured by the covering. The deceased had a distinctive tattoo on both forearms and the wedding band on the left hand was also patterned and quite unusual. These were the only parts of the victim's body that they could allow a relative to view, all that would be identifiable.

Tom found himself wondering what was running through her mind, at which stage of the grief process she was at. She wavered and he stepped forward, fearing for a moment that she was about to faint but she steadied herself, casting a sideways glance towards him and indicating she was okay. That moment broke her fixation on the body and she turned away. Tom held out an open hand and guided her from the room and back into the adjoining corridor. A young man in his teens, her son, rose from a plastic chair where he'd been waiting and approached expectantly. The expression on his face was hopeful but this was extinguished by his mother's demeanour.

"Mum?" he asked. She looked down, not wanting to say the words and could only manage a nod. Andrew Lewis's son was crestfallen and he put his hands together in front of his face, shaking his head. His father was dead.

"I know this is a terrible moment, Mrs Lewis," Tom said, drawing her attention. "But we need to ask you some questions about your husband. It will help us establish our investigation and track down who did this. Do you think you're up to it?"

"Yes, of course, Inspector. Anything I can do to help."

Tom led them along the corridor and into a family waiting area. It was little more than a group of padded chairs set out in a U shape with a collection of magazines laid out on a nearby table. They sat down, mother and son side by side and holding hands to support one another.

"When did you last see your husband, Mrs Lewis?"

"Sophie, please," she said. Tom nodded. "Not for a few days. We're separated you see, have been for the past six months. I mean, it's not official or anything. We are…" She glanced at him. "Were doing it on a trial basis. To see if a bit of space could help work things out."

"I see. But you still talked regularly?"

"Yes, of course. We saw each other a couple of times a week. Probably more than that recently," she said, addressing him with a nervous smile. "Andy was so excited about the future, about our future."

"What was he excited about?"

"Andy felt that we had turned a corner and that tied in with his work which was also going well."

"What did he do?"

"He's a bit of an entrepreneur," Sophie said, meeting his eye and chuckling as she shook her head. "Just don't ask me what he did, buying and selling. He used to talk about *drop shipping* whatever that is. It's all nonsense to me but Andy seemed to know what he was doing. I've no idea how he learnt to though. It was such a shift for him after leaving the army."

Her son, James, smiled at that comment. "Dad was never likely to manage a hedge fund or anything but he always said he played the percentages and things usually worked out for him."

"It's true," Sophie added. "Sometimes Andy would be on such a poor run, I would get worried but then he'd manage to turn it around as if out of nowhere. The amount of celebratory meals we used to go out for…"

"How long had he been doing that?" Tom asked. He wanted to build up a picture by letting them talk but guide them along the way to draw out the information he was after.

"Since he came out," Sophie said.

"Of the army?"

"Yes," she nodded. "He was in the cavalry. That was a far cry from playing the markets or whatever it was that he did. It seems like another life now, watching him go off on deployment."

"How did he find his time in the military?" Tom asked, controlling the direction of the conversation.

"He loved it, I think. It suited him when he was younger. Some of the lads were understandably anxious about going into a war zone but Andy loved the thrill of it. That was part of his excitement to me as well, if I'm honest. He cut quite a dashing figure as a soldier. He came through all that without a scratch… physically, anyway." She glanced at her son, smiling weakly. James squeezed her hand a little tighter, a gesture she appreciated.

"What about mentally?"

She nodded slowly, turning her gaze back to him.

"Yes. Andy struggled when he got home. I think Afghanistan was hard for him, even harder when he wasn't in theatre. Over there he had purpose. He was surrounded by his friends and they looked out for each other. It was when he got home, when he had time to think that it really troubled him."

"Did he seek help from the army?"

"Oh yes, eventually. To begin with they were very supportive but in the end they suggested, or at least his counsellor suggested, that perhaps it would be for the best if he left the army. And it was then that things really fell apart." Sophie looked at James apologetically. Something passed between mother and son, shared experience perhaps, and then she looked back at Tom.

"What happened then?"

"Andy lost his purpose, his whole reason for being," Sophie said. "Or that's what he thought, anyway. I thought that being safely at home with me... and the boys, should be enough for him. Naive really. It took me a long time before I realised that though, Inspector. Things were hard for a while, Andy suffering from mood swings, chronic anxiety and insomnia. Once that support network was gone, he just tried to hide, block everything out. Do you know what I mean?"

"Yes, I've met people along the way who have done the same."

"Then you'll know how hard it is to see someone you love disappear into a bottle. You do everything you can to try and stop it but end up hurting them as much as they hurt you."

"Is that how you came to be separated?"

Sophie thought about it, her face a picture of concentration. "We were on and off for some time. Andy would come and go, we would fight." She looked at James again and he smiled supportively. "But as I said, things have been better recently. Andy seemed like he was on the up. I've heard it many times before but this time, it was different somehow. Andy used to talk about his work in terms of *sure things* and when we needed him to come through, he always managed it. I guess I should never have doubted his lucky streak seeing as he made it out of Afghanistan unscathed."

"You said he was part of the cavalry, right?" Tom asked. She nodded. "Did he ever talk about it, what he went through out there? I know a lot of guys don't."

Sophie inclined her head to one side. "Not in any great detail, no. The occasional story that he thought might raise a smile, that sort of thing."

"He used to joke about them being one of the twenty-minuters," James said, smiling.

"The twenty-minuters?" Tom asked.

"Yeah, from Blackadder."

"The television series?"

"Yeah," James said, his smile broadening to a grin. "You remember the air corps episode where they were nicknamed the *twenty-minuters* because that was their average life expectancy?"

Tom smiled, recollecting the episode. "Yes, I remember."

"Well, Dad used to joke that every time his troop left a base they'd be in a contact within twenty minutes." James spoke with very obvious pride in his father's service record. "They were a forward reconnaissance unit in Helmand. He always joked they were a bullet magnet for the Taliban."

Tom smiled warmly. James's eyes glazed over and he touched his hand to one of them to ensure no tears slipped out.

"Did Andy remain close with anyone from the service, after he came out?" Tom asked.

"Yes. He still saw a number of guys from his old troop. Many of them are still around here. Andy always said that once you'd served together in a combat situation, you really knew who you could count on in life and they'd be with him forever."

"Was he close with Fred Mayes?"

"Freddie? Yes, absolutely," Sophie said, nodding enthusiastically. "Freddie was something of a rock to Andy. To many of the guys, I reckon. He kept them all together. Sometimes I thought he held too much sway over my Andy."

"How so?"

"Well... Andy was too quick to do whatever Freddie asked of him. I guess it doesn't really matter now but it used to grate on me a bit."

"What did?"

"That I couldn't get him to fix a cupboard door for weeks but all Freddie, or any of the others for that matter, had to do was pick up the phone and he'd be off like a shot! Infuriating is an understatement, Inspector."

Hearing the nature of the relationship between Andy Lewis and Freddie Mayes made it quite conceivable that Lewis would be willing to meet his friend in such an obscure location at that time of the night. Someone else knew that too and lured him to his death.

"Did Andy mention any problems he was having recently? You've mentioned his drinking habits along with his PTSD but is there anything you can point to recently that was troubling him? Any relationship issues with friends or business acquaintances?"

Sophie looked to her son and he met her eye with a blank expression. She turned back to Tom, shaking her head.

"No. I'm sorry, I can't. The last time we spoke, he was so enthusiastic about the future. I remember him saying it's all paid off and now was the time when everything was going to come good. Another one of his *sure things*."

"Any idea what he may have been referring to?"

Again, Sophie shook her head. "I assumed it was his work, that it was going well and he'd made some good investments or something."

Tom made an effort to hide his disappointment. Andy Lewis felt as if he was on the up, that his future held promise but someone else had other plans for him. For both him and Freddie Mayes. It was starting to look like Cassie's theory was sound. The connection must be the military service or what they'd done since they came out and settled back into Norfolk life.

"Tell me, Sophie. Where was Andy living at the moment? We still have him registered at your house but clearly he's been staying elsewhere."

"He rented a flat not far from us in Hunstanton."

"Great. Can you give me the address please?"

James sat upright, reaching into his pocket. "I can do better than that. Dad gave me a set of keys."

He took a set of keys from his coat pocket. They were held on two rings and he disconnected a bunch of three from the others and made to pass it across. At the last moment, he hesitated, withdrawing his hand and removing one of three keys that were on the ring.

"Sorry," James said, passing Tom the remaining two keys which he accepted gratefully.

"When was the last time you were there, James?" Tom asked.

James's brow furrowed as he thought about it. "Not for a while. Dad gave me the key in case I ever wanted to use his place and he wasn't around, but I've never really had the need. I figured he gave them to me just so that I knew he wanted me around. Symbolic, you know?"

Tom nodded. "I'll get these back to you. In the meantime, I'll have a car run the two of you home. We can always speak again."

He offered his condolences once more before standing up and leaving the two of them together in the family area. Cassie joined him.

"There's a uniform car waiting outside to run them home," she said quietly. "The pathologist is waiting. He wants a word."

CHAPTER ELEVEN

TOM NOTED the departure of Sophie Lewis and her son, accompanied by a uniformed constable. He then fell into step alongside Cassie as she led them through a set of doors and came to the first office on the left. She knocked and they were bidden to enter. Inside, waiting patiently for them, was a studious-looking man in his late fifties. Tom hadn't met him before despite being broadly familiar with the team from Norwich who staffed the pathology departments.

"Michael Roberts," the man said, standing up from behind a spartanly furnished desk and offering his hand.

Tom accepted it, introducing himself. The pathologist offered them both a seat and they sat down. Usually, the body, in this case that of Freddie Mayes, would be shipped down to Norwich for the autopsy but at Tom's request the initial examination had been expedited and the pathologist travelled up to the coast.

"I can see your team is doing its level best to keep me at the seaside for a little while longer, Inspector Janssen," Dr Roberts said dryly.

"It might seem that way, yes."

"Seeing as you were here, I thought we may as well discuss my initial assessment of Mr Mayes," Roberts continued, opening a folder on his desk in front of him. "I understand you witnessed the victim's fall from the cliff; is that correct?"

"Unfortunately, yes I did."

"Well, it will come as no surprise to you that the fall was certainly the cause of death. No prizes for guessing there," Roberts said, adjusting the glasses, perched on the end of his nose, as he peered over them to make eye contact before returning to his notes. "Death was by a massive depressed fracture to the cranium. He landed head first, Inspector. Death would have been instantaneous and, under the circumstances, possibly something of a blessed release."

"The burns?" Tom queried and the doctor nodded.

"Yes, quite extensive to the exposed parts of the body. Mr Mayes suffered third-degree burns to thirty-six percent of his body," Roberts said, once again consulting his notes. "I'm sure you will be unsurprised to hear the most extensive damage was to the extremities; the head, including the face, nine percent, the hands, another nine and then the front of the trunk, predominantly his upper chest and shoulder area suffered the remainder. Nasty business."

"Have you been able to determine what started the fire?"

"Not for absolute certainty, no. Without a doubt he was doused in some form of accelerant. My guess would lean towards your readily available petrol rather than anything exotic. The smell of such is still noticeable on the victim's clothing, that which didn't burn due to him coming to rest flat in the sand. The heat and flame burned upwards, protecting the rear of his torso from the worst of the damage. Obviously, this will all be confirmed by the laboratory once the samples are returned."

"I managed to send off blood samples both for toxicological and identification purposes. Once you established the military connection, I had the victim's records drawn from the Ministry of Defence database for comparison purposes."

"Is this Freddie Mayes?" Tom asked, sitting forward in his seat.

"Oh, absolutely. Without a doubt," Roberts said. "Mr Mayes

underwent several procedures during his time in the army along with vaccinations for his deployment overseas. You will also be interested to hear about the tox screening we did. He had a high level of diazepam in his blood stream, far higher than one might expect to be prescribed to a sufferer of depression, stress or anxiety for instance. As far as you're aware, was Mr Mayes undergoing treatment for any of those conditions or for associated insomnia or the like?"

"That's not our understanding at this time, no," Tom said. "When you say high levels, could you elaborate on that, please."

Dr Roberts flapped his hand in the air, swatting away a fly or other insect bothering him. "High enough to impair him physically. From the accounts of the moments prior to his death, it would imply the tranquilisers were wearing off, although it would be reasonable to presume the heightened adrenalin production in the body's natural response to burning could have inhibited the effects of the diazepam. That would be a subjective view however."

Tom exchanged a glance with Cassie. Freddie's whereabouts were unknown from the Thursday night through to his appearance on Saturday evening when he died. Keeping him topped up with tranquilisers would have made the task of detaining him much easier.

"Is there any chance of tracing where the drug may have come from?" Cassie asked, hoping the answer would lead to an easily traceable supplier.

"Diazepam is quite accessible, I'm afraid," Roberts said glumly. "I wish I could offer you more help with that but it is one of the go-to choices for medical practitioners up and down the country. The best you can realistically hope for is to identify a suspect and then see if they have access to the drug but that in itself will prove little. Diazepam is one of the most prescribed drugs for treatment of stress and depression."

"Meaning any suspect we find will have a strong likelihood of having someone they know who has access to it," Tom said, clarifying the doctor's point. Roberts nodded, placing his elbows on the table and interlocking his fingers in front of him.

"I'm sorry I can't be of more use with that one," Roberts said. "However, I did find evidence of abrasions and incisions in both the wrists and ankles. Notably so in the latter due to there being far less damage to that area of the body. The marks were uniform, less than ten millimetres across, and broke the skin in several places."

"Cable ties?" Tom asked.

"That would be my thoughts also, yes, and would have been present on the body for some time causing an immense amount of discomfort I should imagine. Not as much as the burning in itself, though, which would have been excruciating. The clothing he wore, due to its composition of both man-made and natural fibres, will have magnified the heat generated." The doctor paused, clearly reading their solemn expressions. "As I said, a nasty business."

"Thank you, Dr Roberts. Have you been able to take a look at the body recovered from the crime scene this morning?"

"Only by way of a cursory examination. I'm required to give evidence in court tomorrow morning and therefore will need to transfer this one back to Norwich today."

"I understand," Tom said. "Can you offer us anything to go on?"

"As long as you don't hold me to it should things change after I conduct the examination," Roberts said. Tom nodded. "I think the cause of death will be quite apparent to you, Inspector. I should imagine the first shot would have been enough to kill him. If not from the initial wound, then I'm certain he would have bled out within ten to fifteen minutes. If he was still conscious when the second shot was fired, no doubt at closer range than the first, he wouldn't have known much about it. I observed the next of kin's response via the viewing window and I expect the identity of the deceased will be confirmed in due course in much the same way as with Freddie Mayes."

"Thank you, Doctor Roberts," Tom said, glancing at Cassie and rising from his seat. "We'll let you get on with arranging the transfer back to Norwich. I appreciate you coming up on such short notice to accommodate us in the Mayes case."

"One thing I would say, Inspector," Roberts said. Tom turned back on his way to the door. "Speaking with your DS here," he indicated Cassie, "I'm perhaps reading between the lines a little and wouldn't want to overstep my brief, but I think both of these cases are indicative of a high level of premeditation on the part of the killer."

Tom looked at Cassie but her facial expression made it clear she hadn't voiced their discussions on these cases being connected.

"And, judging by how few murders you have in these parts, the waiting for a bus analogy doesn't escape my consideration but I find the coincidence unlikely. I dare say, should you not make headway in this case soon, I wouldn't be surprised to find myself back on the coast... how should I put this, sooner rather than later?"

Tom smiled politely. He wasn't used to medical examiners expressing opinions on a killer's motivation but, he had to admit, the man was very astute.

"Thank you for your time, Doctor," he said, opening the door and allowing Cassie to leave first.

"WHERE DO you think we should go from here, Tom?" Cassie asked as they left the building and descended the steps to the car park. "Should we canvas the other members of Freddie's troop and give them the heads up?"

Tom stopped, hands thrust into his pockets as he looked around, thinking hard. After a moment, he shook his head. "No, I don't want to do that. Let's work out who and where they are and start talking to them but be careful what we say. At the moment, let's be honest, we've no idea as to why our killer targeted these two. Yes, the link between them is their service together but the killer could just as easily be one of their troop as someone who has an issue with it. It might play favourably to the investigation not to let on that we're investigating that angle."

"And what if another one of them turns up dead in the meantime? We'll be up to our necks in it," Cassie said.

Tom recognised the concern in her tone. It was more for any potential victim than for herself, he was quite sure.

"I hear what you're saying."

"But you disagree?"

"Not necessarily," Tom said, frowning. "Have Eric run down a list of people who served with Mayes and Lewis, cross-referenced with those living locally. That way we will know how many people we're working with. Then we need to get among them, shake the tree a little and see what comes from it. I agree with Dr Roberts. Whoever did this was angry... and not at the wider society. For my mind, it was personal. Premeditated. Sadistic."

"You could say planned with military precision," Cassie added.

"Which is why I don't want to tip our hand. When you speak to Eric have him also run down Andy Lewis's financials. While he's doing that, you and I will go and take a look at his flat.

CHAPTER TWELVE

TOM JANSSEN STOPPED outside the communal entrance to the block. It was a wide, squat building, only four stories high but occupied a prominent position overlooking the sea and had a direct line of sight along the promenade towards the town. It wasn't a particularly new building, constructed in an uninspiring sixties style.

Cassie finished parking the car alongside the square, a patch of ground between this and the parallel street that was a mix of lawn and trees, all carefully managed. It was a great location. The streets here were laid out in a grid with wide roads and paths; even with lines of car parking, they still seemed spacious. All of which was in stark contrast to those of the nearby Victorian old town with its narrow patchwork of roads and tight angles. The old town was built before the onset of the motoring age which made it difficult for both residents and visitors alike.

"Ready?" Cassie asked, coming to join him.

He nodded and turned, taking the set of keys from his pocket. There were two keys on the ring and both were standard Yale keys. He tried the first in the lock and it slipped in easily. The door opened and they passed through, seeing stairs on the far side of the lobby. There were no lifts and they headed up the stairs, the sound of their footsteps echoing throughout the stairwell on the polished surfaces. The block was well maintained, if a little tired. Andy Lewis's flat was on the third floor and located to the front of the building.

Coming to the flat, Tom hammered his fist on the door. To their knowledge, Lewis lived alone but they couldn't be certain. They waited but, as expected, no one came to the door and Tom unlocked the door with the second Yale key given to him by James, Lewis's son. Remembering the third key that James removed from the ring before handing them over, he momentarily considered what that was a key to. He wondered if he would find out in the flat. A distinctive smell of stale air came to them as they entered. The flat was warm, the central heating was on, but it wasn't stifling. The flat had a central corridor leading from one end to the other where it opened out into a living room with dual-aspect windows offering a panoramic view of both Hunstanton and the seafront. Off the corridor was access to a small kitchen, a bathroom and two bedrooms.

One of the bedrooms was made up for guests with minimal furniture and the fitted wardrobes stood empty. This room had a musty smell that reminded Tom of the upstairs to his grandmother's house for some reason. Maybe it was the smell of an unused room. She had several of them in her house, particularly once she became infirm and unable to use the stairs.

Entering the kitchen, he was greeted by a mess. The sink was full of dirty crockery, a small saucepan sitting on top half-filled with what looked like a mixture of water and remnants of a curry. The work surfaces were in a similar state with no spare space to be had. A stack of aluminium takeaway food cartons lay to the left of the sink in a white plastic bag. Much of the limited space remaining in the small area was taken up with empty bottles of spirits, wine and cans of beer. These must have been there for several days or more, giving off the stagnant aroma you usually expected when standing beside a bottle bank. He recalled that Lewis told Sophie he had turned a corner in his life but apparently not so when it came to his alcohol consumption. Tom didn't drink any more but he used to and, even in his youth, he would have struggled to rack up this number of empties. Cassie joined him having completed her inspection of the hallway cupboard, indicating she'd found nothing of any note. She glanced at the empty bottles, raising a knowing eyebrow before opening the fridge and stepping back as she examined the interior.

"Typical bachelor pad," she said, recoiling from the contents of a plastic tub she'd just taken from the fridge and smelled. "What on earth is this anyway?" she asked, angling it towards Tom so he could also see the contents. He frowned and she hastily put it back on the shelf where she'd found it and closed the door.

"Not all bachelors live like this," he said, with a wry smile.

"Ah, but you're house trained," she said with a wink. "I don't know who trained you, but they did a reasonable job of it."

"Reasonable?"

She laughed and Tom turned, squeezed past her and headed back out into the central corridor. Cassie's mobile rang and she held back, answering the call and silently mouthing *Eric* to him. He nodded and continued on. The next room was the master bedroom. It was larger than the guest room and overlooked the square. These wardrobes had clothes either hanging or folded neatly on shelves. Not many though. Andy Lewis had fewer choices of what to wear than he did himself and Tom knew he was far from a clothes horse. Alice was frequently trying to adapt his dress sense, not to style him as such, but to broaden what he chose to wear. She was still trying.

He leafed through the hanging shirts to see what else, if anything, was behind them in the wardrobe but apart from a set of trainers and dress shoes, there was nothing to find. He found the dresser offered similar spoils. Most of the drawers were empty aside from underwear or socks. He closed the last drawer, the runners shrieking in protest. Lowering himself to the floor, he looked under the bed, but all he managed to do was dislodge a significant amount of dust that irritated his eyes and nose. Returning to the corridor, he headed to his right and into the living room. This room ran the full width of the apartment. A large television stood at one end with two sofas set out in front of it. At the other were a round dining table and four chairs. None of the furniture was particularly fancy and the flat as a whole looked much as one might expect from a rental: functional and without frills.

Crossing to the sofa he found a collection of magazines lying on a small coffee table. They were themed around films and music, nothing of any interest. He heard Cassie saying goodbye to Eric as she entered the room, tucking her mobile back into her pocket.

"This is all a bit odd," Tom said.

Cassie looked around. "What is?"

"All of this. Does it strike you as the home of someone who is on the up?"

"Not really," she said.

"And if he's running a business from here, surely he'd have the associated kit to do so. I haven't even come across so much as a laptop."

"But then again," she said thoughtfully, "some people are a bit delusional. Maybe he was just trying to sell himself to his wife to get on her good side, trying to get them back together. He wouldn't be the first bloke to try and pull the wool over his wife's eyes, would he?"

"You're too young to be so cynical."

She laughed. "Doesn't mean I'm not right though, mind you. Eric's just come back to me having run down Lewis's assets and accounts."

"Anything of note?"

"More notable by the absence than anything else."

Tom's brow furrowed. "I don't understand."

"He started by running down his bank account. It's a standard current account with a balance just shy of three hundred quid.

Eric says the balance hasn't been above a thousand in the last three years. No monthly salary paying in, no direct debits leaving to cover cost of utilities or the like."

"He must have another account somewhere?"

"Yeah, that's what I said too," Cassie explained, opening up her note-book. "Eric swears he's checked. There are no other accounts held in Andy Lewis's name."

"Shared account with his wife?"

Cassie shook her head. "Eric checked there too. Their joint account was transferred solely into Sophie's name a while back. She probably didn't trust him."

"What about a business account? He'd need one to be buying and selling. Dropshippers operate virtually, they don't hold stock and are the middlemen between buyer and seller. He couldn't do it with cash."

"Again, nothing. Eric ran down Lewis's name in the register of directors at Companies House and he's not listed." She looked around. "I think we can safely say he wasn't trading from here. Maybe he has an office somewhere else?"

Tom took a deep breath, scanning the room. "Maybe. What about finance, loans, that type of thing. Maybe he's a Walter Mitty character."

"Nothing that Eric has been able to find so far. The car he was driving last night is registered to him and a hire purchase check revealed no payments are outstanding or loans secured against it. Andy Lewis isn't listed on the PAYE register with HMRC nor has he filed any self-assessment tax returns in the last three years. By all accounts, this guy should be considered almost penniless."

"We'll have to widen the search criteria. Look into relatives, elderly ones whose accounts he may have approval to draw from. Also, start searching council tax records and business rates to see if he has ownership or liabilities to any other property. Sophie told me he always came good financially when she needed it, that he always struck lucky when required. This here..." he made a circular motion with one hand to indicate the flat, "doesn't fit with that description. Unless Sophie was lying, which wasn't my impression, this doesn't add up."

"Eric was ahead of you, Tom. He's been into the Land Registry this morning. This flat changed ownership last year into the name of a Mabel Reid. Using the historical records on the web, Eric contacted the agent who brokered the deal. They said it was a straightforward purchase, no chain and without a mortgage requirement. They don't recall meeting the buyer and the agent who would have done the viewings no longer works for them."

"A cash buy?"

Cassie nodded. "It went through once the land searches were completed, took less than five weeks according to the agent. Mabel Reid must be linked to Lewis somehow if he's living here. We haven't located her yet but ID must have been shown in order to satisfy money-laundering regs."

"So where was he getting his money from?"

"My thoughts exactly," Cassie said. "Maybe he did everything off the books. You know, dodging tax. If he kept his operation small enough then he might not have drawn attention to himself."

"In which case there will still be a trail of sorts; accounts, computers… something."

"Maybe one of his friends will be able to tell us more in light of his demise."

"Let's hope so but, in the meantime, make sure Eric keeps digging. So far, all we have to go on is a functioning alcoholic with dubious finances and the fact that Freddie Mayes liked to put it about a bit but was otherwise a decent bloke who looked after his friends. Something tells me we've barely scratched the surface on this one." Tom's brow furrowed. "It might be worth speaking to James Lewis again as well. He seemed eager to help and he had a key to this place. Maybe his father was a bit more open with his son than with his wife."

"Worth a shout," Cassie agreed.

"First off, let's go and speak with another of Freddie's closest friends, Eddie Drew. See what he has to say for himself."

CHAPTER THIRTEEN

"Good afternoon," the lady sitting behind the desk said, greeting them with a broad smile. She was what Tom Janssen would describe as highly polished. She was dressed in a business suit and her hair and make-up were fastidiously well presented. "How can I help you today?"

The smile never left her face, it was so well practised it must have become second nature. Tom took out his identification and discreetly showed her his warrant card.

"We would like to speak with Mr Edward Drew if he's available."

She glanced over her shoulder and up towards a window overlooking the showroom from a mezzanine above. Returning her attention to them, she tilted her head to one side, maintaining her smile.

"I'll need to see if he's available."

Tom returned her smile. "Thank you. We'll wait."

He stepped away from the reception desk and joined Cassie who was eyeing a convertible coupe which was the centrepiece of the display. Every vehicle was a high-end marque. The showroom was almost cavernous, bordered on three sides by double-height walls of glass and the floor was high-gloss black porcelain. At one end were a selection of SUV models, then came a selection of family saloons and estates and ended up with the sports models where they now stood. Cassie was leaning over and examining the interior of one as he came alongside.

Tom lowered his voice. He wasn't concerned with being overheard but the environment seemed to lend itself to quiet reflection.

"See yourself in one of these?"

She glanced up at him, smiling. "I don't think my salary would stretch to one. Unless you want to give me a pay rise."

"Maybe something a bit older," he said, turning his gaze to the lines of used cars outside. Even these would most likely be beyond her reach, not one of them looked to be over three years old.

"Nah," Cassie said, bringing herself upright. "They're all a bit too flash. It's not really me, is it?"

The receptionist appeared before he could reply.

"Mr Drew will see you now," she said, indicating towards a set of stairs nearby in one corner of the building.

The stairs were partially enclosed, opening out onto a landing overlooking the showroom beyond. Only one door was present and it opened as they approached. They were met by a man in his forties. He cut quite a smart figure in an expensively tailored shirt and trousers. His tie was centred, the knot precise. His hair was swept back from his head, by way of far too much product, and meticulously crafted. He spoke in such a way as to convey calm authority, his voice resonating.

"Detectives. Edward Drew," he said, introducing himself and offering Tom his hand. They shook and Tom introduced Cassie who bobbed her head by way of a greeting but kept her hands by her side. "Please, come through."

Drew led them into his office, stepping aside to allow them to pass before closing the door.

"What is it I can do for Norfolk's finest?" he asked, offering them both a seat in front of his desk. Only one was present and he swiftly picked up another from the edge of the room and brought it across, placing it down in front of Cassie and gesturing for her to sit down with an open palm. She smiled politely but waited for Drew to head around to the other side of the desk before she sat down.

Tom took his seat as Drew sank into his high-backed leather faced chair. Turning back to them, he placed his elbows on the desk in front of him, clasping his hands together and interlocking his fingers.

Tom glanced at Cassie who was already taking out her notebook and a pen.

"We understand you are good friends with Freddie Mayes," Tom said.

"Yes, Freddie and I go way back," Drew said, his pleasant demeanour dissipating at mention of the name. "Katrina called me yesterday. What a nightmare this has been for her. For all of us. Are you any closer to understanding who did this to him?"

"Enquiries are ongoing," Tom said. Drew's dissatisfaction with the reply was evident.

"Well whoever is responsible should be strung up!"

Tom inclined his head to one side. "I appreciate the sentiment—"

"Sentiment?" Drew said, not making any effort to tone down his response. "Freddie was a decent man, served his country. To go out like that is a disgrace."

"Perhaps you could help us understand Freddie's life a little? It might help us track down his killer."

"Yes, yes, of course. Anything I can do to help."

"We're trying to establish a motive for his murder. So far, everyone seems to hold Freddie in high esteem."

"Quite right. He was one of the good guys."

"There has been the suggestion that Freddie had a weakness, that he was… somewhat promiscuous in his personal life. Is that something you can comment on?"

Drew sat upright, folding his arms across his chest and took a deep breath. "Look, nobody's perfect. Do you think that might be why he was targeted?"

"It's possible," Tom said. "Was he seeing anyone in particular?"

Drew sank back into his chair, slowly shaking his head. "I suppose Katrina probably knew, she's not daft. It's likely to come out anyway."

"What is?"

"That Freddie used to enjoy casual relationships. I mean, it was common knowledge among us, his friends. The rate he went at it, Katrina would need to be blind to have missed it."

"Do you have any names?"

Drew shook his head. "He used one of those dating apps." He chuckled dryly. "I say dating, it was a hook up app. I don't think anyone was under any illusion that it would be something long lasting. Certainly not Freddie, at any rate."

"Is it possible that one of these women thought differently or they had a partner who might not have cared for what Freddie was up to?"

Drew's lips rattled as he exhaled through them. "Who knows? He never told me about any problems. I know a couple of them he was involved with were married though, Freddie said so, so I suppose that's quite possible."

"But no names?"

Drew shook his head. "No, no names. Sorry."

Tom's gaze drifted to a framed photograph on the desk to Drew's left. It was a shot Tom had seen before, at Freddie's house. Drew noticed, scooping it up and holding it in front of him.

"Years of service, multiple tours… and to end up dying in sleepy old Norfolk," Drew said, shaking his head and passing the picture frame across to Tom who accepted it. He examined the photo. "Each of the boys has this shot, Inspector. It serves as a constant reminder for us."

"A reminder of what?" Tom asked passing it back.

Drew held it in one hand, staring at the image. "Have you ever been in the forces?" Tom shook his head. "Well, let me tell you, over there in Helmand it was something else entirely. You wouldn't believe it. We depended on one another to make it through each day alive. No exaggeration. Sorry, I don't mean to patronise you, Inspector. I imagine you've had similar times in your job where you have to rely on the man, or woman," he said, eyeing Cassie, "standing next to you. It's not an experience you forget."

"You remain close to your unit?"

"The troop, yes," Drew said, subtly correcting Tom's description.

"Do you have any idea who might wish harm on Freddie?"

Drew sat forward, meeting Tom's eye and shaking his head. "I really can't, no."

"How's business?" Tom asked, changing tack.

Drew bobbed his head. "Business is good."

"And the others?" Tom asked, flicking a casual hand towards the picture frame they'd just looked at. Drew picked it up again, smiling as he scanned the faces.

"Some better than others," he said. "Harry Oakes is doing all right. Me and Freddie too. We lost Woody a while back. That was a shame."

"Woody?" Tom asked. It wasn't a name they'd heard mentioned.

"Carl," Drew said, turning the photograph in Tom's direction and pointing to one of the two figures kneeling in the shot. "Carl Woodly, here on the left."

"Woodly. Is he any relation to Joe by any chance?"

Drew nodded. "Yes. Joe is Carl's younger brother although the name is about the only comparison you can draw between the two of them."

"You don't hold Joe in high regard then?"

Drew smiled. "No. Joe's a bit of a waster, always has been. Carl used to talk about trying to keep his brother on the straight and narrow, finding him work, stepping in between Joe and their father but he never made much headway with him from what I can tell."

"Right. What did you say happened to Carl?"

Drew inhaled deeply, turning the picture back and staring hard at it. "He died... oh, a year or two back now," he said frowning. "I'm not sure exactly." His eyes flicked up at Tom and then Cassie before he set the picture back on his desk where it belonged. "House fire. Carl was asleep inside, didn't stand a chance."

"I see." Tom exchanged a brief look with Cassie. "Are you aware of the shooting that happened late last night?"

"I heard a body had been found," Drew said, his brow furrowing. "But I wasn't aware of it being a shooting though."

"We confirmed the identity of the victim earlier today. It was Andy Lewis."

Tom fixed his gaze on Drew, watching for a reaction. Drew's lips parted and his eyes widened, his self-assuredness escaping him. This was news to him.

"Andy? Are you sure?" he asked. "I mean... really sure?"

"He has been positively identified by his next of kin."

"My God," Drew said quietly, his head dipping forward as he brought a hand to his face, covering his mouth and nose. "I had no idea."

"Someone lured him out there on a false pretence and then shot him, point blank. It looks very much like they did similar with Freddie Mayes last week. Any idea why someone might be targeting your old troop, Mr Drew?"

Drew brought his hands together as if in prayer before his face, forefingers touching the tip of his nose. He exhaled slowly before his eyes flicked across at Tom.

"No," he said softly, removing his hands from his face. "I wish I did."

"It's curious to me, Mr Drew," Tom said, fixing him with a stare, "how every person we speak with about you and your friends all cite how close you are to one another and yet, it appears someone has taken great exception to you without justifiable cause. For all we know this person may well be looking to pick you off one by one. But none of you seem to have a clue as to why that might be."

Drew held Tom's gaze. "I can see how that might be puzzling for you, Inspector. Believe me, if I knew what was going on I would say so."

"Would you? I truly hope so, Mr Drew. I really do. You see, you might be next on the list."

Drew laughed at the comment throwing his head back as he did so. It struck Tom as theatrical, too theatrical to be genuine.

"I don't think it's a laughing matter," Tom said. "If I were you, I would look at taking precautions."

Drew brought himself upright. "I think I'm quite capable of taking care of myself, Inspector Janssen. Believe me."

"I wonder if both Freddie and Andy would have said the same if I'd spoken to them this time last week."

Drew sniffed hard before exhaling audibly. "You might be right, but somehow I doubt it. Besides, I've got an advantage they didn't have."

"Which is?"

"Thanks to you, I'll be able to see it coming." Drew said coolly. "Although, I still don't see it. Andy and Freddie were great guys, the kind you would want by your side. After all, I would know. I reckon you're on the wrong path there but... I can see why you're asking the question."

"Nonetheless, we will be speaking to every member of the troop who lives locally," Tom said. "Which appears to be most of you. Wouldn't you say that was unusual? For you all to choose Norfolk to live in having left the forces, I mean."

Drew cocked his head, turning the corners of his mouth down. "Maybe so, I couldn't really speak for anyone else but, as I said, Inspector, we were under immense pressure over there. It wasn't usual times, you know. I saw when I was back home how people viewed the war in Afghanistan and, believe me, it wasn't anywhere near as organised as you probably think. For large parts of our tours we were pretty much on our own out there. It stands to reason that we'd stick together afterwards. I doubt it's something you can really understand unless you've been through it."

Tom nodded, glancing at Cassie. She indicated she had nothing to add and Tom turned back to Drew, reaching into his pocket and taking out one of his contact cards. He handed it across and Drew took it, glancing at the details.

"I admire your confidence but should you see anything unusual or out of place, do call us, Mr Drew. It remains to be seen if your troop are indeed the targets but you should be careful nevertheless."

Drew held the card up and tipped his head in Tom's direction. "I will bear it in mind, thank you. And you'll keep me abreast of any developments?"

"If there's anything we think you need to know, then we'll be in touch."

"I'd appreciate it, Inspector."

They bid him goodbye and Drew walked them to the door, holding it open for them as they passed through. They heard the door closing before they'd reached the stairs. Cassie cast a sideways glance at Tom as they descended.

"For a bunch of guys who have stayed so close to one another, they seem remarkably blind as to what's going on around them. Interesting about Carl Woodly, too. I think we should have a look at this house fire that he died in."

He was inclined to agree. He lowered his voice as they reached the showroom floor, their shoes squeaking on the polished porcelain surface as they walked.

"I wonder how many more of them will have to die before someone starts to talk?"

CHAPTER FOURTEEN

EDDIE DREW PARTED the blinds of his office window with the fingers of his right hand. He watched the detectives as they crossed the showroom floor and left through the double doors, disappearing from view. Releasing the blinds, they closed and he walked back to his desk. Perching himself on the end, he folded his arms across his chest, thinking hard about what he should do. Detective Inspector Janssen struck him as a shrewd investigator. He didn't appear to say everything that came to mind. The sergeant was another one who seemed to pay close attention. Several times he'd caught her watching him, reading his body language. They weren't fools but at the same time he didn't get the impression they were lying to him. They were genuinely perplexed about the circumstances surrounding Freddie and Andy's deaths.

Turning, he picked up his mobile from his desk and unlocked it, tapping the tile for one of those he had set up on speed dial on the home screen. The call connected and was answered almost immediately.

"Eddie, how are you?" a jovial voice said.

"I'm all good," Eddie replied, intentionally lightening his tone.

"Listen, I'm sorry I haven't got back to you since you called me on Sunday but it's been… a little manic."

"That's okay. I was calling about Freddie."

"Yeah, I figured," Drew said, stepping away from his desk and pacing the office, thrusting his free hand into his pocket. "It's not good. I've just had the police here asking about it."

"What did you say?"

"What the hell could I say?" Drew countered. "I hadn't seen him since the middle of last week. As far as I knew, everything was cool. How about you?"

"No, I didn't realise anything was wrong either."

Drew took a breath. "From what they said to me, it sounded like they've already spoken to some of the troop."

"I should expect a visit then. What are they like?"

"Sharp. Serious," Drew said. "Don't try and bluff them. They don't seem the type. From what I could gather, I reckon they're working their way through all of us but, at the moment, they haven't got a clue what's going on."

"What do *you* think is going on?"

The tone had changed. He was concerned, it was obvious.

"You don't know about Andy, do you?"

"What about him?"

"He's dead."

There was silence at the other end of the line. It lasted for at least half a minute before he spoke again.

"How?"

"Somebody ambushed him. They lured him out to the middle of nowhere and shot him." He could hear the tension in his voice, feel the tightness in his chest. "The police just told me. It's definitely Andy but I don't think they've gone public with it yet."

"Anything else?"

"Yeah, they were asking about the rest of the troop… and about Joe."

"Woody's brother?"

"Yeah. They must have come across Joe but I don't know how. Their ears pricked up when I mentioned Woody. Maybe it was that whole thing last month with Catton," Drew said.

"Didn't Freddie say that was all sorted?"

"Yeah... but I'm not so sure now. I mean, how can we be?" He waited, letting the information sink in before asking the question. "What do you think we should do?"

"I think we need to meet, thrash it out."

Drew felt uncertain. "Are you sure that's a good idea under the circumstances?"

"Yes, of course. It would be unusual if we didn't meet under the circumstances, don't you think? Besides, we need to try and figure this out and it'd probably be better done in person than by keeping digital records."

"Good point," Drew said. "I'll drop by Harry's place, make sure he's on board."

"Let's keep it casual. Meet for a drink like we often do, usual place, same time. It'll draw less attention that way."

"All right. I'll see you there," Drew said. He was about to hang up before quickly adding, "Greg, have you seen anything... odd going on around your way recently?"

"No, I can't say I have. Don't tell me you're getting all paranoid about this."

"Two of the guys are dead, so yeah, I'm a bit worried. I think that's normal."

"The police have rattled you, Eddie, that's all. This is nothing we can't handle. We've been through far worse. I'm sure there's nothing to it and so there's nothing to worry about."

"Freddie said that last month, remember? Now he's dead," Drew said, regretting his aggressive tone as soon as he spoke the words.

"Like I said, you're rattled. I get that. Take a breath, go and speak with Harry and, whatever else you do, stay calm. All right?"

Drew looked to the ceiling, taking a deep breath and closing his eyes.

"Okay. I'll have a word with Harry and we'll meet as normal."

He hung up, slipping the mobile into his pocket. Greg was right, he was rattled. When Katrina called he'd been concerned, wondering what Freddie had got himself into. Now there was Andy. This was all coming too close to home.

Crossing the office, he opened the door to the cupboard. Mounted on the wall to the back of the top shelf was a laptop safe. Briefly glancing over his shoulder at the door to make sure it was closed, he turned back and tapped the six-digit code into the keypad. Each number beeped as he pressed them, then a longer beep sounded to signify it was unlocked. He drew the heavy metal door open and reached inside. His fingers curled around the grip of the pistol and he withdrew it. The feel of the weapon in his hand was reassuring. Moving the slide, he checked that a round was chambered and then tucked it into the rear waistband of his trousers.

Closing the safe, he slid his jacket from the hanger on the back of the office door and put it on. Grasping the door handle with his right hand, he paused, placing the flat of his left hand on the face of the door and leaning in to rest his forehead against it too. He stood there for a moment taking two or three measured breaths and seeking to calm his mind. The desk phone rang snapping him out of his search for solace but he ignored it, pulling open the door. Voices carried from below and he made his way downstairs.

Reaching the showroom, Natalie, on the reception desk, removed the phone from her ear and called out to him.

"Mr Drew, I have a call for you!"

"Take a message," he said without looking. Instead, he strode outside and crossed the lot to where his car was parked. The vehicle detected his presence and unlocked as he approached. Taking off his jacket, he tossed it onto the passenger seat and looked back towards the showroom. The mechanics were busy in the service bay and no one was present on the lot. Taking the weapon from his waistband, he placed it in the pocket of the driver's door and got in, pressing the engine start button. Drawing his seatbelt across his chest, he engaged first gear and drove the short distance across the lot to the highway.

Nothing was coming from either left or right and he was about to pull out when a figure stepped in front of the car. He slammed on the brakes, bringing the car to such an abrupt stop that the engine stuttered and stalled. The man stood in front of the car, barring the way. It took a moment for Drew to recognise him. The last time they'd seen one another, he didn't look like this. His hair hung to his shoulders and he had weeks of unrestrained growth of facial hair. He looked dirty and unkempt but the eyes were still the same, cold and piercing, as he stared directly into his own. The man leaned forward, placing both palms flat on the bonnet of the car but he said nothing. His facial expression was fixed and the eyes met Drew's, glaring at him. The wildness in them scared him.

Drew reached for his gun, then hurriedly the door handle, only to be restrained by the seatbelt which engaged, locking him in place. By the time he'd undone it and clambered out the man was on the far side of the road and passing through the undergrowth of the tree line beyond the verge. Drew broke into a run, nearly being struck by a passing van he hadn't seen coming. The driver swerved to avoid him and then reactively blasted the horn but Drew paid no attention as he cannoned through the bushes in his pursuit.

Branches scratched at his face and he nearly lost his footing twice in quick succession on the uneven ground before the vegetation thinned enough for him to look around in search of his quarry. He found himself in a small clearing. It must be around twenty metres away from the road because the sound of passing traffic was muffled by the surrounding brush and trees. Nothing moved aside from the branches overhead, swaying gently in the breeze. Crows cawed from above and he heard rustling in nearby bushes but he couldn't make out what had caused it. A fallen tree lay off to his right whereas to the left the brush was largely impenetrable, marking natural barriers to his field of vision.

Despite the pistol in his hands he felt vulnerable, his headlong chase into the trees had been foolish and now he stood alone, unsure of his quarry's position or intention. Discretion seemed a better course of action and he took a step backwards, seeking to retrace his route back to the road. A stick cracked away to his right and he spun in that direction, bringing the weapon to bear. He released the safety catch and waited, staring into the undergrowth and willing himself to see beyond what he could.

"I see you, Catton!" he shouted. He waited but no response was forthcoming. Listening intently, he scanned the undergrowth keeping his weapon trained on wherever his eyes went. "We all see you!"

His voice carried, silencing the birds in the trees overhead. Still there was no reply.

"Come near me again and I'll have you," he barked. "Do you hear me, Catton? I'll have you!"

Retreating several steps from his position, he reapplied the safety and tucked the weapon back into his waistband. He was almost certain Catton was long gone but it felt reassuring to voice the threat. Once he reached the edge of the clearing, he used both hands to ease the branches aside realising then that at least one of them had gashed the side of his cheek on his previous pass. He cursed his own stupidity. Within five minutes of ending the telephone call he'd done exactly what he'd been instructed not to do. He had allowed himself to be baited.

This time, he'd got away with it. Maybe next time he wouldn't.

─────────

BARELY TEN METRES away from where Drew had been standing, John Catton emerged from behind a large sycamore tree where he'd been safely shielded from view. He could see the back of Drew's white shirt passing through the undergrowth heading towards the road. Leaning back, he rested his head against the tree, his eyes scanning the canopy above observing the passing clouds through the only break in the foliage. Only now did he breathe easy. Eddie Drew was going to get what he deserved.

It was just a matter of time.

CHAPTER FIFTEEN

Tom Janssen pulled the car into the kerb and switched off the engine. The parking lights remained on and he glanced towards the house. It was dark now, despite being only a quarter to seven in the evening. The days would lengthen from here on in but for now, with rolling clouds above, it felt later than it was. Having called in on his boat to collect his mail, he was heading over to Alice's where he'd been spending more and more time of late but, before doing so, chose to call in on the Woodly residence. It was between his place and Alice's anyway and both Cassie and Eric found the discussion with Joe Woodly interesting. This took place prior to learning of his brother Carl serving alongside Freddie Mayes and the rest of the troop.

Curious to understand how the ties never came up in the conversation, he was itching to meet Joe. It was his altercation with Freddie Mayes that was the only blot on the recent life of the ex-serviceman. No one else had a bad word to say about him, aside from some as yet unidentified potentially angry husbands.

Much of the house was in darkness with only a single light on in a downstairs room to the rear. The pull-up garage door was open, however, and bathed in fluorescent light. A figure moved inside and it wasn't likely to be Joe. This man was much older, probably his father. He got out of the car and walked up the drive. The man didn't hear his approach, the sound of a radio masking his footsteps. The man was in his mid-fifties, heavy set and with a receding hairline. He was dressed very much for tinkering in a garage; paint-flecked overalls and old trainers held together by a wing and a prayer.

"Hello," Tom said, stepping into the light, still with his hands in his pockets to avoid the cut of the evening breeze. The man was startled. He looked at Tom, a piece of sandpaper in his hand, his eyes narrowing. Tom withdrew his ID but the man turned away from him, focussing on the wood clamped in the vice mounted on the workbench in front of him.

"Police. Yeah, I guessed as much," he said, running the coarse paper down the length of the wood with two even passes before bending down to inspect the smoothness. He ran a thumb slowly along the edge. "Sheila told me you'd been round for Joe." He looked at Tom, tossing the paper aside and brushing the sawdust from his palms. "She said he hadn't done anything but I told her you'd be back. It was only a matter of time."

"It was my detectives who spoke with your son yesterday," Tom said. "I just wanted to go over a couple of things. Your son isn't a suspect."

"Perhaps not yet," he said, stepping towards him and offering his hand. Tom took it. "Paul Woodly," he said with a smile.

"DI Tom Janssen."

Woodly raised an eyebrow. "At this rate we'll have the chief constable around here by the end of the week."

Tom smiled politely.

"Is Joe in?"

Paul shook his head. "Not seen him since I got home. I don't think he's been back here since your lot spoke to him."

"Is that unusual? Where does he stay if not here?"

Paul shrugged, turning back to his vice and releasing the strip of wood he'd been preparing. To Tom it looked like a spindle for a balustrade although it was too short for that. "He stays out with friends… no idea who or where to be honest. I can't keep up with that boy. What's this about anyway?"

Tom glanced around the garage which resembled more of a workshop with benches lining the walls and the variety of equipment on show. A lathe was set off to the left, sawdust piled at the foot of it. "He had an altercation with a man last month. I need to clarify a couple of things," Tom said, keeping the reason for his visit intentionally vague. He nodded towards the machine. "What are you working on?"

Paul glanced at the lathe, then back to Tom. "A dining set; table and chairs." He gestured towards the rear and encouraged Tom to follow him further into the garage.

The building was split in two with the greater area given over to finishing space and separated by a partition wall. In this area, a number of pieces of furniture were in different stages of finishing. A table top was leaned against the far wall, shrouded in a protective shrink wrap with cast-iron legs alongside it. These too were already wrapped for transport. Four chairs were set out side by side and by the looks of them were waiting a finishing coat of either wood stain or varnish.

"Bespoke woodwork," Paul said proudly as Tom eyed the detail work of the chairs. "You can walk into any showroom in the country and buy a dining set but not if you want something unique."

Tom had to admit the craftsmanship was excellent.

"It's beautiful," Tom said, admiring the man's efforts. "I could do with you visiting my boat. There's a ton of work needed there."

"My order book is pretty full for the next couple of months but, after that, I'd be happy to take more on. I love doing the speciality jobs."

"Maybe I'll do that," Tom said, smiling.

"That altercation you mentioned. Was it that thing with Freddie Mayes last month?"

Tom nodded. "Yes. What can you tell me about it?"

"Not a lot really," Paul said, frowning. "Joe didn't want to talk about it. Probably wouldn't have even known about it if it hadn't been seen by someone the wife knows. He's hardly likely to mention it to me."

"Why not?" Tom asked.

Paul's frown deepened. "He doesn't speak much does Joe. You have to drag stuff out of him at the best of times. Hasn't always been that way or, at least, not that bad. Don't get me wrong, he was always a quiet kid, very much in the shadow of his brother."

"Carl?"

Paul met his eye, nodding silently.

"Presumably, Joe knew Freddie Mayes through his brother. Is that right?"

"Yeah, of course. Joe knew Freddie really well. We all do. Carl and the others stayed close."

"Band of brothers type thing?" Tom asked.

Paul's eyes narrowed as if he thought Tom was somehow mocking him and he felt uncomfortable with the scrutiny.

"You've never served, have you?"

Tom shook his head.

"Then you wouldn't understand. What you see as some kind of cheesy camaraderie goes much deeper in reality. If you've trusted people with your life and they you with theirs, it lasts a lifetime. Believe me, it counts for something."

"I didn't mean to imply anything to the contrary. I take you have served yourself then?"

Paul nodded. "Cavalry; three tours of Iraq straddling both campaigns in the Gulf as well as a stint peacekeeping in Bosnia. Fair to say Carl followed in my footsteps; the boy did me proud too." His expression saddened at mention of his son and he became pensive. "Damn I miss that boy. I wish he was still around to help us out with Joe."

"Carl would be a stabilising influence on his brother?"

Paul's expression lightened and he smiled, shaking his head at the same time. "Yeah, you could say that. They were like day and night, those two. To this day I can't see how two boys could grow up side by side, same parents, schooling... and turn out so different. Looking back, Joe was always a little withdrawn but he followed his big brother like he was his shadow. When Carl joined up and went off on deployment, Joe seemed to disappear inside himself."

"He didn't think to sign up as well?"

Paul laughed. "No way. Joe's not the sort. I knew that early on. Way too soft." He looked over his shoulder through the window towards the house. The light was on in the kitchen and Tom could see a woman busy inside. "Sheila will disagree but that's the crux of it. Joe wasn't cut from the same cloth as Carl."

"You've had your problems with Joe," Tom said.

Paul nodded. "I'm sure you've been through his record. He was a decent kid, still is underneath it all, but fell in with the wrong crowd. I know it sounds like an excuse, one you probably hear a lot in your business but it's true. I feel guilty about it to be honest. I was always away... Sheila, home on her own with the boys. By the time I came out it was too late. Joe was well down the wrong path. Not that we didn't try." Paul leaned back against a bench, folding his arms across his chest. "Carl did too. Joe had never managed to hold a job down since leaving school, drifted around a bit. Carl found him work through his friends."

"Freddie Mayes by any chance?"

Paul nodded. "Among others, yes. Eddie Drew, Greg... even Harry found some odd jobs for him to do over at the nurseries for a while. Carl pulled in favours from all over but it didn't do any good. Like I said, you'll have read his file. My youngest is a walking disaster zone, Inspector."

"And you've no idea what the issue was between him and Freddie Mayes that day?"

Paul shook his head. "Knowing Joe, he was probably tapping up Freddie for some money and it pains me to say that. It's what he does, leeches off of people day by day. Once they get sick of him he moves on to the next and keeps going until he comes full circle hoping they have short memories. He must be talented because he's still going although his reputation precedes him."

Tom thought about that. This area wasn't particularly large and word got around. Once a reputation was established, it became difficult to shake.

"What was Carl like?"

Paul's demeanour visibly changed, his arms coming to his sides and disappearing into pockets. He was more comfortable talking about his other son.

"Strong, brave and very sharp," Paul said, smiling proudly. "Didn't get any of that from me, it's all from his mum. He was a bit of a tearaway in his teens but the army sorted him out. It changed him, brought him back a different man. It was the making of him."

"I understand he died in a house fire, is that correct?"

Paul nodded, turning melancholic. "Dodgy electrics and a gas leak. One of those things that just shouldn't happen." He sighed deeply, running his tongue across the edge of his lower lip as he shook his head. "I told him to buy a new build, not trust these old houses and he took my advice. Maybe he would have been better going for one of those older places and fixing it up himself. I guess you can get loose wiring anywhere, can't you."

"That was the cause?" Tom asked.

Paul bobbed his head. "Carl had been out on the tiles. The explosion was so big... happened so fast that he wouldn't have felt a thing, which is something."

"I thought I heard voices," a woman's voice said from behind them. Neither man heard her approach.

"Sorry love," Paul said. "This is Inspector Janssen." Tom smiled at the introduction, Sheila returned it. "He's looking for Joe... again."

"I don't know where he's got to," she said.

"The inspector was asking about Carl," Paul said, the pitch of his tone softening. His wife's face dropped momentarily, the burden of grief still evident.

"I'm sorry," Tom said, reading her expression. "I'm not looking to open old wounds."

"No, no, please don't apologise," Sheila said breaking into a nervous smile. "Sometimes I think we don't bring Carl's name up enough these days. You should come inside, see his room." She beckoned Tom towards the house, her smile broadening.

"Sheila, I'm sure the inspector has better things—"

"No, I'd love to," Tom said, "if that's okay with you, of course?"

Paul exhaled, spreading his palms wide. "Feel free."

Sheila excitedly encouraged Tom to follow and set off towards the house with a spring in her step.

CHAPTER SIXTEEN

SHEILA WOODLY HELD the back door open for Tom and once he crossed the threshold, he took the weight of it and she hurried to the hob, turning two of the burners to a lower setting. A mixture of fragrant spices filled the room and Tom felt guilty for intruding.

"If this is a bad time..." he began but she waved away his comment, instead turning and walking out of the kitchen and once again, encouraged him to follow.

He glanced over his shoulder and saw the form of Paul Woodly returning to his work in the garage. He caught up with Sheila as she mounted the stairs. The carpeted treads squeaked underfoot as they went up, the banister shaking as he took a hold of it. The landing was narrow with four doors off it. One room was a bathroom to the front of the house and he could see a double bed through the next. There was a definite sky-blue theme going on in that particular bedroom. Sheila led them to one of the two rooms overlooking the rear garden. Both doors were closed and she hesitated as she grasped the handle of the one to the right.

The moment passed and she opened it, stepping aside and allowing him to enter. She followed a half step behind him. The first thing that struck him was the adolescent presentation. Posters hung on the walls, stuck up with tack and they were sagging under the weight. They must have been put up years ago. They were a mix of feature films, none recent, football players, and a host of military-themed images that seemed more like shoot-em-up computer games rather than actual combat stills.

On one wall was a series of shelves and these were adorned with sporting trophies, medals hanging from hooks attached beneath them. Tom crossed over and examined them. They all had small brass-effect plaques with inscriptions upon them. The trophies themselves were made of plastic and partly wrapped in foil. He had seen many of these over the years, teenage prizes handed out by schools and sports teams.

"Carl was always a winner," Sheila said from behind him. He glanced over his shoulder, smiling. "Picking up awards left, right and centre."

Alongside the bed was a small desk. Sitting on top was a games console. Tom didn't have one, gaming wasn't his thing but again, this seemed old technology. The bed was a single and placed sideways up against the wall beneath the window to ensure the small room maximised the available space for the incumbent. The bed appeared to have been slept in recently. Sheila noticed his lingering gaze as she absently toyed with her necklace.

"I sleep in here occasionally," she said quietly. He looked at her and she seemed embarrassed by the revelation and he wondered why she felt the need to share it. "I feel closer to him that way."

No appropriate words came to mind, so he said nothing, merely smiled and looked away.

"Does that seem odd to you, Inspector?"

The tone of the question piqued his curiosity. It wasn't a challenge as such, coming across more as a request for affirmation than anything else. Again, he didn't know what to say. Sheila Woodly hadn't come to terms with the loss of her son. This wasn't a level of grief he could easily relate to.

"I imagine we could all cling to anything that reminds us of someone we've lost should the circumstances arise," he said. He glanced around the room again. "I was under the impression, from speaking with your husband, that Carl had his own place."

"He did," she confirmed, sitting down on the end of the bed, placing her hands together in her lap. "Once Carl left for his basic training, he never lived here again, not really. He would come home on leave from time to time but more often than not he'd head away with his mates. The army opened his mind to the possibilities that the world had to offer. He didn't see that here in Norfolk."

Tom inclined his head to one side. This he could relate to.

"How old was he when he left?"

"Oh, Carl would have signed up on his sixteenth birthday if I had let him. His father was all for it, unsurprising I suppose seeing as he talked about nothing but the army the whole time the boys were growing up. I knew Carl would follow the same path, it was obvious from when he was seven years old." Sheila's face took on a faraway look. Then she appeared to shake herself back to the present. "I relented when he turned seventeen. I figured he was going to anyway and hanging around doing nothing after he left school wasn't doing him any good. If he hadn't joined, he might have gone the same way as his brother."

"But he didn't go straight on active service, did he?" Tom asked, thinking on the lad's age.

"Oh no, he couldn't until he was eighteen at least. When he came out, I was so pleased that he chose to come home. Well, to Norfolk at least."

"Were you surprised?" he asked. "Bearing in mind what you just said about broadening his horizons."

Sheila thought about it for a moment, her brow furrowing. "Yes and no. When his visits home became more infrequent, I figured he would never come back. There was nothing for him here. After all, most of his friends from school left in search of work or entertainment but he did and I was grateful for that."

"How old must he have been then, when he came home?"

"He was twenty-six when he came out."

Tom looked around the room. She guessed what he was thinking.

"This is pretty much how he left his room when he joined up, Inspector. As I said, he hardly stayed here after that and, when he did, he wasn't bothered about the posters or whatever. He'd outgrown it all," she said, looking around the room. "He'd outgrown the room, this house, all of his friends." She shook her head. "But this is the time I choose to remember when I think about him. I can still see the teenager who was so excited about ploughing his own furrow, taking on the world, rather than the haunted, jaded shell that came back from Afghanistan."

Paul hadn't mentioned anything of this which surprised him. Perhaps it wasn't only Sheila struggling to come to terms with the loss of their son.

"Sometimes," Sheila continued, "I think that's part of the reason he came back to Norfolk, to come back to where he felt safe. It was dull but he was always safe. I can see from the look on your face this is all news to you, Inspector."

"I didn't realise I was so easy to read," he replied.

She laughed but it was bitter. "I'm afraid my husband doesn't want to confront that reality. He holds so much of his own experience in such high regard that he can't recognise his son's experience differed so much. Don't get me wrong, I'm incredibly proud of Carl, we all are, but being out there... it changed him. Maybe he would have found himself again in time but... it wasn't to be."

"Tell me, did Carl ever speak about the other members of his troop? Those who also came to Norfolk after they left."

"Yes, all of the time. They were all very close," she said. "I assume you are asking for a reason."

"Did he ever express any concerns about them, speak about any problems or issues he was having?"

"No!" Paul said, standing in the doorway.

Neither of them heard him coming up the stairs and Tom wondered how long he'd been on the landing before choosing to enter.

"No," Paul reiterated, lowering his voice. "They were a tight group, always looking out for one another, like I told you earlier."

"Yes, you did," Tom said, not breaking step. "You mentioned some of them by name. How well did you know them personally?"

Paul took another step inside the room. With the three of them in there, despite Sheila sitting on the bed, the room felt cramped and small. Paul looked around as if he was coming in for the first time. Maybe it had been a while since he'd last been in there.

"It's a close community. Everyone knows everyone," Paul said.

"Have you seen any of them recently?"

"Not really, no," Paul said. Sheila didn't look likely to speak and, in any event, he continued. "I saw Freddie a couple of times earlier in the year. He was trying to throw some work Joe's way again. I was pleased with Freddie for doing that, what with Joe letting him down so badly before. I reckon he did it out of respect for Carl. Likewise with Greg."

"Greg Ellis?" Tom clarified.

Paul nodded. "He came by at the tail end of last summer with an offer of work for Joe."

"Doing what?"

Paul shrugged. "At the clubhouse of his golf course I think. It might have been in the bar or the kitchens, I'm not sure. But it didn't last."

"Greg had to let him go," Sheila said, drawing a scowl from her husband. She looked him straight in the eye. "Well, there's no point glossing over it, is there? The inspector will only go and ask Greg himself!"

Paul sighed, shaking his head. "Yes. That's true." He turned to Tom. "Joe was caught stealing."

"From the till?" Tom asked.

"No, worse. From the customers," Paul said, looking deflated. "Greg smoothed it over with them but he wasn't happy. I mean, you can't blame him. He managed to keep your lot out of it which we were grateful for." He cast a look at his wife who half-heartedly smiled her support. "Joe has a lot of problems, Inspector. Carl's death hit him hard… very hard. I don't think we realised, did we, love?"

Sheila shook her head. "We were so caught up in ourselves that we didn't see how bad it was for Joe. He had his problems before but Carl's death just seemed to magnify everything. I don't think we've got a grip of it yet either."

"We make too many excuses for the lad, Inspector," Paul said, drawing himself upright, the military rigidity of his earlier career showing through in that moment. "But I fear it's too late now."

Tom looked between the two of them, each drifting over their own memories.

"How about the others, have they been in touch?"

Paul shook his head. "No, I can't say they have. I remember a number of them calling by in the days and weeks after Carl… after the fire. But other than Greg and Freddie—"

"What about John?" Sheila said, her head coming up. "He was here a couple of times."

"John?" Tom asked.

"John Catton," Sheila said, turning from him to her husband. "You remember, Paul."

"Yes, come to think of it, he did stop by," Paul said, his eyes looking up as he sought to remember. "A few months back, before Christmas, I think."

"No, it must have been more recent than that," Sheila said. The correction irritated her husband. "It was New Year, I'm sure."

Paul screwed up his face, thinking hard. "You could be right but he wasn't here for long. I sent him on his way quick smart."

"Why?" Tom asked. "What did he want?"

"I'm afraid I didn't give him much time to explain, Inspector. You see, John Catton is a strange one. I remember Carl bringing him around soon after they redeployed back to the UK. John was an oddball back then. Some people can handle active service and others... well, they can't maintain what's needed for the length of time required. I saw it myself in the Balkans. It's not their fault, I should add, but living like that, under those conditions, can destabilise some people."

"Are you saying John Catton is mentally unstable?"

"As clear a case as you're ever likely to see, yes. The boy needed help and... I sure hope he's got it by now, otherwise I fear for him, I really do."

"And you've no idea what he wanted?"

"Money, I should imagine by the look of him," Paul said. "Looked like he'd been sleeping rough. He was in a hell of a state."

"We should have helped him, Paul. Not sent him away like that," Sheila said.

"I did what I thought was best," Paul said, emphasising the comment and tilting his head in her direction but not meeting her eye. "John being as he was... would have upset Joe and he's got enough to deal with as it is... we all do."

"Any idea where I can find him, Catton?" Tom asked, making a note of the name. He looked between the two of them. They looked at one another before they both shook their heads.

"I'm sorry, Inspector," Paul said, shrugging. "You could trawl the pubs... or the hostels maybe. Try your luck. He's not from around here and so he may have moved on. Who knows?"

"Okay, thanks. Where is he from?"

"Scotland," Paul said. "Central belt. Fife, if I remember right from what Carl told me but that was a long time ago."

"Can you describe him to me?"

"Just shy of six foot, slim guy, especially now. Brown hair, wild eyes... you'd know him if you came across him, that's for certain."

"Okay, thanks very much," Tom said. He took out one of his contact cards and handed it to Paul. "If he shows up again, please could you give me a call and I'll still need to speak to Joe again as well. It would be great if he called me rather than me chasing him down. As I said, he's not a suspect but I do need to speak with him."

The couple both nodded and Paul tilted the card in Tom's direction.

"I'll do my best for you, Inspector."

CHAPTER SEVENTEEN

PAUL WOODLY STEPPED BACK from the porch and into the house, closing the front door behind him. Sheila waited for him at the bottom of the stairs, her arms folded defiantly across her chest. He paused, momentarily meeting her eye, but no words were exchanged and instead he took a breath before walking back towards the kitchen.

"You should have said more."

Paul stopped in his tracks, hesitating at the entrance to the kitchen. He didn't turn around but could feel the heat of her stare on his back.

"And what would you have me say... to the police of all people?"

"You could start by telling the truth."

He turned, she was opposite him now at the end of the hall, her back to the front door. She still held her arms tight across her midriff. Her stance irritated him. Her entire attitude irritated him but he suppressed the first comments that came to mind.

"And what do you mean by that?

"You know full well," she said, allowing her arms to fall by her side. "You know Johnny came here not so long ago. Why on earth did you bother to lie about that?"

"I didn't lie," Paul replied although he recognised the lack of conviction in his tone. He shook his head. "It slipped my mind, that's all."

His wife stared at him, cocking her head to one side. She knew him better than anyone, she always had.

"What did he want, Johnny, I mean?"

"I told you, money. Catton's a shadow of his former self and would probably spend anything we gave him on drugs. He's not the same lad Carl introduced us to, Sheila, you should see that.

"You still should have helped him," Sheila said, looking away. "For Carl's sake, if for no other reason."

Her tone was less aggressive, no longer in search of a confrontation. He was grateful for that.

"Whatever we did for him, it would never have been enough. Don't you see that?"

Sheila sighed, rolling her eyes as she was prone to do when disagreeing with him.

"Besides," he continued, "you're a fine one to talk about telling the truth."

"Meaning?"

The defiance was back.

"You still cling to this rose-tinted view of Carl. He isn't what you make him out to be, not any more."

"That's because he's dead, Dad."

Paul turned to see Joe standing behind him. How long he'd been there he hadn't a clue. Under his father's watchful eye, Joe wilted, nervously shifting his weight between his feet. Paul's gaze narrowed, focussing on his younger son as he stepped from the hall into the kitchen towards him. Joe took a half step back in response to his father's advance.

"I'm well aware of that, boy," he said. "I remember that every day when I open my eyes… and again when I look at you."

"That's enough, Paul!" Sheila said, entering the kitchen behind him.

"Is it?" Paul said, turning to her. He slowly raised a pointed finger back at their son without looking over his shoulder. "Carl wasn't the same when he came back, not after Afghanistan. But he was still twice the man that this one will ever be."

Sheila looked past him to Joe, who shrunk even further within himself.

"That's not fair," she said, "and you know it."

"No, what's not fair is how I have to listen…" He glanced at Joe. "How *we have* to listen to you reminding us of how great Carl was every day. It isn't true now and it probably never was."

"You loved him!"

"Yes, I did… and I still do, Sheila, but talking him up all the time…" he gestured to the upstairs, "and maintaining a bloody shrine to him is utter nonsense. We need to move on. He's not coming back, you know. You need to take more of your tablets, woman."

Sheila stepped forward and slapped him across the face. A flash of anger reared within him and he advanced on her, raising his own hand. Someone grasped his wrist, restraining him and stopping his retaliation. He spun on Joe, who immediately released his grip and stepped back.

"Don't, Dad," he said meekly, averting his eyes.

Paul recognised the fear in them but at the same time saw his mother's defiance. He definitely took after her side of the family, not his own. He lowered his raised hand, turning back to his wife, feeling his anger dissipate to be replaced with shame for almost losing his temper.

"Nothing good can come from looking back all the time," he said quietly. He turned away from her and shot a glance towards Joe. "Don't worry about any dinner for me. I'm not hungry. I'll be in the garage if anyone wants me."

He moved off, stopping as he came alongside Joe. Fishing out the contact card Tom Janssen gave him from his pocket, he handed it to Joe who accepted with obvious reluctance.

"What's this?" Joe asked.

"The inspector wants a word with you," he said coldly. "I'd

suggest you call him sooner rather than later. And be mindful of what you say, boy. He's smart. Way smarter than you."

Joe glanced at the card in his hand, at his mother and then towards the departing form of his father's back. Paul reached the back door, looking over his shoulder as he placed a hand on the frame.

"I think they're looking for someone to pin Freddie's death on," he said, meeting Joe's eye. "There would be nothing simpler than finding a junkie with an axe to grind."

Joe looked away and Paul left the kitchen without another word. Maybe he'd been too hard on Joe, both today and in the past, expecting him to be more like his older brother. That wasn't fair. The two of them weren't cut from the same cloth and Joe just didn't have it in him. He had the same drive and determination, certainly, but he channelled it into other aspects of his personality, manifesting in supreme levels of deceit, manipulation and self-delusion. Self-serving traits to be found in drug addicts the world over. Entering the garage, he pulled the door closed allowing it to slam.

Coming to stand before one of his workbenches, he picked up a stray rag lying among the sawdust. He shook it clear before screwing it up and tossing it to the far side of the bench. Placing both palms flat on the bench, he looked down at the floor between his feet, closing his eyes.

"What did you leave us for, Carl?" he whispered quietly to himself.

CHAPTER EIGHTEEN

Tom Janssen placed the flat of his palms against the temporary fencing, hooking his fingertips through the links and scanned the area beyond. The fenced off area was pretty large, roughly half an acre he guessed. It was mostly scrub strewn with stones and broken brick. Weeds grew sporadically across the site, some of which were easily two-feet high and flowering; probably a result of the curiously alternating weather they'd been having recently swinging between winter chill and unseasonal warmth.

The fence panels were a token gesture of both safety and security. There was nothing present worth stealing; piles of rubble were of no value and no one was likely to set up camp and squat here. He lifted the end of one panel from the concrete block it was set into and slipped between it and the next, walking onto the site. Looking back to where the car was parked, Cassie Knight hung up on her call, glancing at the screen on her handset before slipping it back into her pocket and walking up the slope to join him. He directed her to the access point between panels with a flick of his hand and soon she was alongside him.

"Nice spot," she said, turning and following his gaze.

She was right. From where they stood, at what would have

been the entrance to the property, they had a view of the sea and the coast extending towards the north. There was a strong breeze today, coming in off the North Sea. It had driven the overcast skies greeting them first thing inland. Presently the sky was clear and they were bathed in sunlight even if they couldn't feel the warmth due to the wind chill.

"What did you get from the agents?" he asked.

The site had several *For Sale* signs mounted on the perimeter fencing. The plot was in a prime location with fantastic coastal views but had apparently remained unsold for nearly two years now.

"There's been interest and they reckon it'll be under offer soon enough," she said, reading her notes.

"Any word on the delay? A plot like this is usually sold long before it even hits the open market."

Planning permission was tricky to come by in Norfolk. The dominance of agricultural land-holding and small communities limited the spread of development. Each local council had a development plan, but permissions were often sought but not necessarily granted in order to contain the urban spread. Cassie looked around.

"There was a hold up with the litigation. Seemingly, Carl hadn't sourced adequate insurance cover for the building works and that led to a dispute between the bank and solicitors representing the executors of Carl's estate."

"What kind of dispute?"

"Carl sourced a self-build mortgage, one where the lender advances you stage payments to get you through the building process. Somewhere along the line, someone didn't check the right documentation and sign things off properly," Cassie said, reviewing her notes. "It probably would have gone unnoticed had he continued to meet his repayments but the subsequent fire, along with Carl's death, put paid to that."

Tom stepped through the rubble, little more than piles of dried earth and hardcore. The outline of the foundations was still recognisable but the majority of the building's structure had been razed to the ground, no doubt deemed unsafe after the fire.

"What do we know about the fire?" he asked.

Cassie didn't follow as he patrolled what would have been the interior of the house. She put her notebook away and thrust her hands into her pockets, bracing against the chilling breeze.

"There's some debate about that as well," she said. "The investigator from the fire brigade recorded it as most likely caused by an electrical fault that flashed over in the fuse board at some point in the early hours of that night. The fire that followed took hold and ignited the mains gas connection. The explosion that followed destroyed a significant proportion of the house prior to the arrival of the emergency services."

"What did the coroner rule on Carl's death? Was it caused by the explosion or the fire?"

"Impossible to say. There wasn't enough left of him to carry out a post mortem. The master bedroom was above the utility room where the explosion occurred. DNA samples were obtained from what was left of the house once the fire was brought under control. That's how they concluded he was in the building along with eye-witness accounts to say they saw him inside shortly beforehand."

"So there were no physical remains to speak of?"

Cassie shook her head.

"You said there was a debate."

"Yes, the coroner ruled Carl Woodly's death as accidental due to the fire and explosion. The insurance should have paid out, covering mortgage and rebuilding costs, but they wanted to carry out their own investigation. Unsurprising as they were on the hook for the better part of half a million when it all comes together. Their independent investigation raised the suspicion of arson and they withheld the pay-out. What was the police view at the time, do you know?"

Tom shrugged. "Before my time here. Eric looked into it for me earlier and there wasn't an investigation. He vaguely remembers it but he was still in uniform then. The fire brigade saw it as accidental and so there was nothing to investigate. Tell me, could they back up the arson with anything concrete?"

"There was enough of a grey area for them. They've stuck to their guns. A complaint has been lodged with the Financial Conduct Authority, the ombudsman, by the estate but, in the meantime, the property was subject to a repossession order acquired by the lender. This was granted by the courts last month and that's why the plot is up for sale."

Tom rubbed absently at his chin, eyeing the site.

"A plot like this… must be worth upwards of two hundred thousand pounds, right?" he said.

Cassie nodded. "The agents reckon they'll get more because it comes with services already attached. Why? What are you thinking?"

Tom met her eye, frowning. "How does an ex-trooper like Carl Woodly fund a building project like this? As I understand it, even with a self-build mortgage you still need to have significant finance up front. They won't cover the entire outlay, it's too much of a risk."

"I wonder if Freddie Mayes had anything to do with it," Cassie said. This piqued his interest and he raised a questioning eyebrow. "Freddie's building firm was the main contractor."

"Mate's rates… and fudged the figures?" Tom said.

Cassie inclined her head to one side. "It's certainly possible. They were tight. Freddie offering Joe work and so on. It's quite plausible."

"As is the possibility of cutting corners to cut costs."

"The paper trail shows Building Control signed every stage off and all connections of services were done by qualified contractors. The timings of it seemed to raise suspicions. The ink was barely dry on the sign-offs prior to the fire."

"They thought it was a fraud," Tom said, thinking aloud. "Who was the beneficiary?"

"Only Carl... or his next of kin in the event of his death."

"Did he leave a will?"

Cassie shook her head. "I'll have to check. But I do know he was unmarried and lived alone. That's one reason they were confident it was him inside. Everyone said he lived alone and wasn't dating."

"In light of recent events, I think the investigation into the house fire needs to be reviewed," he said, chewing on his bottom lip. "We've lost Freddie Mayes and Andy Lewis. Prior to that, Carl dies in an event like this. That makes three... they're an unlucky bunch aren't they."

"There's a bit of distance between them though, in both time frame and MO. I mean, Mayes and Lewis were killed close together and in a very public manner in comparison to dying quietly in a domestic fire, if you see what I mean?"

Tom nodded slowly. "Yeah, I see that. But what if our killer was building up to it, gathering confidence or maybe Carl's death didn't deliver the satisfaction they craved. You must have been there at one time in your life where you couldn't wait to get one over someone else, only to eventually manage it and find the expected satisfaction didn't follow."

"So they got more creative, you think?"

"Possibly," he said, drawing breath. "Besides, it looks like something of an assumption that Carl was even present when the explosion took place. I wouldn't mind seeing how much of a sample they found in order to run the DNA test."

Cassie's eyes narrowed as she fixed him with a stare. "What are you thinking; that Carl wasn't inside?" She appeared thoughtful, considering the implications. "The next thing you'll be suggesting Carl Woodly's back seeking revenge from beyond the grave."

Tom smiled at the suggestion but didn't dismiss it. Cassie's lips parted.

"You're not serious?"

"Let's cover all the bases. Run down Carl's financial records and check how he funded all this," he said, making a circular motion with his hand. "While you're at it, double check his current account, savings, credit cards, mobile phone records... everything. Ensure he didn't pop up sometime later when he was supposed to be dead. It's a fact that a ghost returning from the grave would be more of a suspect than we currently have at the moment."

"You *are* serious," Cassie said.

"Damn right," Tom replied. "Remember *canoe man*?"

Cassie had to admit it was possible. That case shocked the nation, a man supposedly dead whose life insurance paid out only for him to turn up alive and well, living a new life in Panama years later. He had faked his death at sea with the help of his wife. Even their children had been kept in the dark.

"If we're looking back at Carl Woodly's finances, do you think we should evaluate the remaining members of the troop as well? If there is a financial motive behind all of this, it would stand to reason that the others would be connected."

Tom thought about it. "There is one trooper who doesn't appear to have access to much finance."

"You're thinking of this Catton character, aren't you?" Cassie asked, glancing up from scribbling in her notebook. "I told Eric to go back to Sheringham where the fight occurred in search of some footage. Uniform didn't bother as no one was seeking to press charges and they were both served a caution. It happened in broad daylight in the centre of town. There must have been someone who captured something on camera in this day and age."

Tom looked at his watch. With a bit of luck, Eric would have achieved just that.

"HERE THEY COME NOW," Eric said, pointing at the screen.

Tom and Cassie entered the ops room to find Eric hunched over his screen. He was keen for them to review the footage.

"That's definitely Joe Woodly," Tom said, resting a hand on the desk beside the detective constable as he leaned in to see. The footage wasn't great, recorded on a low-resolution camera positioned across the street resulting in a grainy black and white picture. They were at least forty yards away, probably more. "Who's he talking to?"

Eric shook his head. "No idea, but look at the state of him. He stands out."

Even with the poor quality, it was clear the man Joe was talking to was distinctive. His hair was long, shoulder length and curly, standing up from his head in every direction. His overall appearance was scruffy and unkempt.

"Do you think this could be the guy the Woodlys were talking about, John Catton?" Cassie asked.

"He certainly fits the description," Tom said.

"This is it coming up," Eric said, interrupting. "Here's Freddie now."

At that moment, Freddie Mayes entered the shot from the right. He was already gesticulating towards them the moment he was in frame across the other side of the street. They watched as he marched straight up to the other two and aggressively pushed Joe away. The latter didn't attempt to stand his ground and was immediately thrown off balance, drawing both arms in front of himself to protect his body from attack. The attack didn't come however.

"Wow. Freddie isn't holding back," Cassie muttered.

Freddie Mayes then turned on the other man, grabbing the front of his coat with both hands and hauling him closer despite the latter's attempts to free himself. Mayes was much larger than either of the others and easily had the advantage.

"What's Joe doing there?" Tom asked. Joe backed away, watching the scuffle unfolding before him but he didn't make any attempt to intervene.

"That's not what he told us the other day," Cassie said. "He said Freddie was roughing up a homeless guy and he felt he had to step in."

"Looks more like they knew each other and Freddie took a dislike to the conversation," Tom said.

"Yeah," Eric said, pausing the footage and pointing at the two men locked together. "He and Mayes are exchanging words. They know each other, must do. Likewise, so does Joe. They were on camera talking for a few minutes before Mayes shows up. They definitely knew each other, you can tell."

Tom lifted himself upright. "It would make sense if this was Catton. It would explain them knowing one another. Have you looked Catton up yet?"

Eric reached to his left, retrieving a folder from the tray next to his screen. Opening it, he scanned the front page.

"John Eoghan Catton, born in the Kingdom of Fife. He served in a forward reconnaissance role during the Afghan war. No priors, no convictions."

"Do we have an address for him?"

"No," Eric shook his head. "But I asked around some of my friends last night after you called. There's this guy who lives up at the old traveller site, you know the one up the old track from Brancaster."

Tom nodded. He was impressed. Eric had generated the lead from their basic conversation following his visit to the Woodlys' house the previous evening and done so by talking to a few friends. His local connections never ceased to amaze him. "Yeah, I thought that was abandoned."

"Me too, but apparently not. This guy's a veteran and he's got a bit of a reputation in the town."

"Reputation for what?" Tom asked.

"For being… a bit off the wall, not that he's ever done anything specific. At least, no one could recount him getting up to anything. Some of the lads refer to him as *Homicidal John*."

"That's interesting seeing as we're in the homicide business," Cassie said with a rueful smile.

"I'm thinking it's got to be one and the same guy, right?" Eric said, glancing between them.

"Likely, yes," Tom said. "Let's go and see what he has to say for himself."

CHAPTER NINETEEN

Tom Janssen pulled the car into the kerb and switched off the engine. Glancing across at Cassie, he smiled.

"We walk from here."

Cassie Knight looked around. They were surrounded on all sides by small bungalows, sixties built, laid out side by side with well-tended lawns and each one a reproduction of the last. She looked confused.

"Where are we?" she asked.

They'd driven to Brancaster, one of the small villages to be found on the main coast road. Tom was familiar with the area and knew exactly the location of where Eric was describing as soon as he mentioned it.

"Come on," he said, cracking open the door. Cassie followed suit and Tom indicated towards a path running between two properties. It was less of a path and more of a track, one chewed up in the past by farm machinery but didn't appear so recently. Grass was now growing in the ruts gouged out by tractors and, judging by the lack of wear to the track, it was dog walkers and mountain bikers who more commonly passed this way these days.

The route wound its way behind the houses and within a

couple of minutes they were enclosed on each side by open farmland. The track was bordered by hedgerows and headed up a shallow incline. Rounding a bend, the track became more or less straight and continued on lined with trees and hedges. The coastal road ran close to sea level with the nature reserve between it and the sea, but to the south side of the road this steady incline rose to a prominent ridge running east to west.

A small group of derelict agricultural barns came into view on their left, shielded by centuries-old trees. Cassie glanced in their direction and Tom stopped to look back the way they'd come. From their vantage point they could now see the water, sunlight glittering off the whitecaps in the distance. Resuming their walk, they approached their destination.

Not quite at the top of the ridge, in a sheltered position surrounded by trees, they could see the makeshift encampment set off to one side of the track. There were only five vehicles, none of them in a roadworthy condition. The tyres on most were flat and they looked like they hadn't moved in years. The windows were mostly covered in green algae, coated in dried leaves, many with moss growing at the base of the windows and along the wiper blades. The first vehicle they came to was an old Nissan hatchback. The vinyl-lined seats were split with the padding visible. An assortment of rubbish lay about the interior, a mixture of old packaging bleached clean of the identifiable labels by years of exposure to the sun.

The next was an old post office delivery van. It was a high-sided vehicle, the traditional red of the Royal Mail now faded and discoloured by time. Any official markings had been removed, most likely when it was decommissioned and sold off. It must have been last seen on the road in the late fifties or early sixties because Tom couldn't recall ever having seen its like on the road in his lifetime. Behind this was a small caravan. Net curtains hung across the windows, they were stained brown and would once have been ivory or perhaps even white. They obscured the interior from view. Beyond the caravan were two other cars, a saloon and a mini-van, and both were in a similar dilapidated condition. The two of them exchanged glances.

Cassie raised her eyebrows and blew out her cheeks. "Is this it? I expected more to be honest."

"What did you envisage, tied-up ponies and kids playing tag?" he asked.

Her face split a broad smile. "Well, now that you mention it that'd be more like it, yeah."

Tom grinned. A rustling in a nearby bush off to their right drew their attention as a small dog appeared. It was predominantly white with a black and brown face and looked like a Jack Russell, only longer in the leg. It was probably a cross but what with, Tom had no idea. It stopped, cocking its head and examining them for a second before yapping broadly in their direction before turning tail and scurrying under the caravan, disappearing from view.

Tom approached the caravan and raised a clenched fist to knock on the door. Before he could connect, it creaked open and a man appeared from within eyeing them warily. Tom took his measure. He was tall, slim and fair. He had several weeks of growth in his facial hair and his general appearance was dishevelled and dirty, looking like he hadn't slept properly in weeks. He sniffed hard, his eyes searching Tom before moving to Cassie behind Tom and to his left.

"John Catton?" Tom asked, confident enough that this was their man from the CCTV footage. The man's eyes came back to Tom and he swallowed hard, nodding.

"Aye. What of it?"

"Police," Tom said, reaching for his identification.

"Yeah, that's obvious," Catton replied. Tom and Cassie exchanged a glance. "You don't exactly look like ramblers, you ken, and I don't see many people walking their dugs around here in suits like. Plus, I dinnae see a dug. At least, not one that isn't mine."

The terrier appeared from under the caravan at that very

moment, ignoring Tom and bounding up the step and through Catton's legs, vanishing into the interior. Tom revealed his warrant card.

"I guess not. DI Tom Janssen." He indicated to Cassie. "This is DS Knight. Cute dog."

Catton glanced over his shoulder inside, presumably at the dog but Tom couldn't see. "Aye, I guess so right enough."

"What's its name?" Tom asked casually.

"Man's Best Friend."

"That the name or a statement?"

Catton raised a single eyebrow. "Both."

Tom nodded. It was unconventional but, looking around at the dilapidated site, so was everything here. "We'd like a word, if that's okay?"

"Whatever it was, I want it on record that I didn't do it, right." Catton looked at each of them in turn, his brow furrowing as he spoke.

"Can we speak inside?" Tom asked.

Catton looked over his shoulder and into the interior, his body obstructing Tom's view. He shook his head, reaching for a coat and stepping down from the caravan.

"Nah. I wasn't expecting company. The housekeeper's not been round yet, so probably best to speak out here."

He closed the door to the caravan and walked to the rear. There was a collapsible camping chair set out before a makeshift brazier, little more than an old metal drum resting upon bricks with multiple holes punched in the side to allow passage of air through to feed the fire. The exterior was severely corroded with rust and the lining on the inside blackened by soot.

Tom glanced around. "I thought this place was abandoned long ago."

"Not quite," Catton said. "Last man standing... sitting... whatever." He inclined his head to one side and smiled at his own joke. Cassie came to join them, leaning against the rear of the old Royal Mail van, keeping her hands in her pockets. Catton's gaze drifted to her and she met it but neither spoke. He looked back at Tom. "So what can I do for the polis?"

"You were involved in a scuffle with Freddie Mayes last month. You remember that?"

Catton's eyes narrowed and he angled his head up to the sky as if to feel the sunshine on his face. "Freddie, aye. So?"

"What was it about?"

"Nothing much," he said, turning his attention back to Tom. "Just Freddie being Freddie."

"Meaning?"

"Ach… you know," Catton said waving his right hand dismissively as he sank back into his seat. "Freddie was always looking to organise the troop. Old habits die hard." Tom fixed him with a stare, an expression indicating the answer wasn't good enough. Catton splayed his hands wide apologetically. "Freddie took exception to how I live ma life, okay?" He sat forward, resting his elbows on his knees. "Freddie was never a man to let things go."

"You know he's dead, don't you?" Tom asked.

Catton held Tom's gaze. "Aye. I might live like a hermit but I still talk to people, like." His eyes crossed over to Cassie, still watching from her position behind the van. Catton sniffed, wagging a forefinger towards her. "Now, I'm getting the impression she does nae like me very much."

Tom followed his gaze. Cassie raised her eyebrows and half-smiled. Catton looked at him.

"Is she like bad cop to your good?" he asked.

Tom shook his head. "Where were you last Saturday evening?"

"When Freddie was killed?" Catton asked. Tom nodded. Catton looked around them, pursing his lips as he appeared to contemplate his reply. "I could say I was in the town watching the Viking guys do their thing, along with the rest of Norfolk…" His eyes fell on Tom. "But… I was here… alone, before you ask. And I don't need an alibi."

"Why not?"

"Because I didnae kill him," Catton said, cocking his head to one side with an overenthusiastic smile.

"Good to know," Tom said. "But I didn't ask."

"You were going to though… either in a minute or a couple of days," Catton said, frowning and scratching at an itch on his forearm. "But I didnae do it. I might not have any time for Freddie Mayes but I'm done with killing."

"I've heard that elsewhere recently," Tom said. Catton raised his eyebrows in a gesture of curiosity. "From another member of your old troop."

"Not surprised," Catton said, sitting back and exhaling deeply. "Some people thrive on what we did. Others, the sensible ones, see enough and don't want to go back."

"Are you talking about your experiences in Helmand?"

"Aye, right," Catton said, adopting a faraway expression. "We were part of the BRF attached to 3 Commando. It was pretty rough, you know, a rolling rotation of six months on, one off. Brutal."

"I'm sorry, that doesn't mean much to me. What's the BRF?"

"Brigade Reconnaissance Force. *The Viking Group*, fast mechanised infantry operating forward of established lines. Eyes and ears if you like," Catton said, sniffing and brushing the end of his nose with the back of his hand. "That was back in the fun days, early on, around '07… It was like the wild west out there back then." He laughed but it was a sound tinged with bitterness. "Take thousands of men, a shed-load of equipment and drop it in Afghanistan and tell them to get on with it! Proper mental. You guys want a drink?" he said, standing up. Tom shook his head and Cassie didn't answer. He walked to the Nissan and popped the boot open with some difficulty, levering it up with some force. The dampers appeared shot.

Tom looked around. "Must be a bit lonely out here."

"Suits me just fine," Catton said, rummaging through some bags in the boot of the old Nissan. He returned with a can of beer, opening it as he sat down and taking a sip.

"What do you do for heating, cooking and light. Can't be easy?"

"Not as hard as you think. I can handle a campfire and I've got a wee genny for when I need a bit more, like, you know."

Tom spied a small generator between the caravan and the hedgerow with a metal jerry can standing off to one side. He wondered if it ran on petrol or diesel.

"How long were you in the cavalry?"

"Ten years, give or take. Good times," Catton said with a grin.

"From what you described it sounds like it was pretty chaotic," Tom said.

"Aye, and the rest," Catton said, bobbing his head enthusiastically. "We were what's known as a *Brigade Asset*, man, which made it doubly fun for us."

Tom inclined his head, signalling both that he didn't understand and at the same time encouraging him to continue.

"Because of our rotation, we were inherited by whichever brigade arrived for the next tour. Now one thing you should know about the British army is that they like to document everything. Every deployment arrived fully equipped, or not as was often the case, with everything they needed… but, and here's the kicker," he said pointedly, extending his forefinger from the side of his beer can and jabbing it towards Tom and then Cassie, "because we weren't officially part of their deployment, they didn't bring anything for us."

"Sounds unfair," Tom said, imagining the situation as best he could.

"Aye, definitely. Now the negative aspect to all this was no one wanted to take responsibility for us. They barely had enough kit for their own troops as it was so they didn't want to supply us as well."

"So what did you do?" Tom asked, curious.

"We improvised," Catton said with a shrug. "Every time we saw a logistics convoy passing through, we'd strip it clean of whatever we needed, be it water, food or ammunition."

"Didn't they object?"

Catton burst out laughing, a genuine reaction. He waved away the question. "Nah man, they were out in the wilds, my friend! We gave them protection in exchange, security that they otherwise wouldn't have. They loved us. Who cares if they arrive at the Forward Operating Base a little light on kit. They got there in one piece."

Tom smiled at the thought. "Was that one of the positives? You mentioned the negatives."

"Aye, one of them yeah, the other being a lack of accountability. If you don't want to be responsible for us, then you're not going to be accountable for us either… Pretty much did what we wanted back in those days."

Catton sank back into his chair, raising the can in a silent salutation before moving it to his lips.

"Like I say… mental."

"That does sound like quite an experience," Tom said. Catton nodded his agreement, grinning. "I would imagine the bonds of friendship formed there would last a lifetime."

"Aye, you'd think so."

"Is that why you all came back here, to live in Norfolk?" Tom asked. "I mean, it is unusual wouldn't you say? I would have thought you'd all go your separate ways once back on civvy street, certainly not all come here to live in sleepy Norfolk."

Catton smiled, meeting Tom's eye. He held the gaze for a few seconds before bobbing his head deferentially.

"Fair point, aye. There's nothing for me back home. Ma parents are long gone, as are ma mates. Everyone's moved on you know. What's there to go back to? Here's as good a place as any. The sun shines regularly," he said, raising his can in Tom's direction.

"You have no other relatives?"

Catton shrugged. "I've got a brother in Glasgow but we don't get on. You know how it is."

Tom nodded. "Only child myself."

"Probably a blessing if you had a brother like mine," he said smiling.

"What do you do for work," Tom asked, looking around. "Doesn't seem like much is going on around here."

"Ah, I do okay. There's a bit of casual agricultural work floating around seasonally. It's back-breaking stuff but not exactly mentally taxing. It gets me by. Look around you." He held his arms out wide, the smile broadening further. "I don't exactly have a lot of outgoings."

"Right… and what about the rest of the troop, do you see any of them?"

"Nah, not these days," Catton said, staring Tom straight in the eye. "They've chosen their paths and… I've chosen mine."

"Did you also know Andrew Lewis was murdered earlier this week?" Tom asked, watching him intently for a reaction.

Catton placed his hands in his lap, cupping the can with both.

"No, I hadn't heard," he said quietly.

They hadn't released Andy's name to the media yet, so if Catton had known then he may have inadvertently given himself away. As it was, his ignorance appeared genuine. Tom lowered himself to his haunches so he was at eye level with Catton who met his gaze.

"It looks like someone may well be targeting members of your troop. Any ideas as to who or why that might be the case?"

Catton exhaled in a controlled release, his eyes darting to Cassie and then back to Tom. He slowly shook his head. "No. I can't help you there."

"I see," Tom said. "It's funny…"

"What is?"

"No one seems able to help. No one has a clue as to why someone might be coming after all of you."

"Freddie and Andy is hardly *all of us* though is it?" Catton said, shaking his head. "Are you possibly being a bit overdramatic?"

"What about Carl Woodly?"

"Woody?" Catton said, his eyes narrowing. He slowly bobbed

his head forward. "Good guy was Woody. I miss him. Shame for him to go out that way."

"It's a tragedy for sure," Tom said. "You and he must be roughly the same age."

"Aye, a year apart that's true. Helmand was my first deployment. Woody already had a few months under his belt by then."

"Did Woody have an issue with anyone?"

"How do you mean?" Catton asked.

"Well, did he fall out with Freddie or any of the others… like you have?"

Catton shrugged, looking at his feet.

"Dumb luck… a gas explosion in a new-build house," Tom said. "To go through what you all did in the war only to die in an accident like that. Freddie Mayes built it… the house, didn't he?"

Catton glanced at him and then away. "Yeah, so I understand it."

Nothing else was forthcoming and Tom switched tack, standing up.

"You know, if your troop is under threat whoever is behind it could come for you next."

Catton sighed, looking up at him. "Let them come," he said, indicating their surroundings with a sweeping gesture, splashing a little beer on the back of his hand in the process. "Let them relieve me of all that I own." He grinned.

"You said Woody was a good guy."

Catton nodded, the grin dissipating. "Aye, the best."

"What about the others? Freddie aside, obviously."

"Ah… man, Freddie was all right… once upon a time. They were all good guys… but things change."

"What changed them?" Tom asked.

Catton stared at him with an unreadable expression.

"Time."

CHAPTER TWENTY

A FIGURE WAS STANDING outside the police station as Tom Janssen turned off the main road and entered the car park. The man was leaning against the railing lining the path to the front door smoking a cigarette. He eyed them as they passed, pulling into a nearby bay. He was well dressed, in his forties and heavy set with close-cropped hair which was shot through with grey. Tom switched off the engine, and leaning forward he glanced past Cassie to see the man watching their car.

"I'd say we have a visitor," he said, nodding in the man's direction.

"I wonder who he is?" Cassie replied, following Tom's gaze. "I've not come across him before."

"Me neither," he said, opening his door.

A blast of cold air struck him as he got out. The day had started grey and overcast with threatening clouds coming in off the sea but the wind having cleared them away, was now cutting into them. Cassie fell into step alongside him and they walked towards the station. The man cast the butt of his cigarette to the floor, placing his hand in his pocket and stepping away from the railing to intercept them.

"Detective Inspector Janssen?" he asked. His accent had a

London edge to it. Tom nodded. "Thought so. Harry described you to me."

"Harry Oakes?" Tom asked, narrowing his gaze as he drew closer. The man had a dark and swarthy appearance and when he smiled his teeth radiated polished white. He was more powerful than Tom first imagined, nowhere near as tall as he was himself, probably five ten but stocky. A man with this size frame would have to work out four or five times a week. The physique wasn't possible to maintain otherwise.

"What can I do for you?"

"Greg Ellis," the man said, offering his hand as his smile broadened. The crow's feet rippled around his eyes which were a startling shade of green. Tom took the offered hand.

"You served with Harry Oakes and Freddie Mayes," Tom said. "I was planning to have a word with you."

"I figured as much," Ellis said. "I thought I would spare you the trip. Is this a good time to talk?"

Tom glanced at Cassie and a silent communication passed between them. She nodded and smiled.

"I'll catch up with Eric," she said, tipping her head to Ellis, who inclined his own, before heading indoors.

"Take a walk?" Ellis asked.

A rumble of thunder sounded and Tom glanced in the direction of the dark clouds harbouring off the coast.

"We'll be all right, Inspector," Ellis said, eyeing the clouds in the distance. "It'll be a while before they come our way."

They walked side by side, Tom drawing his coat around him and turning the collar up.

"You spoke with Harry Oakes, you say?" Tom said, glancing sideways. Greg Ellis stared straight ahead as they walked, his angular features set in stone.

"I did, among others. We're a tight group, Inspector," he said, shrugging as he met Tom's eye. "I expect you've already figured that out. After you visited Harry, he called me to let me know what had happened to Freddie." He sighed, shaking his head.

"Shocking thing to happen. Whatever he's done in this life, he didn't deserve to go that way."

"No one does," Tom echoed the sentiment. "So what brought you here today?"

Ellis stopped, turning to face him.

"Is it true that you think someone's targeting the troop?"

Tom assessed him. Recollecting his conversation with Harry Oakes, they didn't know about Andy Lewis then, so he hadn't mentioned the theory. Greg Ellis seemed to be able to read his thoughts.

"I also had a call from Eddie Drew," he said, reaching up and scratching at the side of his head as he spoke. "To be frank... well, you rattled him to say the least. Easily spooked is Eddie."

"That's probably not a trait that goes well with a combat soldier, is it?"

Ellis smiled, inclining his head and moving off. Tom easily kept pace with him. "That's true, Inspector. None of us have served for a few years now. Our last tour ended a couple of years before ISAF scaled things back over there. We've all been out for varying lengths of time and Eddie, for all of his positive attributes, was always a little highly strung."

Tom found that assessment curious. "He didn't come across that way to me when we spoke."

Ellis laughed. "Yes, Eddie's quite the salesman. He won't let you see it unless he wants you to. Never buy a car off him by the way," he winked at Tom as he spoke the last.

"You don't trust him?"

"I wouldn't go that far, no," Ellis said, cocking his head, "unless he's trying to sell me something. Eddie would sell his own mother if he thought he could make a profit out of it. So, is it true? Should we be worried?"

Tom was pensive, considering how best to frame his response. "Are you worried?"

"I'd be lying if I said it hadn't crossed my mind," Ellis said. "I mean, when two of your mates are murdered it's reasonable for you to start asking questions."

"Everyone else seems to dismiss the notion," Tom said. Ellis cast him a sideways glance but said nothing.

They both stopped. From here the path became a muddy track passing through open farmland heading towards the coast. They had a view of the sea here with the approaching storm on the horizon. Ellis looked Tom square in the eye.

"I was the lads' sergeant... they're looking at me to take their lead from, you know. What is it I'm supposed to tell them, Inspector?"

Tom ignored the question. "What was Freddie Mayes involved in?"

"I don't know what you mean?"

"You're their sergeant. They come to you for guidance and you know them better than anybody else, isn't that how it works? So you tell me," Tom said, fixing Ellis with a stare and studying him. "Help us out and then I'll be in a better position to help you."

Ellis broke away from the scrutiny of Tom's gaze, shaking his head as he absently kicked something invisible away with the toe of his boot.

"Come on," Tom pressed. "Both Freddie Mayes and Andy Lewis were killed in a personal way. They were executions; Freddie's in particular was brutal and very public, so you tell me why someone would do that?"

Tom intentionally didn't mention his doubts surrounding the death of Carl Woodly. At this time it was only a suspicion.

"Is there anyone you fell out with, not local, maybe back during your time in service who could be holding a vendetta against you and your men?"

"No, there's nothing like that."

"You're sure?"

Ellis met his gaze. "Absolutely certain."

"What about John Catton?" Tom asked.

Ellis reacted, brushing the suggestion aside with a flick of his hand. "Catton's off the wall these days, yeah, but as for killing Freddie or Andy... you must be joking. Have you seen him recently?"

Tom nodded. "We've spoken with him."

"Then you'll know you'll get no sense out of him at all. He still living out at that old gypo site?"

"I thought you guys were tight," Tom countered, not confirming anything. "If the man's struggling, I figured you'd be all out trying to help him, not dismissing him."

"Yeah," Ellis said, turning his eye back to the view and seemingly scanning the coastline. "But you don't know him like we do. And don't judge us too harshly," he said, glancing sideways at Tom, "it's not like we haven't tried you know. I couldn't have him working at my place, not quite the right look, you know? But I know some of the lads tried to step in and help... found him work, offered him somewhere to stay and that. Every time, he threw it back in their faces. Have you ever had someone in your life who repeatedly did that to you, Inspector?"

Tom inclined his head to one side. "I've met all kinds."

"Then you'll understand. You can only go so far before... before you throw in the towel and walk away. For the sake of your own sanity if not for theirs."

In Tom's mind, there was visible anguish in the man's expression and that was hard to fake if one chose to. He thought back on what Paul Woodly told him about Carl's friends offering work to Joe. They did appear to try and help out their own.

"Did you put yourselves out for Catton like you did for Joe Woodly?"

Ellis's expression lightened at the mention of Joe and he nodded.

"We did a lot for Joe," Ellis said. "Both prior to Woody's death and after. I tell you, it's an odd thing how one apple can fall so far from the tree in comparison to another."

Tom's curiosity was piqued. "Joe and Carl?"

"Yeah. Woody... Carl... was a top man, dependable. You knew

where you stood with him whereas Joe... was at the other end of the scale."

Ellis took out his packet of cigarettes, offering the open box to Tom who declined with a flick of the head. Ellis cupped his hands in front of his chest, turning to use his body to shield the lighter from the prevailing wind and lit up. Exhaling the first drag, he slipped the packet back into his coat pocket and ran his tongue along the edge of his lower lip.

"You were saying," Tom said, "about Joe Woodly."

"Right, yeah. Joe's something of a special case. Normally I wouldn't have bothered, knowing he'd be a waste of time and effort, but with him being Woody's brother and all we had to. He did a stint with Harry at the nursery but plants weren't his thing. Not ones you can't harvest and smoke anyway," he said with a wink. "Eddie tried as well."

"Selling cars?"

Ellis shook his head. "No, Joe's not exactly customer-facing material, at least that's the description Eddie used." He laughed at that, taking another steep draw. "Eddie had him detailing."

"Cleaning the cars then," Tom said.

Ellis smiled, nodding. "Yeah. Joe didn't last long. I guess it's not exciting work but it was steady and Eddie paid him far more than the going rate. In any event, he didn't turn up much and when he did he was often late. I found that out myself too."

"So you gave him a job?"

"Yep," Ellis said, looking glum. "Several. I knew I shouldn't but... Woody was gone, the parents were a wreck and Joe was going to end up another statistic if someone didn't step in. I gave that boy so many chances it got ridiculous in the end. I had to let him go when I caught him thieving. He'd already had his hand in the till behind the bar so I took the temptation away by having him working in the kitchens and clearing tables. But then I found him going through the members' coats in the cloakroom, seeing what he could find." Ellis shook his head, frowning. "He left me no choice. If the club members couldn't trust the staff looking after them then they'd go elsewhere. Let's face it, there are enough golf courses around these parts."

"How did he take it, being fired I mean?"

"About as well as you can imagine," Ellis said, flicking the ash from the end of his cigarette. "No one likes to get the sack, even from a job you hate."

"Have you had anything to do with him since?"

Ellis blew out his cheeks. "No, can't say I've come across him recently."

"What was his fight with Freddie Mayes about last month?" Tom asked, focussing hard on his reaction. Greg Ellis didn't flinch. "John Catton was involved as well."

Ellis didn't answer for a moment, instead he drew another intake from his cigarette before casting it to the floor and stepping on it. Tom watched him do it but Ellis didn't notice the disapproval in his expression. "Freddie said something about it. He took quite a dislike to Catton in the end. I mean, they were never best of mates anyway but Freddie was quite fixed in his views and Catton riled him."

"How so?"

"The way he chose to live, to present himself... pretty much any measure you can think of. They were opposites and always likely to clash."

"But that particular day, that was different."

Ellis shrugged. "Not as far as I know. I heard it all second hand as it happens, so I can't really tell you."

"Who from?"

"Andy Lewis."

"Right," Tom said, disappointed that the only witness who could confirm this account was also dead. "A bit of a switch for you isn't it, from mechanised infantry to running a golf course. How did that come about?"

Ellis laughed. "You're not wrong but we were trained to adapt and I figured a golf course would be easy money. Around here, a captive audience, lots of space. As it happens, turns out I was way off the mark. Competition is fierce for memberships and the upkeep costs are something else. Probably why I got the business for a song."

"Is that so?"

"Yes. The previous owners mortgaged themselves up to the hilt and then couldn't meet their commitments. They had to sell in a hurry and the local planners would never allow commercial development of the land, so it was destined to remain a golf course. There weren't many takers at that time, so I guess I was in the right place at the right time or the wrong place... depending on how you see it."

"In your opinion, both Mayes and Lewis were doing well?"

Ellis nodded. "No complaints as far as I know."

"I gather Freddie had a roving eye when it came to women." Ellis bobbed his head. "Anyone special?"

"No, not as far as I know. Freddie was never looking for anything serious."

"Were his conquests married?"

"More often than not, yes," Ellis said. "Let's face it when you reach a certain age the unattached women are old enough to be your daughters, and wouldn't find Freddie a catch, so it stands to reason his partners would be married."

"Anyone you know?"

"No, sorry. Freddie didn't bother with recanting names... deeds, yes, but not names. That's the type of guy he was."

"Classy," Tom said in an uncharacteristic judgement before he was able to catch himself. Ellis stared hard at him.

"We're all flawed human beings, Inspector. Freddie was no different."

"Eric," Tom called as soon as he entered the ops room. The detective constable's head appeared from behind his computer screen like a meerkat. "What have you got on at the moment?"

"I'm redoing the financials of both Mayes and Lewis."

"Turn up anything useful?"

Eric shook his head. "No, I still can't find anything registered to Lewis besides his car. The owner of the flat he lived in was Mabel Reid, who is his aunt on his mother's side."

"Has anyone spoken to her yet?"

"No. She's living in a local care home. Andy Lewis had power of attorney regarding her affairs," Eric said. "I spoke with the home, she has advanced dementia and Lewis is her only known living relative, although he hadn't visited her in the last twelve months. Not that she would be aware of that."

Cassie came to join them. "We've put in a request for the aunt's bank accounts but we need a court order for that. Just waiting on a magistrate."

"Good," Tom said, turning back to Eric. "If that comes back today, Cassie can pick it up for you. I want you to drop what you're doing and focus on Greg Ellis. You haven't met him I take it?" Eric shook his head. "That'll help. Stick to him like glue. The wall of silence around these guys is starting to irritate me. Someone knows more than they are telling us, maybe they all do, and if they won't volunteer it then we'll have to get in amongst them and keep picking at the threads until something unravels. And it will unravel. I just hope it's before another body turns up."

Eric glanced at the clock. Tom noticed.

"I'm sorry about whatever you had planned, Eric. I promise I'll make it up to you. I've just left Greg Ellis outside. I don't know where he's headed but you'll either find him at home or his golf club I imagine."

"No problem," Eric said, shutting down his computer and picking his jacket up from where it was hanging on the back of his chair. "I'll call Becca on the way, she'll understand."

"And Eric," Tom said, as the DC scooped up his car keys. "Pay attention. Ellis could be a target… or indeed a suspect, so be careful and keep in touch."

Eric nodded coolly. Cassie offered him a supportive wink and Eric left. She turned to Tom.

"So Ellis has caught your eye then?"

"He was the troop sergeant," Tom explained. "By his own words they all look to him for guidance. I don't see why now is any different. He came here fishing for information to see what we knew, not to offer us any realistic help in catching a killer. If anyone knows what the hell this is all about, it's going to be him."

"What are we going to do now?" Cassie asked.

"I want you to try and find out where Andy Lewis hid his money and how he earned it. If nothing turns up we'll go and see the estranged wife and son again. In the meantime, I'm going to speak to the DCI."

"Oooo… tell Tamara I say hi and I can't wait to see her new pad," Cassie said clapping her hands together with a big smile.

"Will do," Tom said, making to leave. Reaching the door, he glanced back. "Keep in touch with Eric. We still don't know what we're dealing with here."

CHAPTER TWENTY-ONE

Tom Janssen almost missed the entrance, braking heavily in order not to overshoot it. Located just before a bend, and with thick shrubbery and mature trees to either side of the property, it was well hidden from the road. The bungalow was set back from the road on quite a large plot, not overlooked by any of the neighbours. It seemed expansive to him. Mind you, almost every house he visited had that feeling these days. The mooring where he lived was right alongside a public footpath and almost every passer-by found it an irresistible draw to see what living on the water looked like.

Pulling up near to the front door, he noted the interior was in darkness. The light was already failing as he left the station, drizzle was falling and the ominous threat of a stormy night was still present. He got out and approached the front door, pressing the bell and stepping back to wait. There was no movement and he looked around. Tamara's car, her everyday car at least, was parked in the drive.

He stepped to his left and cupped a hand against the window looking through to a front reception room. No curtains were hanging yet and all he could see were removal boxes stacked alongside one another. It didn't look like she had made inroads into unpacking yet. The gardens were so wide that they wrapped around the entire building and were not separated by any fencing. Tom headed around the side of the house towards the rear, following the course of the driveway.

Coming to the back garden he found the house was still in darkness but the gravel drive led up to a double garage. One of the up-and-over doors was open and light streamed out from inside. He should have known. The stones crunched underfoot and he thought she must hear him coming. Reaching the garage, he looked inside to see Tamara Greave's old Austin Healey with the bonnet up, lit by overhead strip lighting but no sign of Tamara.

"Hello the camp!" he called, walking forward.

"Tom, is that you?" Tamara called.

The voice sounded detached, coming from below and he dropped to his haunches, realising that she was standing in a pit beneath the vehicle. He peered through the gap between the car and the floor to see a grimy face looking up at him. He couldn't see her mouth but he could tell she was smiling. He stood up and moved to the rear of the car. Tamara came up the steps from beneath, hanging a portable light on the bumper of the car as she passed.

"Now I can understand why you haven't unpacked yet," he said smiling.

He hadn't seen DCI Tamara Greave for over a week. She'd finally made the move to a permanent address having spent months living in and out of hotels or other temporary holiday-let accommodation. This had been a period of great upheaval in her life, splitting from her long-term partner and taking on a promotion at the same time. She'd earned this time off to get herself settled and Janssen immediately felt guilty for coming to see her.

Tamara was in an old dark blue boiler suit that seemed far too large for her but she'd rolled up the sleeves and turned up the legs to make it fit. She'd tied her hair up, loose strands falling to her shoulders on each side. She rubbed an old rag between her hands, but seemingly only managed to smear whatever was on her hands rather than clean them. Throwing the rag aside she greeted him.

"Oil leak," she said, grinning. "Now I can get underneath to see it, I can fix it."

"Pretty nifty, the garage coming with an inspection pit."

"Why do you think I bought the house?" she said. "I'm sorry I've not been in touch but it's all been a little crazy. Seriously, I swear solicitors make it harder than it has to be on purpose."

"Tell me about it," Tom said, shaking his head. "I've finally got my liberation paperwork through this week."

"The divorce?"

He nodded. "Yes. It's taken a while but Samantha finally put pen to paper. Once the house is sold, I'll be free and clear. Well... free at any rate."

"I know what you mean. It's taking me a while to get used to it as well," Tamara said, crossing to a workbench that had a variety of tools hanging in position alongside plastic boxes of different-sized nuts and bolts, rawlplugs and other kit which was neatly arranged and labelled.

"Was all this left here for you?" he asked, scanning everything laid out.

"No, I've done that this week," she said.

Tom raised his eyebrows. "Priorities, I guess."

"Alice must be pleased to hear you've managed to finally sever your past."

"Ah... yeah, well I haven't told her yet."

She smiled, folding her arms across her chest and cocking her head to one side.

"You better had because if she finds out by accident you'll be in it up to your neck!"

"I know, I know," he said, holding his hands up in surrender. "I've got to get my head around it first."

"Second thoughts?"

"No, no, nothing like that," Tom said, brushing off the

suggestion. "It's just that I've waited a couple of years for it to happen and now it's here I don't feel like it's something to celebrate. Can you understand that?" He looked at her. Tamara's expression had taken on a faraway look. Suddenly he remembered her situation. She hadn't had several years to come to terms with her own decision yet. The feeling of guilt returned. "I'm sorry. This is the last thing you'll want to be talking about."

"No matter," she said, snapping out of it and smiling weakly in his direction. "So, how is the investigation going?"

Tom frowned.

"I'm an experienced detective, Tom. I don't see a housewarming plant in your hands and the weight of the world is reflected in your face."

"Am I that obvious?" he asked. "I'm sorry. I did plan to get you something."

"It'd only die anyway," she said, waving away the apology. "Besides, the chief super called me this morning."

She read the irritation in his expression.

"He was considering recalling me from my annual leave." Tom was about to protest but she held up a hand, cutting off the complaint before he aired it. "I told him you and the team could handle it and you'd say so if you thought you needed help. I must admit after what happened at the festival last Saturday, I almost cancelled my holiday myself."

"Why?"

"As horrific as it is, I reckon it's more interesting than many of the cases that come our way. But, like I told the super, I'm sure you've got it in hand."

He appreciated the vote of confidence but the irritation at their superior's intervention remained.

"It's one of those cases," Tom said, looking up into the rafters overhead. "No one in and around the victims knows anything and yet I feel almost all of them know something."

"You've linked the two murders then?"

"Not officially," Tom said. "The MO is different with each and it's just the personal relationship linking them, but in my mind they're definitely related. There could be a third death as well from a couple of years back that slipped by as an accidental death. It was in a house fire."

"The chief super didn't mention that."

Tom shook his head, pulling himself upright and taking a deep breath. "That's because I haven't told him yet. I don't want to until I have some evidence. It was investigated back in the day, the insurance company got wind that something wasn't right and didn't pay out."

"Did we conduct an investigation?"

Tom shook his head. "Fire investigator ruled it as an electrical fault but it was a new build and constructed, incidentally, by Freddie Mayes."

"Neat," Tamara said, perching herself on the front wing of the Healey. "Bit coincidental."

"That's what we think too. I've had Eric trawling through the financial backgrounds of both victims. Mayes seems above board. His business is well respected, as is he by all accounts. The other one, Lewis, is another matter. His wife and son fingered him as a wheeler-dealer but that seems wide of the mark. Plenty of money floating around but no sign of how he came by it. It looks like he might have been routing it through an elderly relative, which stinks of laundering to me."

"You've widened the investigation to include their former service buddies, I understand?" Tom nodded. "What do they have to say for themselves?"

"Not a lot," Tom sighed. "Mayes played fast and loose in his personal life but so far that hasn't garnered any suspects and, if that was the case, how does Andy Lewis tie in? No," he said, shaking his head thoughtfully, "it's much more likely to be linked to their extended group or their shared past. I find that unlikely though, bearing in mind how many years have passed since they came out. I think whatever is behind all of this, they brought it to Norfolk with them. It's a hunch, I'll admit. So far, they're all smiles and offers of help but they're saying nothing."

Tamara's brow furrowed as she processed the information. After a few moments of silence, she met his eye.

"Do you want my opinion?"

He nodded. "That's why I'm here."

"Press all of them. Expand your interest into all of their finances," she said wagging a forefinger for emphasis. "If one of them is laundering money then some of them will be aware, maybe even part of it. The construction industry is one that's easy to accommodate inflated prices on the books and plenty of them as well. All of which can be done to avoid scrutiny."

"Good call," Tom said approvingly.

"I'd also squeeze them publicly as well, make them think you've got a lead on them even though you haven't."

"I already have Eric following one of them, Greg Ellis," Tom said, chewing his lower lip. "He stands out as the one they all look to. He's not hiding. Quite the opposite, he's already tried to draw out whatever we have on them. He's got a lot of front, I'll give him that, but he did little other than draw me to him."

"That could be your lever," Tamara said. Tom cocked his head inquisitively. "His self-belief that he's smarter than you. I'll bet he thinks he can get the better of us simple folk. After all, we're just police officers. Push him... hard. Make it public, the more eyes on him the better. If the others start to question his leadership it might make them nervous. Just pick your moment carefully to maximise the effect and it could lead to a mistake."

"Sounds good," Tom said. "I'm going to revisit Andy Lewis's family as well. I genuinely think the wife is in the dark but something tells me their son might know a bit more than he's letting on. You know when I do drop the suggestion that this is a three-murder investigation they'll want you back in the office, regardless of how much faith you have in me."

Tamara screwed her face into a mock grimace. "You're

probably right. Just make sure you've done most of the work before I come back though, could you?"

Tom smiled. "Any chance of a cup of tea before I go?"

"Sure," Tamara said, looking over her shoulder towards the house. "I have a kettle. I vaguely remember packing it too. It must be in there somewhere."

CHAPTER TWENTY-TWO

TOM JANSSEN LEANED against his car, pressing the mobile to his ear. The call was answered quickly. Her voice sounded hollow and distant, unsurprising due to the week she'd had. He tried to sound upbeat, hoping to allay any anxiety his call may generate.

"Mrs Lewis, it's DI Tom Janssen. We met—"

"Hello, Inspector," she said, her tone elevating as she spoke. "I remember."

"How are you and James?" He regretted the question as soon as he asked. Her husband had been murdered, she was very much in a state of shock.

"I'm okay," she said sighing. "All things considered. They've told me they can't release Andy's body. Is that right?"

He felt for her. This was a sudden event and she was forced into a response. A fleeting memory passed through his mind of when his father died when he was still a teenager. It, too, had been unexpected although very much from natural causes. His mother had wanted to get everything arranged as soon as possible, not because she was in a great hurry to move on with her life but because she needed something to occupy her mind, to distract her from facing the reality.

He wondered if Sophie Lewis was going through something

similar. Arranging a funeral, notifying friends and relatives of the date gave a sense of purpose; anything rather than face the raw emotion of losing someone, particularly in such brutal circumstances. That would come in the end, it always did.

"I'm afraid that is the way with these cases. Your husband's body is..." he struggled to find the words that wouldn't come across as cold and shallow.

"You can say it, Inspector Janssen."

"Evidence," he finished, gritting his teeth having said it. It was tough to hear but it was the truth. "I'm sure you will be able to lay Andy to rest as soon as it's possible."

"I understand," she said softly, almost inaudibly. Were it not for the lack of ambient noise near to Tamara's new home, he wouldn't have heard her. "What can I do for you?"

"I was hoping to have a word with James if he is at home," Tom said. "In person preferably."

"He's not here," Sophie said. "I think it has all been a bit much for him. He's gone out to see his friends this evening. In search of a touch of normality, I think. Who can blame him, right? Is everything okay?"

He heard the fear in her voice, exactly what he'd hoped to avoid by calling ahead rather than knocking on the door unannounced.

"It's nothing to worry about, I assure you, but I do need to have a word with him. Have you any idea which friend he will have gone to visit?"

"No, not really," she said. "Let me think. They usually like to gather on the green around by the arcade. I'm sure you know it."

She was right, he did. It was a popular hang-out for kids at all times of the day and night. Even without money to play the arcade machines, there was still the promenade and sea wall to hang out by and the beach itself when the tide was out. Hunstanton wasn't a big town. He was confident he'd find him.

"Thanks for your help, Mrs Lewis."

"I could call him for you on his mobile… tell him to come home—"

"No, please don't do that. I have to pass through Hunstanton on my way home." He lied. "And it'll be no trouble to stop by there and have a word. No need to ruin his evening out if he needs to see his friends."

"Okay… if you're sure."

She sounded uncertain, as if she doubted him. He did his best to put her mind at rest.

"It's related to your late husband's flat and how things were left there. James has been inside recently and so could probably answer a few questions for me. That's all."

It was the most plausible idea that came to mind and seemed to do the trick.

"Oh, right. Yes, I'm sure James will be happy to help with that."

"Thanks again, Mrs Lewis."

"Sophie, please."

"Thank you, Sophie. We'll be in touch again soon."

He hung up and got into the car to make the short drive along the coast to Hunstanton.

THE OLD VICTORIAN seaside town of Hunstanton was a place Tom was familiar with. He knew where he was likely to find James Lewis; the teenagers had always gravitated to the pier amusements on the seafront. Coming in from the Old Hunstanton side of town, the road descended down almost to sea level from Cliff Parade with the bowling greens to his right and the amusement arcade in front of him. When he reached the green, he took a right turn on a little road that wound down to a small parking area alongside the sea wall with the cliffs at its rear.

Getting out of the car, he drew his coat around him and fastened it up. Night had fallen and any residual warmth from the winter sun had been displaced by a bitter wind coming in off the sea. He headed towards the amusement arcade. It was far more modern than he remembered from his youth, the original having burnt down around the turn of the century to be replaced by this incarnation. Even the old building from before was a replacement at the location of the original pier which was itself destroyed by fire decades previously. Now the curved roof and wall of glass facing the town lit up the green with flashing lights and neon, acting like a magnet to those looking for entertainment. The kids loved it here, irrespective of whether they had money in their pockets. It was a place to congregate with their friends.

The bitter snap to the weather seemed to have kept the numbers low, however, in the teens rather than amassing dozens. That would no doubt change as the more clement weather of spring arrived. Walking up the set of steps to the front of the building, facing the green, he scanned the assembled teenagers. They were split into three groups, not one of them looked above twenty. A few faces glanced at him as he passed through in his search but he couldn't see James Lewis. He approached a group of four standing alongside the entrance to the amusements, reaching for his identification as he did. They eyed him warily as he spoke. It must be unusual for them to find someone of his age among them. They relaxed when he revealed his warrant card although a flash of nervousness crossed the face of one boy in particular. Tom figured he probably had a bag of cannabis on him judging by the dark shadows around his eyes. It was something of a giveaway.

"Have you seen James Lewis tonight?" he asked. "His mum told me he was likely to be hanging around down here."

The boys immediately shook their heads, too quickly in Tom's opinion, whereas the girls glanced at one another. One shrugged and the other hesitated, drawing his full attention to her.

"Have you seen him tonight?" he pressed. "James isn't in trouble. I just need a word."

Her lips parted but she didn't say anything. Instead her eyes flicked to something behind Tom and to his left. Instinctively, he glanced over his shoulder to see James walking out of another set of doors a few metres away. At the same moment he looked, James glanced towards them, meeting Tom's eye. There was a moment of recognition and he stopped dead in his tracks, hesitating. Tom turned towards him and that was the teenager's cue. A burst of energy saw James Lewis take off in the opposite direction, frantically seeking to put space between them.

Such was the speed of his flight that it caught Tom unawares but he gave chase, calling after the fleeing teen. James descended the stairs to the promenade almost colliding with a couple coming the other way. They protested but stood aside as Tom rushed through in James's wake. *Why was he running?* James looked over his shoulder back at Tom, his expression panic-stricken but didn't let up.

Tom knew he was in good shape and had always managed a pretty mean time when it came to a lung-bursting prolonged sprint but, apparently, so was James Lewis who managed to open up a gap between the two of them. He thought about ordering him to stop again but realised it would only use up more of his breath. He conserved his energy and tried his best to keep up with the younger man's pace. James would tire eventually and where did he think he was going?

Dog walkers and those out for an evening stroll were perplexed as the two figures ran past. The promenade stretched from Hunstanton around the coast to Heacham. Surely James wouldn't keep going. Their pace did appear to be slowing, a fact Tom was grateful for but the distance remained. Coming to the end of the sea defences protecting the town, James cut left and into the funfair, disappearing among the rides and stalls that made up the permanent visitor attraction.

Reaching the entrance, Tom pulled up, desperately searching for sight lines through the rides and trying to pick up James's path. He knew the fair well. It was small and enclosed on all sides. In high season there were four entrances and exits from the fair but at present only two of them were open. If he was careful then he should be able to keep both in sight. However, an athletic person could probably climb the perimeter fence if required to. Tom was grateful for the lower footfall at this time of year because there were fewer visitors present. Those who did venture in numbered similar to the staff which was a blessing. During peak season, you would be shoulder to shoulder all the way around.

Tom moved through the fair at a measured pace, constantly alert to those around him. A couple of times he thought he caught sight of James only to have his hopes dashed but he carried on. The various tunes playing from the rides sounded odd with so few people around, sad and pitiful when unaccompanied by shrieks of joy and laughter, when normally they would bring a smile to your face.

The doors to the ghost train burst open as a cart thundered out on rails, the occupants giggling at the experience, just as the music to the carousel began and the machine started up.

A flash of movement in the corner of his eye saw Tom react. He stepped up onto the carousel as it started to pick up speed, the horses moving up and down in unison. He shifted his weight between his feet to maintain balance and moved through the ranks of brightly-coloured horses, all the while watching the exterior for signs of James. Shouts came from above as a spinning G-force ride lifted into the sky before tilting to one side and then down towards the ground, the caged participants screaming in both terror and delight.

The operator of the carousel stepped forward to challenge him but Tom ignored him, pushing past and lining up his exit from the ride. His idea worked. By leaving a clear route to the exit, he'd hoped to draw out the teenager. Timing his movement just right, Tom pushed off from where he stood. His momentum carried him forward faster than he could have managed under his own steam and he was catapulted from the ride connecting with a slow-moving James Lewis who was inching his way along between the carousel and the ghost train.

The teenager was so intent on the search for his hunter he

hadn't paid attention to the rides around him. Tom clattered into him and the two went sprawling to the ground.

Tom was first to react, having braced himself for the impact, he came to tower over the teenager who was doubled over and clutching his side. Tom righted himself and took a firm grasp on him, hauling him upright despite his protestations.

"Man, I swear you've broken my ribs!" James moaned, grimacing, still clutching his side. Tom ignored him, spinning him and pushing him up against the wall of the ghost train where he came face to face with the mural of a clown, six feet tall. Tom swiftly pulled both arms behind his back and placed him in handcuffs. He didn't want a repeat of that chase. It was cold and he was dressed appropriately for it but was now uncomfortable, sweating profusely as a result of the pursuit. James was similarly out of breath and, due to how he was standing, was also struggling to gather himself. Once Tom was sure the teenager was suitably restrained, he took him by the shoulder and turned him so they were face to face once more.

"Why on earth were you running, James?"

The teenager averted his eyes from Tom's gaze, slowly shaking his head. Tom saw it more as a gesture related to being caught rather than a dismissal of the question.

"Have you got anything on you that you shouldn't have?" Tom asked. James looked up this time and met Tom's eye before rolling his own.

"No… not really," he said quietly.

"Not really?" Tom repeated, starting to root through his charge's pockets. Everything that came out of the pockets that wasn't interesting, Tom casually dropped on the floor at their feet.

There was little of interest in the jeans aside from a small press seal bag with what looked like cannabis resin inside. This was backed up by the next pocket with a pouch of hand-rolling tobacco along with a pack of orange cigarette papers where several chunks had been carefully torn from the flap, the pack having been 'roached' as smokers would say. Tom held the bag up, cocking his head to one side and raising his eyebrows questioningly.

"Hardly worth the mad dash was it?"

James looked away without comment and Tom tucked the bag into his coat pocket before continuing the search. Patting down James's coat he felt a significant bulge in the inside right. Unzipping the coat, he stared hard at the young man who, once again, looked away. Tom pushed aside the coat and reached in to retrieve the contents from the pocket. The feel of it was familiar and he knew what it was before his eyes got to see it.

Holding the bundle of notes out in front of James, he placed a restraining hand on the teen's chest before angling the find so he could better judge the value. It was at least a thousand pounds in used twenty pound notes. Tom figured they'd been around for quite some time too, not just because of their slightly dog-eared condition but because it was still paper money as opposed to the new polymer notes in circulation since the previous year. This wasn't new money and he was intrigued. It had to be the reason James ran.

"Well, well, well… how did you come by this?" Tom asked, studying the young man's expression. He looked utterly dejected. "And don't tell me you've been down the bookies because I'm not buying it."

James Lewis sighed, staring at the notes before his eyes flitted at Tom.

"Well?" Tom asked again.

"I'll show you," James said with obvious reluctance.

CHAPTER TWENTY-THREE

THE DOOR SHRIEKED in protest as Tom pulled on the handle. The up-and-over door to the garage juddered as he raised it, illuminated by the torch Cassie Knight held aloft. They were in a small block of a dozen garages owned and used by the residents of the flats located nearby off Cliff Parade, a couple of minutes' walk from where Andy Lewis lived. Andy's son, James, was sitting quietly in an interview room back at the station having given Tom the location. Thinking back, James removed the key to this garage from the ring when he handed the set over at the mortuary. Did he know then what was here? Had he planned ahead? If so, the cold callous nature of the decision would say a lot about the young man.

"I swear I didn't know!"

James's words after he'd been detained echoed in his mind. He donned a pair of nitrile gloves and looked around. A pull cord hung next to the entrance and he tried it. The fixture clicked reassuringly but the strip light didn't come on. Cassie stepped forward and passed the light over the interior. To the casual eye, there was little here that would be unexpected.

It looked like the overflow of personal items and furniture that could occur when downsizing from a house to a flat. Much of it appeared to be junk; there was nothing of any real value. Two old bicycles were propped up against one wall looking very much like they hadn't seen the light of day in years. A two-seater sofa was stood on its end in the far corner alongside several cardboard boxes stamped with the name of a national removal firm. These ones in particular were leaning precariously, the bottom box having got damp at some point, weakening the structure and destabilising the stack. They could collapse at any moment. It was impossible to know what was contained within them.

The detectives entered, Tom scanning some camping equipment on the left. It too appeared not to have been used for a long time. The overriding smell was one of damp. Unsurprising considering these blocks were only single-skin brick and therefore very prone to the elements. An old three-bar electric fire stood alone against one wall and Cassie inspected it.

"Looks like this has been used," she said. "There's not a lot of dust or grime on it."

Tom glanced across. It was an old contraption, pretty much a death trap under current regulations but he could see it being used for occasional heat in a place such as this. Why anyone would spend enough time here to require heating was an interesting consideration.

"Where did he say he found it?" Cassie asked, sweeping the beam of her torch across the interior again.

"We're looking for an MFO box."

"Say again?" Cassie asked, turning the beam on him.

"A Mobile Forces Overseas box," Tom said softly, still casting an eye over the contents of the garage. "Every soldier stationed overseas gets one to transport their kit. Think of a large wooden packing crate."

"Like this one?" Cassie said. He crossed to where she'd knelt down, lifting the corner of an old fabric dust sheet that was spotted with paint and the grime from decades of use. Beneath the sheet was a wooden box stamped with three capital letters – MFO.

"Just like that," Tom said, pulling back the sheet while Cassie kept the light on it.

The lid of the box wasn't fastened down and he lifted it off with ease, resting it gently behind the crate and leaning it against the wall. Cassie stepped closer, angling the light towards the interior. They exchanged a glance.

"This will explain how Andy Lewis always managed to come through financially for his wife whenever the need arose," Tom said, reaching in and lifting out one of the packets contained in the box.

It was tightly wrapped in cling film, so much so that you almost couldn't make out what was inside. Tom took out his mobile and, having first ensured Cassie provided enough light, snapped a few photographs. Then he began to unfurl the wrapping. Inside were bundles of cash in used twenty pound notes. In this one packet alone he guessed there must be somewhere north of ten thousand. He looked back into the interior of the crate. It was jam packed with similar bundles.

"Why use so much of the cling film?" Cassie asked.

Tom looked around them and then up at the roof. The garages were built side by side with flat, felt-lined roofs. Over time these were prone to failure making the interior susceptible to the elements.

"Damp for one," he said, meeting her eye. "Plus vermin would happily chew their way through this lot to make a nest, I should imagine."

"There must be tens of thousands of pounds in here, maybe even six figures," Cassie said, astonished. "I mean, where the hell did it come from?"

Tom shook his head slowly. He didn't have the first clue.

"James Lewis claimed his father told him if anything ever happened to him that he should come here to the garage," Tom said, rewrapping the bundle of cash and putting it back where he found it, "but he never told him why."

"So he says," Cassie said, clearly doubting the truth of the claim.

"Yes, so he says," Tom repeated. "If he already knew what was here then it stands to reason he might know how his father came by it, too."

"What are the odds of his father's friends knowing where it all comes from?" Cassie said.

"I wouldn't mind asking that very question. Speaking of whom, have you heard from Eric?"

"Not for a while," she said, reaching for her mobile. She passed him the torch before typing out a short message to Eric. Whilst tailing Greg Ellis, it would be much safer for Eric to subtly read a text message than for him to receive a telephone call.

CHAPTER TWENTY-FOUR

HARRY OAKES PUSHED the door open and entered the pub. It wasn't busy and he easily spotted them sitting in a corner booth near to the open fire. He smiled to the landlord, who gave him a wave and pointed towards his friends. Silently communicating his thanks with a nod, he crossed the bar.

Two men in their sixties were having a game of darts, the thrower currently receiving a fair amount of sledging from his fellow player and there was another man, younger, most likely in his twenties, sitting at a table alone tapping away into his mobile and nursing a pint. A woman's laugh carried from the adjoining room and he could see across the bar to where two or three people were enjoying an evening's drinking whilst chatting to the bar staff. Aside from these few, the pub was empty. It was often the case in the off season. That would change.

Approaching the table, the two men greeted him and one slid a pint of bitter across towards him. He took off his coat, folding it and placing it neatly on an unoccupied stool at the end of the table before sliding into the booth. Lifting his pint to his lips, he tipped the drink towards them.

"Cheers," he said, sipping the head off the glass.

"Nice of you to join us, Harry."

"Pleasure, Gregory," Harry replied, ignoring the sarcasm and placing the glass down. He wiped the foam from his top lip with the back of his hand.

"I think what Greg's saying," Eddie Drew said, sitting forward and resting his elbows on the table, "is that you're late."

"I know that, Eddie. I'm not daft but I had to get the girls to bed. If you had kids then you'd understand."

"Hah!" Eddie replied, waving away the excuse. "The bloody girls are always your excuse. Why anyone would want kids is beyond me anyway."

"How about to give yourself purpose or to leave something behind when you're gone," Harry countered. He took another sip of his pint, savouring the taste. It wasn't often that he made it out for a beer. Life was a far cry from what it used to be, a thought that inspired him. "Or maybe just to move on and create something good with your life. You ought to try it."

Eddie Drew bristled, much to his pleasure. It felt good to wind Eddie up. He'd always been a corporal who was too big for his boots and the conversion to civvy street along with running a business had done little to change him; at least, not for the better. As usual, it fell to Greg to be the calming influence.

"Gentlemen," Greg Ellis said, looking between the two of them and gesturing with his hands to calm down. "Let's not get the evening off on the wrong foot."

Eddie sank back in his seat but he still glared across at him. Harry couldn't help but smile, an expression drawing another stern look from Greg. He bobbed his head by way of an apology.

"Sorry, Eddie. I'm sure you'll get some somewhere."

Eddie Drew's solemn face split into a grin and he shook his head. "Yeah, well, your missus called but I knocked her back. I don't want your cast-offs."

He smiled. In the background, over Eddie's shoulder, he thought the lone man at the table was looking in their direction. He watched him, waiting to see if he looked up again but he didn't, remaining fixed on his mobile. He thought nothing more about it, lifting his pint. Greg glanced sideways at him.

"How's the horticultural business?"

It seemed a genuine question. Greg wasn't one to take the mick.

"Prep is going well, building for spring but the renovations..." he sipped at his drink, swallowing hard and putting the glass down, "are damned expensive. I never figured the hothouses would set me back so much."

"Feeling the pinch?"

He looked across the table, this time it was Eddie and the question was serious as well. Very odd, the man must be ill. He nodded.

"It's tight, yeah."

"What about your good lady's family?" Greg asked. "Couldn't they step in?"

He shook his head. "No way, not after they sold it to us the way they did. Besides, Tina wouldn't allow it. She went against her old man and staked her family reputation, and her future for that matter, on me delivering." He shook his head. "Not an option. How about you guys, either of you want to invest in an up and coming nursery?" The question was only asked with mock sincerity. Neither of them recognised that fact.

Eddie grimaced. "You're not alone," he said, swilling the remnants at the base of his glass before draining it in one swallow. "I've got a franchise from a manufacturer who went in heavy on diesel..." he said, sniffing and putting the now empty glass down hard. "And do you know what people don't want to buy these days?"

"Diesel cars." Both Greg and Harry answered in unison.

Eddie smiled, splaying his hands wide. "The antichrist has arisen and it's powered by diesel," he said, sliding out from his seat. He pointed to both their pints in turn. "Same again?"

Harry shook his head for he'd barely touched his but Greg nodded and Eddie left for the bar but first angling his walk towards the gents, looking increasingly unsteady with every step. Harry turned to Greg Ellis.

"How many has he had?"

There were a number of empty pints on the table.

Greg shrugged. "He'd already had a few before I got here."

"How is the golfing world anyway?" Harry asked, changing the subject as he watched Eddie stumble through the door to the toilets. "No shortage of retired white men with terrible dress sense regarding trousers living around these parts. You must be going all right?"

Greg sighed, lifting his glass to his lips. For a second, he thought he was likely to ignore the question but, after a moment's reflection, Greg replied in his usual enigmatic style.

"Plenty of golf courses around too."

Harry watched as Greg's gaze lowered to his pint glass sitting on the table in front of him, cupping it with both hands. His expression was pensive as he contemplated something; something he was reluctant to voice. The moment passed and the melancholic aura surrounding Greg visibly appeared to pass.

"Have you had any more visits from the police?" Greg asked.

He shook his head. "Not expecting any either."

"Don't be so sure," Greg said, fixing him with a stare. There was something in his expression, something unsaid. He felt a knot of anxiety tighten in his stomach.

"I've got more pressing concerns right now," Harry bit back, sounding more aggressive than he'd intended.

Greg's upper lip twitched as it was prone to do when he was irritated. Harry saw fit to row back a little.

"I'm aware, okay. I appreciate what you're saying." He looked to his right seeing Eddie leave the toilets and head for the bar, bumping into an empty table and cussing it as he did so. He inclined his head in Eddie's direction. "I think you should be more concerned about him."

Greg followed his gaze to the bar and slowly nodded his agreement. "Yeah, maybe. He's rattled, right enough."

Harry sat back, raising his glass. "Understandable. Eddie's never been one to manage stress particularly well, has he?"

"No, it's more than that. Johnny's been showing up."

"Johnny?" Harry said, lowering his voice. "Where?"

"All over... hanging around outside his house, the dealership... popping up whenever it's least expected."

Greg fixed him with a stare, that same stare, the one he always hated where Greg was preparing to ask a question that he already knew the answer to but planned to ask it anyway.

"Has he been to yours?"

He met Greg's eye. There was no point in lying, he would know.

"Yeah. A couple of times."

"You never said!" Greg hissed. "When?"

He shook his head. "I don't know, a week or so back... maybe more." Greg's displeasure at the revelation was obvious, his chest heaving as his expression turned to stone. "Look, I didn't see the point in mentioning it. I told him where to go. He's hardly an issue. What's the problem?"

"You know damn well what the—"

Greg Ellis didn't finish the comment as Eddie reappeared by their side with two more drinks, setting one down in front of Greg, spilling some as he did so.

"Ah... sorry mate," Eddie said, sitting down about as smoothly as one might imagine he would.

Greg dismissed the need for the apology with a shake of his head but his eyes never left Harry's. Greg pulled himself upright, his eyes flitting between the other two.

"We have a bit of a conundrum to deal with," Greg said quietly. "And I think we can kill two birds with one stone while we're at it."

The tone left little to be desired with both Eddie and himself exchanging glances before turning to their old sergeant.

"We thought Freddie had taken care of the situation with Johnny Catton but," Greg said, casting a glance around the bar to ensure they wouldn't be overheard, "it would appear Johnny got the better of him."

Eddie stared down at his pint. Harry knew he wasn't going to comment, he'd never been much of a leader and was always one to follow.

"I thought we agreed not to," Harry said quietly, fearful of inciting Greg's anger. One reason he hadn't mentioned Catton's visits was precisely because he didn't want Greg rocking the boat. Eddie would follow, as always, and then he'd be outvoted, pushed into doing something he thought was too reckless. Even for them. He desperately didn't want to mention how Catton had been to the nursery earlier that day, one of the reasons he was late. "And with everything going on, is now the right time?"

"We did agree but Johnny's upped the ante, hasn't he?" Greg countered, leaning forward. "And he's the weak link, let's not forget that."

He didn't agree. Johnny Catton was a basket case, absolutely, but the weak link was sitting beside him and Greg. Eddie Drew was barely holding things together. That was evident. Johnny Catton turned away from them some time ago and, if push came to shove, he was never likely to have their backs, not any more. Eddie might be a shadow of his former self but Greg could be counted on, just as Andy Lewis and Freddie Mayes could. But the timing… it wasn't great.

"Why not step back and allow the police to handle it?" he said. "Someone like Johnny is bound to flash up sooner or later and then the problem goes away on its own."

"Does it?" Eddie scoffed. "And what about when he starts talking… and he will start talking… eventually. And what if they don't go after him, what then? You fancy what happened to Andy and Freddie happening to you, eh? Fancy one of us explaining to your girls—"

"You stay the hell away from my girls," he growled. It was uncharacteristic of him and both Eddie and Greg seemed taken aback. Eddie looked away but it was clear he didn't appreciate the challenge.

"Now, now, gentlemen," Greg said, "let's keep it down a little. Walls have ears and all that." Greg looked over his shoulder at the same man who'd caught his own eye earlier. The loner glanced up at that point and exchanged eye contact with himself and Greg but soon drifted back to his ever-present mobile phone. "Besides," Greg continued, turning back and lifting his glass, holding it aloft before him, "a little tax might come in useful for all of us."

Greg tipped his glass in their directions and waited, raising his eyebrows questioningly. Eddie slowly raised his own and they touched. Both men then looked at him expectantly. He ran his tongue along the inside of his lower lip. In his mind this seemed unnecessarily provocative, a mistake in the making, but he raised his glass nonetheless. Greg was right. They could all use the money. The three glasses clinked against one another as their eyes met.

"Death or glory," Greg said softly, a glint in his eye as he smiled.

"Death or glory," both of them repeated.

The door to the pub opened and another man entered just as they finished their toast. The newcomer stood by the entrance looking around the room. His eyes fell on them, sitting in the corner and he made a beeline in their direction. Harry bit his lower lip, nudging Greg gently in the ribs to draw his attention. Both Greg and Eddie looked over and the latter's face dropped at sight of Tom Janssen as he came to stand alongside their table.

"Good evening, Inspector," Greg said, not missing a beat. "I didn't know you also drank here."

"I don't drink," Tom replied, taking his mobile out of his pocket and unlocking the screen with his thumb. He laid the handset down in the centre of the table. All three men glanced at the screen. Harry's eyes narrowed as he recognised the MFO box and all three men could see what was inside it. None of them spoke and Harry felt his stomach churn.

"It's interesting what a man leaves behind when he passes on, isn't it?" Tom said.

Greg was the first to sit back. He looked up and met the detective's eye. Harry knew he couldn't do the same, fearing the man would be able to read his deepest thoughts and see straight through him. This was Greg's moment, a situation in which he thrived.

"What exactly are we looking at, Inspector?"

"We found this in Andy Lewis's garage," Tom said. "Look familiar?"

"Wow, that's one hell of a pension," Greg said. "Typical Andy, though, right lads? Always so bloody secretive." Both he and Eddie mumbled agreement. "I wish I'd known. The cheeky sod was always cadging money off me as well. The tight git."

"How do you think he came by it?" Tom asked.

Greg shook his head, turning the corners of his mouth down. "No idea. Andy never talked about his work and now I can see why." Greg looked across at Eddie sitting opposite him. "What about you, Eddie?"

Eddie Drew lifted his pint, turning his gaze to the policeman. "No idea," he said before taking a sip. All of a sudden he looked keenly alert and, more importantly, sober.

He did his part, meeting the detective's eye but first glancing at the young man sitting alone at the table who seemed to be watching what was going on. "I've no idea either, Inspector. I'm sorry. I wish I could help."

The detective held his gaze for a few seconds before casting an eye over all three of them in turn. He knew. It was obvious. How much he knew and whether he could prove any of it, though, was another matter entirely.

"Some might say that it's enough to kill for," Tom said, reaching down and retrieving the mobile.

He glanced at the screen before slipping it back into his coat pocket. Turning away, the detective walked back across the pub towards the exit. He stopped at the door, looking back at them once again. Greg was watching the detective with a look as cold as ice but Harry couldn't look at the inspector, choosing instead to stare at the drink in his hand with as straight a face as he could manage. Then the policeman was gone, back into the night.

The three of them sat there in silence for a couple of minutes. Who knows what the other two were thinking but Harry felt something he hadn't felt for a long time. It was familiar to him, similar to embracing an old friend you hadn't seen for years but one whom you knew better than anyone else.

It was fear. And he was scared. Eventually someone spoke. It was Greg.

"Now… this does complicate things."

CHAPTER TWENTY-FIVE

As he drove home, Tom Janssen ruminated on the image of the three ex-servicemen sitting together in the pub. Playing over the details of the case in his mind, he was certain that the answer lay within the closed circle encompassing these men. Everything about them felt wrong to him. He considered each man in turn. Greg Ellis was the obvious candidate to be the leader, if they still approached things that way. His visit to the station on the pretence of assisting the investigation was in reality nothing more than an attempt to either prise out information in the case or push the inquiry in another direction entirely. At this point, Tom had to admit, he was unsure which.

However, it had been a poor attempt at manipulation if that was indeed the goal. Ellis may well have been a decorated soldier but he'd no idea how they ran a murder inquiry. If Tom was the flame then Ellis was the moth.

Of the remaining two, it was Harry Oakes who he found the most intriguing. He was softly spoken, carried himself well and, from the outside at least, appeared to have turned his back on an adrenalin-fuelled lifestyle, choosing a quieter life in which to raise a family. Tom felt an affinity with the man's choices, Alice and Saffy both coming to mind.

He tried to push thoughts of them aside for the moment, recollecting the discussion he'd had with Tamara. The confirmation of his divorce was likely to change things between himself and Alice. Although she'd never demanded a proposal, he'd offered one anyway which turned out to be an utterly disastrous decision in hindsight. Alice was always looking to the future. Whether or not he was a significant part in that future, he was still unsure. Somehow, he figured he must be otherwise why would she stick around?

He shook off his personal life, forcing his focus back to the case. Eddie Drew seemed very suited to his current role in life. He could quite easily envisage the man convincing a stranger to part with their money for something they didn't necessarily want or need. However, when it came to something he cared about, the tells were quite apparent and you didn't need to be a card sharp in order to spot them.

His own cameo appearance at their little get together this evening threw them; all three, but Drew in particular. Ellis manipulated the conversation with ease displaying a level of arrogance that demonstrated a conscious belief in the superiority of his own intelligence, however misplaced it might turn out to be. Oakes withdrew a little but maintained his nice-guy appearance; maybe it wasn't a routine. Maybe he was the reasonable one, the point of contact Tom could exploit to draw out the truth. Only time would tell with that one.

Eddie Drew... the curt attitude, stony face and his physical rigidity all sought to convey strength and power but, in reality, implied quite the opposite. Tom's appearance scared him. Not only Drew but all three of them, even Ellis despite his best efforts to hide it behind bravado, which was exactly the plan.

The levels of discomfort shown reinforced his belief that these men knew more about how their friends came to die but what he still struggled to understand, beyond merely whether they should be suspects or potential victims, was why they were so set on their vow of silence. Because that's what it was, a choice not to help.

Whatever led to Andy Lewis having stashed away thousands of pounds in cash was unlikely to be legitimate which begged the question, were they all in on it and, if so, was the fear of self-incrimination stronger than that of self-preservation?

Cassie Knight was back at the station running the rule over the three men. All were successful businessmen in their own right, much like Freddie Mayes had been, but were they self-made men or did they receive an injection of funds, off the books, along the way in the same vein as Andy Lewis? A momentary flash of guilt struck him when he thought about Cassie beavering away back at the station. What with Eric still keeping tabs on Greg Ellis, it was only himself who was heading home already, despite it now approaching ten o'clock.

Alice called earlier, around lunchtime, and he promised he would go to hers when he was done, although even he thought he'd have been back long before now. It was the suggestion of Tamara to shake the group up a little that'd changed those plans. Eric's relaying of information to Cassie that they were together in the pub gave him too good an opportunity to miss and he seized it.

How the three reacted now would be key. They might do nothing but, somehow, he didn't think of these men as the type to sit back and let events unfold. They'd been trained to be on the front foot, to take the fight to the enemy and he was convinced that was what they would do. But how and when, he didn't know. Further to that if they were victims, and knew the identity of their would-be killer, how would being on the front foot manifest? Or there was the other possibility, that one or all of them was a murderer. That individual could be playing both the police and the entire group; or as a group, they could be playing everyone else.

The thought occurred that Eric's take on their response after he departed would be revealing. He'd been impressed with the DC. Eric had paid him little attention when he entered the pub, as expected, blending into the background with consummate ease.

Hopefully he'd keep his distance and not push his luck. These men were potentially dangerous and he shouldn't underestimate the threat.

Pulling into Alice's driveway, he stopped the car. Picking up his mobile, he typed out a message to Eric reminding him to be careful. Switching off the engine and releasing his seatbelt, his mobile beeped with a reply. Eric was confident he would be just fine. Tom smiled and cracked open the door.

The downstairs lights were on and he expected Alice to have waited up for him. Just in case she'd fallen asleep on the sofa, something both of them were guilty of on occasion, he let himself in with his key as quietly as he could. The hall and landing lights were on and he heard movement coming from the kitchen at the rear. He headed down the hall, finding Alice emptying the dishwasher.

"I'm so sorry—"

His apology was cut short as she spun to face him, lifting a forefinger to her lips to indicate quiet. She then pointed her finger past him towards the family room. He looked over his shoulder seeing Saffy sound asleep on the sofa. She was in her pyjamas, a blanket laid over and tucked up beneath her armpits. She cradled Mr Snuggleface, her favourite cuddly toy, in her arms.

Tom crossed over to her, lowering himself slowly to his haunches. He gently stroked the hair of her fringe away from her eyes. The colour in her face was paler than usual and the skin seemed red and blotchy in places. He wondered if she'd come down with something but she'd been fine when he'd left for work that morning.

He looked back at Alice and she smiled weakly from where she was in the kitchen. He leaned forward, gently kissing the little girl on the forehead. She stirred momentarily but didn't wake. He rose and walked back to where Alice stood. She had one arm across her waist while the other absently fondled the pendant of her necklace. Something was wrong.

"Is Saffy okay?" he asked in a whisper.

She inclined her head towards the living room and they crept past the sleeping child and entered the adjoining room. Alice pushed the double doors closed behind them, they were glass panelled so they could still keep a watchful eye on Saffy.

"Ade didn't show today," Alice said. The mention of her ex-husband, Adrian, irritated Tom. Whenever his name came up in conversation it was invariably a prelude to something awful, usually surrounding his daughter. Then he remembered, Adrian was supposed to be picking Saffy up from school this week because Alice's shift rota had her finishing late.

"He didn't show up to collect her?"

Alice shook her head. "No, the school gave him half an hour and then called me at work. I had to arrange cover... it was another hour before I was able to get there." Her tone was despondent. "Saffy was distraught when I got to the office."

"I can't believe he'd do that again," Tom said, glancing through the doors at the little girl. He'd been around children on and off, those of friends and acquaintances, and none of them were a patch on Saffy. She was delightful. This wasn't the first time her father had dropped the ball either.

"I know, especially after last time," Alice said. He could hear the anger and frustration subtly present beneath the surface as she spoke. "I've only just been able to get her off to sleep. She got herself so worked up... thinking something dreadful must have happened to him."

"Here's hoping," he said before he was able to catch himself. Alice shot him a dark look. He slipped his coat off, laying it over the arm of the sofa and shrugging defensively. "Well, come on, do you blame me?" he asked, pointing at the sleeping form of the little girl. "Does he have any idea what he's doing to his daughter? I mean, really."

Alice shook her head, averting her eyes from his. "I know. I agree, you know I do but..."

"But what?" Tom said, the thought coming to mind that she was readying a defence of the hapless moron who was supposed to be a father.

"But nothing," she said at last. "I just don't know what to do. I've talked to him until I'm blue in the face and he just doesn't get it..."

"Maybe you need to write something out clearly, so he can understand his responsibilities," Tom said. "Maybe something in crayon."

Alice tilted her head to one side, shoulders sagging with a disapproving expression. "Maybe I need to go back to the court, try and work something out there."

Tom had always found her attitude towards her ex-husband too passive although he'd always done his best to stay out of it, believing his interference would do little more than aggravate the situation. When it came to Saffy however, his instincts encouraged him to get more involved. Up until now he'd managed to suppress those thoughts. Right now, he felt like paying Adrian a visit himself. Alice fixed him with one of her knowing looks. She could read him like a book.

"Don't Tom."

"Don't what?" he asked, smiling nervously under her watchful eye.

"Whatever thought just came into your head... don't. I'll handle it."

"Yeah, okay," he said, looking away from her. *After all, you've done a good job handling it so far*, he thought.

"I'm doing my best," she said.

He looked up at her, realising the last thing she needed was him wading in with his attitude. Alice felt it important for Saffy to keep contact with her father. He understood that. Many others in the same situation would look to do just the opposite, to cut the ex out of their lives entirely, through spite if for no other reason. Perhaps even look to recruit a substitute husband and father figure, but not Alice. She'd always been up front about that. She and Saffy were a package but Adrian was her father and would be an ever-present in their lives. At least until Saffy reached adulthood at any rate.

Still, Tom couldn't help but think the man was a cretin with this little episode doing little to alter the impression he held of him.

"So, how was your day? Have you eaten?" she asked.

Tom frowned. He was hungry and he'd missed both lunch and an evening meal without giving it a thought.

"Come to think of it, I'm famished."

"I saved some dinner for you," Alice said, gesturing for him to come back into the kitchen. "I'll put it in the microwave if you'll take Saffy up?"

He nodded, kneeling down alongside the sleeping girl. Gently sliding both arms beneath her, he lifted Saffy with ease allowing the blanket to fall away. She was seven years old and still felt as light as a feather to him as she settled into his arms. He carefully carried her upstairs to her bedroom. Saffy didn't stir once as he laid her down in her bed and pulled her duvet across her. Tucking Mr Snuggleface in alongside her, he switched on her night light and backed out of the room.

Returning downstairs, he knew now wasn't the time to bring up the finalisation of his divorce. Although he did wonder if there was ever going to be a right time to do so and perhaps he was just taking the easier option by kicking the can further down the road. Alice had plated up the leftovers from dinner and set it out for him at the breakfast bar. Not once had she chastised him for not having been round earlier, something for which he was grateful. The food smelled good and he felt his stomach grumble as he sat down.

"How's the case?" Alice asked, removing the cork from a half-empty bottle of wine she'd retrieved from the fridge and pouring herself a glass. Tom found his food too hot to eat and exhaled heavily.

"It's a weird one, I have to say."

"Aren't they all when it comes down to murder?" she asked, raising the glass to her lips. "I tell you, I've needed this today." Alice eyed the contents of the glass as she placed it down.

Tom smiled and then his phone rang.

CHAPTER TWENTY-SIX

JOHN CATTON HEARD the sirens of the approaching police cars, looked left and saw the pulse of the blue lights reflected in the surrounding trees. Confident he was safely shielded from view, he would stay where he was for the time being. They wouldn't be looking in his direction. Not yet anyway.

Lying very still, he began flexing individual muscles in order to ward off cramp. This was a technique he'd learnt during his time on the sniper training course at Pirbright. Ultimately he'd flunked it at week six but not before picking up a lot of useful skills. It was cold but he could deal with that having got used to it as a kid. His father had left the family home when he was just eight years old and his mother found it tough feeding and raising four children by herself. Heating was often one of the first things to be set aside when things got tight at the end of the month.

From his vantage point, he had a great view of the nurseries. The house was set back from the road but on the far side of both the beds and the hothouses, some distance from where he was now. That was where they'd start, eventually working their way around and in his direction. His only concern was if they'd deploy a canine unit. He figured that was unlikely in the first instance and, even if they did, which scent would they choose to follow?

Even if he drew the short straw, he still fancied his chances of avoiding detection. He'd already planned his exit strategy. A small stream ran barely a quarter of a mile to the south east and he could easily cover that ground more quickly than any of the police, of that he was certain. From there he'd use the water to mask his passage, following the route of the watercourse for a while before cutting back on himself and heading home. No problem. There was a risk but it was a calculated one.

The sirens were off now but the lights were still visible casting dancing shadows in red and blue around the property. How many would come? He didn't know and it mattered little.

He turned his focus back to the hothouse, the third on the property, and the one most in need of some TLC judging from its condition. Many of the roof panes were cracked or missing entirely and of those still present all were covered in grime, obscuring the interior from prying eyes. That was a shame. The temptation to move closer was strong but he resisted.

Having been up against the glass to witness the set-up he knew to go back now would be pushing his luck. Besides, he could recall the scene well enough. Paying attention to detail was something else taught to him at Pirbright. Detail. He was good on detail.

Not for the first time he had a doubt about this one. Of the three remaining, it was Harry who had the potential to do the right thing. He wasn't as selfish as the other two. That's why he'd approached him, giving him one last opportunity to change course. Together they could, perhaps, have taken things another way. Not that it was his call alone but maybe an acknowledgement, some contrition on Harry's part, may have curried favour.

Probably not.

In any event, they were arguably too far gone now. Harry didn't show willing anyway. Now he would come to understand action and consequence.

He felt something different tonight, sitting alongside the

satisfaction of seeing justice served. Was it guilt? Yes, that was it. Guilt. But for whom? Tina and the girls? They didn't deserve this.

Nevertheless, this was still perfectly arranged.

Voices carried to him on the gentle breeze. They weren't close and he couldn't determine how many distinctive voices were present but soon they would be spreading out through the grounds. No doubt they'd proceed cautiously. He still had time.

Easing himself up onto his knees, slowly moving from head to toe, he edged back deeper into the tree line avoiding disturbing the vegetation likely to give away his position as he made the move. The weight of a boot cracking an old branch or catching his coat on the brush were possibilities that might give away his presence and that was the last thing he needed. Retreating into the safety of the woods, he decided not to see this one play out.

Of the three, this was the one he couldn't watch after all.

CHAPTER TWENTY-SEVEN

By the time Tom Janssen arrived at Oakes Nursery, there were a number of liveried police vehicles already present. A young constable stood at the front door, stepping aside as he approached, nodding a greeting as Tom passed. The entrance hall was a tight space, the house being centuries old with low-beamed ceilings and small windows. Glancing over his shoulder at the constable, the officer directed him to the rear of the house. At the end of the hall the building opened out into a rear extension to the original property. Sitting at a casual dining table set just beyond a large island, he found Tina Oakes. Cassie Knight was with her and, as soon as she saw him, she excused herself and crossed the room to where he stood.

"Hi Tom," she said, glancing back at Tina. She was staring straight ahead with her hands before her, nervously wringing them. She was so highly strung she looked likely to crack at any moment. Cassie lowered her voice so only the two of them could hear. "Tina was putting the children to bed. The usual routine, bathing them and reading bedtime stories and the like. She fell asleep with them and, when she woke up, she came down to find this."

Cassie handed him a transparent evidence bag containing a

piece of paper. The message on it had been assembled with letters cut out of newspapers or magazines, quite likely in a crude attempt to avoid identification through handwriting. It read *You and the girls stay inside* and beneath that was a simple four-letter word, assembled *BOOM*. Tom exchanged a glance with Cassie and then looked around in search of the two children. He saw them in the adjoining family room. They were huddled next to each other on a sofa sharing a tablet device in the eldest girl's lap. By the look of the flickering images reflected in their faces, they were watching cartoons.

"Are they okay?" he asked.

Cassie tilted her head to one side. "They don't really know what's going on, so they're coping well enough." She looked at Tina who was in her little world. "But I'm not sure about their mother."

"Has she heard from her husband at all?"

Cassie shook her head. "Not since he left for an evening out with friends. She's repeatedly rung his mobile but it passes straight to voicemail."

"Yes, he was at the pub earlier with Eddie Drew and Greg Ellis. I spoke to him myself. Have you called Eric?"

"Yeah. Harry Oakes left the pub shortly after you did, leaving Drew and Ellis alone," Cassie said. "Eric is sitting outside Ellis's house right now. He went there alone, arriving a little after eleven o'clock."

Tom thought hard, glancing at his watch. It was approaching midnight.

"What about the uniforms," he said, indicating those outside with a flick of his thumb.

"I've just asked them to stay close to the house until we know what we're dealing with here. I mean, it could be a wind up."

"It could," Tom agreed. "But I wouldn't like to find out it's not by way of an unfortunate encounter." He handed her the evidence bag. "Is there anything suspicious lying around?"

"Not that we've seen, no, but it's dark and it's a big site with very little artificial light once you're away from the main house."

"Right, I'll organise a search if you can stay here with Tina and the children."

Cassie nodded and he left the kitchen, stepping out front and calling the assembled officers together. A quick head-count revealed eight uniformed officers were present and Tom split them into pairs. Using a complimentary map to the nurseries depicting the layout of where one could expect to find plants, he assigned each pair to search a different part of the site. They were equipped with torches and instructed not to touch anything but report back if they came across something they perceived as unusual or that looked out of place. He reiterated that point to ensure everyone understood.

The group fanned out and, despite taking great care, Tom had an uneasy feeling growing in the pit of his stomach. Having seen what was done to Freddie Mayes and then Andy Lewis, he was fearful of what they might find. He checked and there was no sign of Harry's car in the car park or towards the rear of the house and it had been at the pub, he saw it himself. Would someone target the business or had Harry met someone on his way home?

Tom checked his own torch was working and headed deeper into the site. Progress was slow as he had to pay close attention when taking each turn or passing through a doorway, all the while wishing that the makeshift warning left for Tina and the girls had been a little more specific. If this turned out to be an elaborate hoax, then all well and good but if, as he expected, this was real then the killer was demonstrating some thought for the innocents. The thought intrigued him. Killers seldom thought about anyone beyond themselves when it came to satisfying their darkest human desires, and for this one to do so made him curious. The targeting seemed ever more personal.

Focussing on the job in hand, Tom left his section of the bedding plants and the comfort of the overhead strip lighting to find himself enveloped by the darkness once again. He was heading towards the old hothouses, as pointed out to him on his first visit when he met Harry Oakes. The entrance to the first was closed off with yellow and black warning tape with a sign hanging beneath, instructing people to keep out. Tom eased the door open and swept the interior with his torch. The beam passed around the interior, only broken by the support pillars. The area was clearly close to being made ready for opening with designated walkways and lighting. Locating a nearby switch panel, he considered testing the lights but thought better of it. The less he touched the better.

Skirting around the glass structure, he came to the next. This was also taped off and appeared to be in a similar condition to the first. They were sited side by side with several points where a person could pass from one to the next but this one was also empty. His radio crackled and he turned up the volume.

"Please repeat," he said. The teams checked in one by one as agreed. No one had found anything. "Okay. Continue the search."

He put the radio back in his pocket and headed to his left where he could see the looming structure of the third and final hothouse. This one was fenced off to ensure no one could accidentally enter. There were strict warnings on display stating it was a building site and dangerous to enter without the appropriate personal protective equipment. Tom walked the line of the fence until he located the entrance point, finding the chain swinging loose. He angled the beam of his torch to it, finding the link had been severed, most likely with bolt cutters.

Turning the beam on the hothouse, he looked for signs of movement but there was nothing to see. The glass panels all around the structure were coated in age-old grime and the light only illuminated this rather than penetrating to the interior. Passing through the gate, he took great care with every step. The first door he came to leading into the hothouse, he inspected closely searching for anything out of place. Once he was happy, he opened it. The hinges were rusty and the door protested as it swung to one side. As before, he passed his beam over the interior only on this occasion he stopped as he eyed a figure apparently sitting in the middle of the complex. The hothouse was roughly sixty metres long and half that distance wide. The figure was facing away from him and slouching, or was slumped, forward. From this distance he couldn't see who it was. Despite the beam of the torch focussing on the person, whoever it was made no attempt to move or speak.

"Hello," Tom called, looking for a reaction. There was none. "Harry Oakes... is that you? It's the police." Still there was no response.

The distance between them was significant and it was dark despite the benefit of his torch. He eyed the ground at his feet to see it was uneven, strewn with shards of glass, presumably from overhead panes that had failed over the years, and covered in detritus. Weeds must have run amok here for a long time before being dealt with. The reality was Tom couldn't see the ground beneath his feet. He didn't fancy crossing the gap. Angling the torch to one side he eyed another entrance along the side of the structure. The door was open or missing, he couldn't really tell. Backing out, he made his way along the front of the hothouse and down the side still taking care where he put his feet. Reaching the door, he found it wedged open. He was now level with the figure who was sitting on the floor barely fifteen metres away.

Once again, he checked the door for signs of a potential booby trap, not really knowing what he should be looking for, but in any event there was nothing that concerned him. He used his radio to announce he'd found something, requesting assistance. The response was affirmative. Sliding the handset back into his pocket, he turned the beam of the torch towards the figure sitting in the dark. He could now clearly see it was Harry Oakes.

Oakes blinked furiously when the light fell on him but he didn't look round to where it originated. Beads of perspiration gathered on his forehead, running down both cheeks and his chest heaved as he struggled to draw air through his nostrils that were themselves bleeding. His mouth had a length of silver gaffer tape stuck across it. He couldn't speak even if he wanted to. Oakes was sitting on the ground with his legs stretched out before him, his arms were also extended to their fullest reach. A length of cord was wrapped around his waist and tied behind a metal pillar supporting the roof structure. In his hands he held a bar, but as the beam of the torch illuminated it Tom saw it wasn't a bar but a hammer. It had an orange and black handle with a rectangular head. It was a medium-sized club hammer, probably weighing a couple of kilos by his best guess. Oakes was struggling to keep his arms upright, they were beginning to vibrate and tremble under the strain. *How long had he been sitting there?*

Cassie appeared at his side along with two uniformed officers, who added their lights to the interior.

"What on earth is going on?" she asked.

"Look," Tom said, slowly moving the beam of his torch to their right and away from Harry Oakes. At first glance it was easy to miss but the light was partially reflected back at them, bouncing off a length of silver wire tightly strung between the handle of the hammer that went up and over a structural support bar and then dropped down to a small green, rectangular box located on the floor four metres away.

"What is that?" Cassie asked. Tom shook his head, examining it under the light of his torch. It was olive green, appeared to be made out of plastic and was old, too, by the look of it. It was roughly ten centimetres high, half that deep and measured almost an elbow to wrist in length and had been mounted in the ground. The light from the torch seemed to pass under it as if it had been stuck in the ground with a couple of pegs.

"My guess is that's the explosive Tina was warned about," Tom said. Cassie made to step forward into the hothouse but Tom grasped her forearm, preventing her from doing so. He directed the torch to their left. Hanging from a nearby support pillar was another homemade message, gently swaying in the draught from the open door. This one said *Danger UXB*. He looked at her, shaking his head.

"We'd better call the bomb squad," Cassie said.

Tom nodded. "Make sure you're clear of here when you do. Spread the word, no radios, no mobiles within a hundred metres of this location. If I'm right, those things can be detonated by radio transmitter and we don't want it going off by accident."

Cassie nodded and left, running back towards the house. Tom turned to the still form of Harry Oakes, desperately holding the hammer aloft in front of him. How long could he keep it up. The wire was attached to the device with no slack at all, should the hammer fall then it logically followed that the device would detonate. What that would entail he didn't know. If the device was live, how much explosive could it contain and how large would the blast radius be? These were questions he couldn't answer. By the look of anguish in Oakes's expression, it didn't appear that he could keep it up much longer. There was little chance of him doing so long enough to enable the team of disposal experts from the Royal Logistic Corps to reach the scene.

Tom stepped out of the hothouse, beckoning the nearest officer to him.

"We need to set up a cordon," he said, looking around. "Minimum fifty metres, no one in or out—"

Sounds of a commotion towards the house came to him, followed by shouts. Tom turned to see a figure sprinting towards him with two officers in pursuit. The closest one managed to lay a hand on the man's shoulder but he shrugged him off with relative ease sending the constable sprawling to the ground. As they came closer, Tom recognised Eddie Drew. He moved to intercept, stepping into his path and planting both his feet and using his height and weight advantage to good effect. Drew hammered into him but Tom was immovable.

Eddie Drew wasn't looking for a fight, only to get past and into the hothouse. Tom rotated his body using Drew's forward momentum to throw him forward and off balance. They both fell to the ground with Tom coming to rest on top of him. Drew lashed out with his elbow, attempting to knock Tom away from him. Tom took the blow to the side of his head and although it hurt he focussed on stopping Drew from going further.

"I need to get in there!" Drew said, desperation edging into his voice as he realised he wasn't going to shake Tom's challenge off as easily as he done the previous officer.

"You can't!" Tom growled, straining his muscles to prevent Drew from getting free.

Despite his advantage, Tom knew how hard it was to restrain one man determined to get free. Even a lone drunk on a Saturday night could require half a dozen officers to subdue them if they really pushed it. More uniforms piled in and the mass of bodies became entangled as one, collapsing to the ground in a heap before order was eventually restored. Drew was handcuffed and hauled to his feet. Tom came to stand in front of him breathing heavily from the exertion of the struggle.

"You can't leave him in there," Drew argued but his expression conveyed he knew he was fighting a lost cause.

"We've got people on the way," Tom said, trying to placate him.

"They'll not make it in time," Drew said, glaring at him. "You know it as well as I do."

Tom looked over his shoulder to see Cassie arrive, an apologetic look on her face. She shook her head, her lower lip was bleeding and her tied-up hair was dishevelled. He realised what must have happened. He turned back to Drew whose attempts to free himself had pretty much ceased as he gave in to the futility of doing so. One officer stood to either side of him, both with a firm hold of his upper arm.

"Set up the cordon and put him on the other side of it," Tom said.

"You can't," Drew hissed as they attempted to remove him. He dug his heels into the ground, pressing back against the officers with renewed vigour. Eventually the officers were forced to call for extra help and, with one taking hold of each arm and leg, Drew was unceremoniously carried away. "You can't do this!" he protested.

"You can't help him," Tom said to the beleaguered man as he passed. Looking into the interior of the hothouse, he knew it was only a matter of time. He looked at Cassie. "We need to get to a safe distance." She understood the unspoken implication of his comment and nodded. Placing a guiding hand on Cassie's shoulder, he turned her and they quickly headed back towards the freshly established cordon, accompanied by Eddie Drew's howls of protest.

Barely had they reached safety when a dull boom sounded. The glass of the hothouse shattered, sending shards of broken glass flying into the air in every direction. The group threw themselves to the ground, Eddie Drew landing awkwardly under the weight of a constable. Fragments of glass landed nearby, sounding like repetitive percussion instruments in a crude orchestra. Then there followed an eerie silence as all those present looked back towards where Harry Oakes had been. Eddie Drew, lying on his side, rolled over face down in the soil and screamed a guttural release of anger.

Footsteps on the path saw Tom rise just in time to catch Tina Oakes as she ran towards the scene. She was barely five-foot four tall, waif-like and he easily managed to restrain her. Initially she battered her closed fists against his chest in frustration only to collapse into his arms as he held her. Without his grip, she would have sunk to the floor. Tina Oakes broke down and Tom held her tightly, making reassuring sounds as she rested her head against his chest, no longer fighting, merely seeking a comforting embrace. He felt utterly helpless as he witnessed her despair.

CHAPTER TWENTY-EIGHT

Tom Janssen recognised the car as it pulled into the customer car park of Oakes Nursery. Greg Ellis met his eye as he pulled up. A uniformed constable stood at the edge of the cordon and was about to issue an instruction for him to leave as soon as he got out of the car but Tom stopped him, allowing Ellis to pass through, crossing the open ground to meet him.

"It's an odd time of night to be making a house call, don't you think?" Tom asked.

Ellis's expression didn't change, it was a mask of concentration. Tom expected a display of calm assurance or arrogance, he wasn't sure which. Ellis didn't provide it.

"Tina called me earlier, left a message. I only just listened to the voicemail," he said, looking past Tom at the number of police vehicles parked around the site. It was a plausible excuse for the delay. Tina had also called Eddie Drew; she had said as much once she'd calmed down after the explosion. Calmed down. Entered a state of shock was more like it. After the explosion, Tom held her as long as she needed before she managed to gather herself. She was indoors now, comforting her two children. How and when she would be able to begin processing the loss of her husband, let alone assist their children, he had no idea. Cassie

Knight was with them. He figured she might object to being handed the task of comforting her but he hadn't made that call because of some vague notion that a woman was predisposed to handle the emotional fall out; he had an ulterior motive and it was cynical. Tina Oakes was at her lowest, ravaged by her loss, and now might just be the time when she lets something slip, something useful. So far, this group had proved adept at closing ranks. Tina being an outsider, facing the loss of her husband, might change things and he wanted someone he trusted nearby just in case.

Ellis wasn't paying Tom a great deal of attention, he was itching to get closer but Tom wasn't willing to let him just yet. Ellis eyed the lorry parked at the far end of the car park. It was a Royal Logistics Corps bomb disposal vehicle. They were always on-call for use in civilian emergencies. More commonly that related to old World War ordnance that was occasionally unearthed on a building site or, in Norfolk's case, washed up on the beaches. They were trained to make things safe or carry out controlled detonations where required. Unfortunately in this case, their arrival was too late for Harry Oakes.

"What's with the EOD?" Ellis asked, pointing towards the lorry. Tom glanced over his shoulder.

"EOD?"

"Explosive Ordnance Disposal," Ellis said. "What's going on?"

Tom ignored his question, the answer was fairly obvious. "What did Tina tell you?"

Ellis was irritated by the question. Perhaps he wasn't used to not being in charge.

"That Harry was missing… and she was worried. I figured it was serious as she's unlikely to call me."

"Why is that do you think?"

Ellis looked away from the vehicle, seeing two soldiers in camouflage fatigues revisit the equipment in the rear before heading back around the building and disappearing from view. Now he was focussed on Tom.

"I don't think she likes me very much," Ellis said. "Nor any of the others really. Not her fault, I guess. We're from a different world to hers. Harry's managed to bridge the gap but I don't think even he's too keen for us to be around much. Now, are you going to tell me what the hell is going on or do I have to go and see Tina myself?"

"Harry's dead, Mr Ellis. He died an hour ago."

Ellis appeared thrown. His fixed expression softened but his eyes narrowed as he broke away from Tom's gaze.

"I… I… but how?"

"In an explosion," Tom said. "What were your movements after leaving the pub earlier?"

Ellis's shock was replaced by anger. "What the hell are you asking me that for? You can't think I was anything to do with this."

"To do with what?"

Ellis gestured towards the scene behind him. "All of that! Harry was my friend for crying out loud."

"I'm just asking you where you were," Tom said softly. "Is that too difficult a question for you to answer?"

"I went home, all right? I left the pub and went home, fell asleep in front of the TV and I was there until I picked up the voicemail message."

That reply tallied with what Eric had already told them. The detective constable would be somewhere nearby, out of sight and keeping his distance in case Tom wanted to maintain the covert surveillance. Ellis lived four miles from here as the crow flies and Tom did a rough calculation in his mind as to whether Ellis could have slipped past Eric, come here and rigged everything up before returning home without being seen. It was not impossible within the time frame but seemed highly unlikely. This event was well planned and perfectly executed. For Ellis to have done so would have required too many variables to go favourably for it to have worked. At least, if he'd done so alone.

Eddie Drew happened upon the scene quickly enough, prior

to Harry's death. Could he fake such raw emotion? Ellis didn't wait for a response, pushing past Tom and heading for the house.

"To hell with this, where's Tina?"

Tom saw fit not to stop him, instead falling into step alongside as they walked.

"You know, it would help me a lot if you were to open up a little."

Ellis stopped, turning on him and raising a pointed finger before his face. "Or maybe you should do your damn job and catch whoever's doing this or…"

"Or what?" Tom asked. Ellis didn't reply, averting his eye from Tom's gaze. He spotted Eddie Drew in the rear of a patrol car, looking the very picture of dejection. Ellis gestured towards him.

"What the bloody hell has he gone and done now?"

Tom looked over just as Drew looked up, seeing the two men watching him. He began to speak but his words were inaudible from within the car.

"Making a nuisance of himself," Tom said.

"He's no harm, really," Ellis said. "Surely you've got better things to do than tie yourself up with an idiot?"

"Assaulting a police officer doesn't go down well."

Ellis rolled his eyes. "Well, he'd had a few earlier, right enough. Probably wasn't thinking straight."

"Yeah," Tom said. "We'll see how it goes. The officer in question might choose not to press charges."

Cassie Knight appeared at the entrance to the house, deep in conversation with another officer. She nodded, looking over at them the whole time before thanking the constable and crossing to speak with them. She ignored Ellis and addressed Tom.

"The military boys say it's safe and they want a word with you."

"Right you are—"

"How are Tina and the girls?" Ellis asked, talking over Tom.

Cassie inclined her head to one side. "Okay, under the circumstances. The kids are asleep. Tina's in shock. We've offered to have a doctor come out, prescribe something to help her sleep but she's knocked it back for now."

"Can I see her?" Ellis asked, his tone dropping the intensity of his earlier interruption. Cassie looked at Tom and he nodded.

"Yeah, sure. I'll take you in," she said, indicating towards the house with her head. Ellis passed Tom and the latter shot Cassie a look to imply she should hold back. "Wait for me at the door and I'll see you in," she said to Ellis, who muttered a thank you but didn't look back. She turned to Tom.

"Keep a close eye on him," Tom said.

"I will."

"And it might be worth releasing Drew at the same time," he said.

Cassie shot him a dark look and appeared ready to protest. Her lower lip was no longer bleeding but it was swollen and looked sore.

"It might be good to see the interaction between the two of them since… since Harry's death."

Her expression of disapproval passed, and she nodded. "Yeah, good thinking," she said, looking towards Eddie Drew in the back of the patrol car, sitting uncomfortably with his hands cuffed behind his back.

Tom set off for the hothouses at the rear where Harry Oakes lost his life. There was a second cordon on the approach to the hothouses at the request of the bomb disposal team. He slipped under the tape, acknowledging the constable who was manning the perimeter. The commanding officer of the RLC team saw his approach and came to meet him.

"Inspector Janssen," Lieutenant Robert Norwood said. His tone was stoic and authoritarian, the military way. "We've made a sweep of the immediate area and confirmed our initial assessment. There was no secondary device present."

"Damn it," Tom whispered, almost inaudibly. That confirmed what he'd already thought likely. The initial explosion didn't trigger a chain of subsequent detonations and he guessed there weren't any more explosives set for them. Tom cast his mind back to the warning sign hanging near to the entrance. Of course, they had no way of knowing at the time but it was clearly designed to give the impression of another booby trap, thereby ensuring no one could go to the aid of the stricken man. He felt guilty then, knowing that he could have taken the weight from Oakes and freed him. The man would still be alive had he moved in or allowed Eddie Drew to do as he wanted. The officer appeared to read his thoughts.

"Don't be too hard on yourself," he said, shaking his head. "There's no way you could have known. I learnt my craft while deployed in Afghanistan and I've seen all manner of IEDs in my time. We've disarmed thousands of set-ups in all manner of guises. You couldn't know, not without taking a detailed assessment of the area. From what your lads tell me," the officer glanced back to the hothouse, now merely a skeletal frame with all the panes blown out, "he'd been there a while. Even if we'd been called immediately, I'm not sure we could have got to him before the detonation."

Tom appreciated the supportive statement but it didn't make him feel any better.

"What can you tell me about the device? I'm guessing it was military."

The officer nodded, gesturing for Tom to join him. They headed towards the hothouse and the door where Tom had earlier stood in, observing Harry Oakes.

"Brace yourself for it's not pretty," Norwood said. Tom frowned, resigned to that prospect.

Reaching the doorway, Tom was concerned with disturbing the crime scene any further. The bomb disposal team needed to carry out a detailed search of the area looking for evidence of trip wires, mines or improvised devices. Their presence, plus the explosion that killed Harry Oakes, had already compromised the scene. Nevertheless, Tom entered but vowed to limit his impact as best he could.

Norwood was right. The scene was shocking. Harry Oakes had been killed by the blast, although now he was unrecognisable. Any exposed area of his body had been struck. The limbs of his upper body, his face, along with all his clothing, appeared to have passed through a shredder and Tom looked away from the face; it was too gruesome to view for any longer than absolutely necessary. No stranger to death, even Tom fought back a gag reflex. Norwood demonstrated his empathy, nodding slowly and slowly sucking air through his teeth.

"That's what they're supposed to do," he said. Tom covered his mouth, meeting the officer's eye.

"Supposed?"

"By design," Norwood stated, crossing near to where the device had been in position and dropping to his haunches. He cast an eye back to where Oakes's body remained, still tied to the pillar. Norwood held both hands up, making the shape of a gun with both forefingers pointing towards the deceased. "It was an anti-personnel mine, designed to kill or wound its target by fragmentation. The thinking is to set them off, either by trip wire or a manual activation of the detonator, and take out those closest but also to incapacitate or injure more combatants in the surrounding area. The casing is packed with just shy of a kilogram of a TNT-based explosive alongside six hundred plus five-point-five millimetre steel balls."

"Geez... that's nasty."

"You're not wrong, Inspector," Norwood said, nodding at Tom's assessment. "The fragmentation alone has a lethal arc of sixty degrees to a range of forty to fifty metres. It's simple stuff really, and highly effective. The casing is waterproof and they are incredibly versatile. You can use them in any type of terrain or climate, completely unaffected by ambient temperatures in the range of minus thirty to fifty degrees Celsius. These metal legs here," he used a pen to indicate two metal legs protruding from the earth, all that was left of the device in the ground, "are used to pin it in place. The casing is a convex rectangle so you can angle the blast where you want it."

"They are often used in conjunction with a blast mine. One end of a detonating cord is inserted into the base of one of these and then taped to the detonating cord of the blast mine. The initial blast mine is activated, killing those nearby and then the fragmentation mine explodes and takes out their mates. Crude but, as I said before, effective. I've even known them to be mounted high up in the trees to ensure a larger fragmentation zone. Very nasty stuff."

"You said it could be manually activated?"

Norwood confirmed with a nod.

"How close would the person holding the detonator need to be?"

The officer thought about it. "Presuming a clear line of sight, they can be command detonated from no more than thirty metres away. They'd need to be using a manual inductor or another electrical power source."

"Any evidence of that?" Tom asked, keen to know if the deck was completely stacked against Harry Oakes or whether he'd stood a chance.

"Not that we found. It wouldn't be a radio frequency transmitter. These are too basic for that. Once the sun comes up, we can have a better look around but I think it was triggered by the victim releasing the strain on the wire."

Tom understood, recalling the sheen of perspiration and effort Harry Oakes was putting in to holding up the hammer. A weight that can easily be held at arm's length for a few seconds could feel like the weight of a car after a prolonged period. Even lowering the hammer a few inches could have been enough to pull the wire from the mine, he need not have actually dropped it to set it off.

"How could someone lay their hands on this type of device?" Tom asked, knowing that it would be hard to come by.

Norwood shook his head. "To be honest, that's not my field of expertise but it wouldn't be easy. I guess anything is available at the right price but…" Tom sensed his reticence.

"What is it?"

Norwood exhaled heavily. "This is military-grade ordnance. You won't come by it anywhere else, you know."

"Any idea about the origin of this particular model?" Tom asked.

"Corporal!" Norwood called, beckoning to one of his colleagues. "Bring us that bit of casing will you."

The corporal came to them, the carpet of broken glass crunching under his weight, passing over a transparent bag. Norwood handed it to Tom. It was an olive-green fragment of plastic, barely an inch across. Even in this poor light, Tom could make out some lettering. For a better look, he angled it towards the temporary lights set up to help examine the scene. He could make out two capital letters, a P and a Y. There looked to be a third before these but there wasn't enough left to determine what it was. He shot an enquiring look at Norwood.

"M P Y," Norwood said. "No doubt we'll find a few more components scattered around when the sun comes up but I think this is pretty old. Out of the eastern bloc, probably an MRUD, former Yugoslav army ordnance. Pretty similar to US Claymores. I don't know how well you know your history, Inspector, but Yugoslavia had a pretty large army back in the day and manufactured a lot of kit that they sold around their allies. They were still in common use in the Bosnian-Serb War and I dare say they haven't changed much over the years and are still in use today."

"You think this is the work of a soldier?" Tom asked.

"I wouldn't say that's necessarily the case," Norwood said. "You don't need any particular expertise to set one of these up, as long as you know what they're supposed to do. After all, it's a pretty simple device. It can be packed into an individual's bergen and safely transportedand it weighs less than a couple of kilos." He looked around the immediate area, raising his eyebrows in a knowing gesture. "And what was done here isn't exactly mission impossible either. A working knowledge of the mine is all that would be needed. It's getting access to the kit that would concern me."

"Okay, thanks," Tom said, the still form of Harry Oakes catching his eye. He was drawn to look, even though he didn't want to, and found himself contemplating what must have gone through his mind as he was sitting there feeling his strength ebbing away. Did he think about his wife and children? Did he realise he was about to die? He found Lieutenant Norwood watching him intently. Tom grimaced and the officer bobbed his head, agreeing with the sentiment.

"The poor sod."

CHAPTER TWENTY-NINE

TOM JANSSEN WAS MET at the front of the main house by Greg Ellis and an animated Eddie Drew who, despite a prolonged spell in handcuffs, alone in a patrol car, seemed unwilling to learn the science behind cause and effect. Tom came into contact with people like this frequently. They were prone to quick reactions rather than calm assessment of a situation. He tried to push past Ellis to come before Tom but a restraining hand stopped him. He shot a dark look at Ellis before checking himself and standing down, albeit against his instincts.

"Is it true?" Ellis asked.

Tom cocked his head. He caught sight of Cassie in the background and she was silently apologetic, mouthing the words and scrunching her face up. It looks like word spread, most likely from another of the disposal team talking to his DS.

"Is what true?" he played dumb. Drew spun on his heel and again tried to push himself to the front, this time Ellis made little effort to rein him in.

"That there wasn't a secondary device," Drew said with a snarl.

Tom confirmed it with a nod. Drew all but exploded, stepping forward but pulling up half a step from him. He was still well inside what would be considered his personal space.

"You let him die!" Drew spat at him, glaring at Tom and puffing out his chest. It was a stance that Tom would usually expect to spurn an assault but Drew remained with a modicum of composure. "You did nothing—"

"We did what we could, under the circumstances," Tom said, taking care to remain calm and not escalate the situation.

"Nah, you just stood there and let him bloody die. I could have got Harry out of there."

"How could we know?" Tom said, but rational thought and logic weren't going to cut any ice.

"I could have—"

"Leave it be, Eddie," Ellis stepped forward, placing a hand on his friend's shoulder. Eddie glared back at him now.

"I could have saved him, Greg. If only this bastard would have let me try."

"Or we might have been scraping you off the floor and walls now," Ellis said, narrowing his eyes. "Along with Harry."

Drew looked ready to argue his point but thought better of it.

"The inspector is right, Eddie. There was no way of knowing and," he said, flicking his eyes at Tom, "if I was in his place, then I reckon I'd have made the same call. This guy got the drop on Harry." He released his hold on Drew who visibly appeared to deflate, and then he turned his attention to Tom. "But he won't get the drop on us."

"Well that probably depends on how the two of you behave," Tom said. "Keeping a clear head and," he looked at Drew, "staying calm are probably the bare minimum required at this stage. Either of you feel like talking?" He looked between them. Ellis met his eye but Drew averted his gaze. For a salesman, someone who arguably lied for a living, Drew wasn't much good when it came to body language.

"This is your world, Inspector Janssen," Ellis said calmly. "It's about time you stepped up and did your job, otherwise…"

"Otherwise what?" Tom asked, moving forward and intentionally standing close to Ellis. He was growing increasingly irritated at the man's obtuse manner hidden behind a veneer of politeness. "That's the second time you've dropped a casual intimation to me. Should I be seeing that as a threat?"

Greg Ellis looked up, meeting Tom's eye. He was a good head and shoulders shorter than Tom but arguably his equal in physical stature.

"We're in your world now, Inspector Janssen," Ellis said, his tone measured but with a hint of malice. "Just see that you don't wander into ours, yeah."

"I'm definitely taking that as a threat," Tom said.

Ellis smiled but the expression didn't reach the eyes. They held an intensity, the likes of which Tom hadn't seen in the man before. He'd always seemed the professional organiser of the group but now his eyes gleamed with an edge that was disconcerting.

"If you cross a line," Tom glanced between the two men, "then mark my words, I will bring every resource we have to bear and I will put them on to you."

Greg Ellis held his gaze, the smile lingering. His upper lip appeared to twitch at the same time as his nose. Whatever he was thinking, he'd resigned himself to holding it in... for now.

"We look after our own, Inspector. That's the way these things work. Make sure you don't stray into my path... they left Harry to sit alone for hours waiting for death and make no mistake, death comes for us all in the end. I'm not a man who's prepared to wait."

"No, I can see that," Tom replied.

Ellis took a step back, the smile fading. Then he nodded to Drew and the two men backed up before turning and striding away. Cassie stepped aside even though there was more than enough room for them to bypass her. She glanced at them as they passed but didn't speak. Tom came to stand beside her.

"I'm sorry, Tom. Drew was hanging around when I was chatting to one of the disposal team. I didn't realise he was within earshot otherwise I—"

"Ah, don't worry about it," Tom said, waving away her

apology as they both watched the men climb into their respective cars.

Both men had been in the pub and the thought that one or both of them might be over the legal limit to drive flashed through his mind but he wanted them out there. The two of them sitting in a cell overnight served him no purpose. Besides, in the early hours there wasn't a lot of traffic around and the situation appeared to have sobered them both up.

"Give Eric a call," Tom said. "He'll be secreted somewhere nearby. Have him stay with Ellis. Wherever he is, I want Eric close by."

"What about Drew?"

Tom shook his head. "He's a hothead and in a pub car park after closing time I reckon he'd pile in without a second thought but tonight? No, he won't flinch unless Ellis gives him the nod. Whatever they plan to do, they'll do it together."

"Gotcha," Cassie said, taking out her mobile as both cars turned out onto the main road and headed off in the same direction.

"And remind him to be careful, yeah," Tom said with a stern look.

Cassie nodded, dialling Eric's mobile while Tom entered the house. The police cars had switched off their lights by now, giving the scene the appearance of calm in light of the Oakes's young children. Tom met the liaison officer at the entrance to the kitchen, a constable by the name of Lisa, who was doing her best to help the family cope with what had befallen them. This was no mean feat.

"How is Tina?" he asked.

"Keeping it together... just about," she said, glancing over her shoulder into the kitchen beyond. Tom followed her gaze, seeing the mother of two sitting on a rug next to a small sofa in the adjoining family room. He could see the two girls asleep on the sofa, the elder child with her arm draped over the younger. They were both probably a year either side of Saffy's age and he couldn't help but think about her, an image of her safely tucked up at home where he'd placed her came to mind. What must the girls be going through? How could they process the loss of their father, particularly in such a savage manner?

"I need to speak with her," Tom said quietly. "Do you think you could sit with the children so that I can?"

Lisa nodded, turning and leading the way. Lisa was a natural in this situation, an experienced constable whose empathy levels were a cut above most others, but who also managed to maintain that distance, just enough to keep her from being overwhelmed by the emotions of those around her. Tom wasn't sure he would do as well.

Tina Oakes saw them approaching. Realising that a senior detective would wish to speak with her, she gently kissed the nearest child on the forehead and stroked the fringe of hair away from the other's eyes before rising slowly to her feet. She appeared unsteady at first but waved away Lisa's offer of a hand.

"My legs have gone to sleep, that's all," Tina said softly, ensuring she wouldn't wake her children.

"This is Tom Janssen," Lisa said, dispensing with the formalities, unaware that Tom had met Tina twice before, albeit briefly on both occasions. "He is investigating what happened and would like a word. Is that okay?"

Tina nodded, looking down at the sleeping forms of her children.

"I'll stay with them," Lisa said. "They'll not be alone."

Tina smiled weakly, nodding her agreement, although it was obvious she was reluctant to depart. Tom held his hand out with an open palm, gesturing for them to head back into the kitchen. Tina tentatively walked ahead of him. As she entered the kitchen, she brought herself upright running both hands through her shoulder-length hair before bringing them to rest on the back of her neck and looking to the ceiling. They stopped at the breakfast bar and Tina pulled out one of the stools, sinking onto it and exhaling as if the emotional exhaustion of the night's events finally caught up with her. She placed her hands out in front of her, palms down, flexing her arms in a stretch before meeting Tom's eye.

"Forgive me, I'm not at my best," she said quietly.

Tom dismissed the need for an apology, taking her measure. The woman looked gaunt, she'd been crying although she'd done her best to disguise that fact but the make-up around her eyes and on her cheeks was both smudged and streaked.

"Has my officer offered to make contact with a friend or relative on your behalf?" Tom asked, glancing back to Lisa who'd taken a seat near to where the children lay.

"Yes, Lisa offered but…"

"But?"

Tina raised her eyes skyward. "But… I'm not exactly on the best of terms with my family right now." She sighed.

"Whatever has gone on, I'm sure it will pale into insignificance under the circumstances," Tom said, frowning.

"Yes… probably," Tina replied, scratching at her forehead and drawing breath sharply. "I just can't face the *I told you so* conversation tonight, that's all."

"They told you about what?"

"Marrying Harry," she said glumly. "My father said it would all end in tears…" She sat up, rubbing at her cheeks with both hands. "I doubt he foresaw any of this but, damn, I hate it when the old bugger is right. What is it you want to know, Inspector?"

"I need to ask you a few questions about today and perhaps the run up to it, if that's okay?"

"Whatever I can do," she said, forcing a polite smile.

"Was there anything unusual today now that you think about it, either around the house or with your husband?"

"Unusual? Such as what?"

"Behaviour, telephone calls…?"

She shook her head. "Not that I can think of, no," she said, her brow furrowing in concentration. "It was much the same as any other recently, dominated by the renovations and pushing the business forward. We have a deadline for reopening, all the leaflets and promotions are booked. It's been tight, a little stressful perhaps but... Harry's been very positive about it all. We were on schedule with all the works. There was only the..." she stared off into the distance at nothing in particular, "the last of the hothouses left to complete."

"How about the past few days, has there been anything odd going on or has Harry been distracted at all?"

Tina thought hard, her brow furrowing. "He's been stressed but that's hardly a surprise. I mean, who wouldn't be with the money we've had going out of the house recently? That's why he went out tonight, to blow off a bit of steam with the guys. He doesn't usually these days, not regularly anyway. Not since we had the girls." Tina's gaze drifted across to her children. Lisa noticed and smiled.

"How have you been funding the work?" Tom asked. "If you don't mind saying. I'm not prying."

Tina waved away his concern. "That's okay. It's been tough. This place," she indicated the house and Tom figured she was also referring to the nursery, "was a gift to us. A wedding present of sorts."

"It belonged to your... grandfather, didn't it? I remember Harry telling me so."

Tina stared at him and then there was a spark of recognition. "Oh yes, of course. You were here before, asking about Harry's time in the army. I remember now. Sorry, I'm terrible with faces most of the time."

He smiled. "Yes, that's right. I came to speak with your husband after Freddie Mayes died. Did Harry ever speak with you about his time in the forces, on active service in particular?"

She shook her head. "No, hardly ever. I don't think he liked to talk about it, at least not with me. I knew he struggled with it from time to time. He'd wake at night sometimes, drenched in perspiration but... he wouldn't speak of it. I respected that. He wanted to put it behind him."

"He's tight with his former comrades though."

"Of course, yes," she said, nodding enthusiastically. "He always referred to them as his brothers."

"How do you find them?"

She inclined her head to one side and he sensed her hesitation.

"I mean, do you get on with them?"

"It's not that... I don't like them, please don't think that but..."

"But?"

Tina pursed her lips, searching for the right words to articulate her feelings.

"They are close, as you said, and it is something of a closed group if you know what I mean."

Tom didn't reply, allowing the silence to grow in the hope of teasing more information out of her. She obliged.

"Harry always said that if we needed them then they'd be there for us, all of us, me and the girls," she said, frowning. "At first, I figured it was some kind of macho soldier... thing," she said shaking her head and making circles in the air with her hands, struggling to detail it and seemingly unhappy with the accuracy of her description. "But Harry would go on about it, drumming it in that we could count on them if anything should happen. Looking back, I found it odd but I put it down to their service together and that Harry doesn't have any family of his own, besides me and the girls of course. They were his family. And that's why I called them tonight. I didn't mean to cause trouble."

"You didn't," Tom said, smiling warmly. "It's understandable. Your husband... was there anything he said today that with hindsight might have appeared a little strange?"

"Like what?"

"Anything. Did he seem out of sorts... withdrawn perhaps or preoccupied?"

"Nothing like that, at least not beyond the normal these days. Like I said, it's been stressful."

"Yes, you mentioned the finances."

"That's right," Tina said, nodding. "The site, along with the house, was a gift but we financed the renovations ourselves. That was the arrangement."

"Arrangement?"

"With my family," Tina said. "It's no secret my father was against our marriage. He was unhappy with my choice of partner, thinking Harry wasn't good enough. Him being from the ranks and all that, although I think it was always more that he hadn't chosen him himself."

"I see," Tom said, sucking air through his teeth.

"What with me being his only daughter as well…" Tina smiled. "My mother was onside though, especially after we had the children. Harry was out of the army by then and we came up with the idea of taking on this place when my grandfather died. Father agreed, as long as we got married and financed it ourselves."

"He wanted things his way, then," Tom said. "How did you finance it?"

Tina laughed dryly. "That's Daddy. We did it through savings. I used to get quite a hefty allowance from my father's estate, although that all stopped when Harry came on the scene. Then Harry had an unexpected inheritance from a distant relative whom he didn't really know."

Tom found his curiosity piqued. "Who was that, can you recall?"

"Oh, it was a great aunt on his mother's side, I believe. She died intestate and one of those tracing companies got in touch with Harry about six months after her death. That was quite a nice surprise," she immediately sought to retract the comment. "I'm sorry, I mean it was awful for her but for us… it couldn't have come at a better time."

"That's okay, I understand. Do you have her name by any chance?"

Tina shook her head. "No, I'm sorry. There were no other relatives and we had already missed the funeral by quite some time. It's sad really, when someone passes away with no one there to see them off." She looked to her right, out of a window overlooking the rear garden. She welled up and Tom felt for her.

"And there was nothing unusual that happened today, or in the past week?"

"No, not… that I can think of…" she shook her head.

Tom's instinct told him that wasn't the case, she was skirting around something, holding back and he decided to apply a little pressure which he hadn't intended on doing.

"Mrs Oakes, whatever it is," he lowered his head to make sure his eyes met hers as she seemed to be trying to avoid his gaze, "I need to know and you're not doing yourself, Harry," he glanced at the sleeping girls, "or your children any good by keeping it to yourself."

She looked up, meeting his eye. Her expression reinforced his instinct and he inclined his head to one side fixing her with a stern look.

"Now's the time to speak up, Tina."

"I'm sure it was nothing," she said, looking down at the surface in front of her.

"Let me be the judge of that, please."

She looked up again, rolling her lower lip beneath the upper as he encouraged her with a flick of his eyebrows. Shaking her head, she spoke softly.

"I saw Harry talking to someone in the car park late this afternoon… an odd-looking chap… all dirty and dishevelled."

"Talking?"

She nodded. "I asked Harry about it afterwards and he said it was just some tramp looking for somewhere to pitch for the night and he'd sent him on his way."

"Did you believe him?"

She shook her head. "It looked more like they were… talking, like they knew one another. I think I've seen him around before as well. Around here, the nurseries, not with Harry but… just around."

Tom ran a hand across his face, thinking hard. He could think of one person in this close-knit circle who fitted that particular description. He took his hand away and eyed Tina Oakes. She was fumbling with her hands in her lap, in his opinion consciously avoiding his gaze.

"Have you told anyone else about this?"

She furtively flicked her eyes up at him and immediately away, not wishing to maintain eye contact.

"Tina. Did you tell anyone else about this tonight?"

Reluctantly she raised her head, staring straight into his eyes and nodding slowly. "I told Greg. Greg Ellis."

CHAPTER THIRTY

Tom Janssen hurried outside, almost colliding with Cassie at the front door. Recognising the seriousness in his expression, she looked taken aback.

"Tom, what is it?"

"Did you get a hold of Eric?"

She nodded.

"Okay, where is he?"

Cassie was momentarily perplexed. "He's outside Greg Ellis's place, as you wanted."

Tom took out his mobile, scrolling through the contacts list for Eric's number. He spoke to her as he did so.

"I want a dog handler up here, as soon as possible," he said, looking around. The night was overcast and what little light was offered by the police presence was easily absorbed by the surrounding woodland. "I want them scanning the tree line of the perimeter."

"What for? I thought the disposal guys ruled out a manual activation," Cassie said.

He nodded. "Yes, that's true but it doesn't mean whoever did this wouldn't stick around. After all, you've gone to such great lengths to set this up, why would you not want to see your efforts bear fruit."

"Right," Cassie said. "I'm on it."

She took out a radio and contacted the control room to request a canine unit be deployed. Tom rang Eric's mobile, his sixth sense tingling as the call connected. Eric answered immediately.

"Hi Boss," he said, sounding both bored and tired, quite an achievement with only two words to help convey it. "What's up?"

"What's going on your end?"

Eric sighed. "All quiet here. I followed Ellis back to his place after he left you at the nurseries. Been here a while now… it's really getting cold. I can't keep the engine running because it'll give me away. Should have brought a sleeping bag but I guess if I get too comfy I'll—"

"What about Drew?" Tom asked, cutting him off. There must have been something in his tone, the directness perhaps, that made Eric sit up and pay attention.

"Yeah, he came this way too," Eric said, alert now. "They both went into the house but he's gone now."

"Drew left?"

"Yes. He was only here for a quarter of an hour before he headed off." Eric sounded concerned now. "Why, what's going on?"

Tom didn't answer immediately. He was thinking through the possibilities. He was a strategist, that was quite apparent. There's no way he'd have sent Drew against Catton alone.

"Tom, you still there?"

"Yeah, yeah, I'm still here, Eric. When Drew left, are you sure he went alone?"

"Definitely. From where I've parked the car I've got a clear line of sight to the front door and both their cars in the drive. Eddie Drew definitely came out alone and got in the car."

"Did you see Ellis… I mean *actually* see him when Drew left the house?"

"Er... no... he saw himself out."

Again, Tom thought about it. Something didn't feel right here. Eric must have sensed the direction of Tom's thinking.

"He drove away and headed down the road but he stopped a little way along," Eric said, filling in the gap. "For a second I thought he'd spotted me but then he pulled off again. I figured he was tuning the stereo or lighting a cigarette."

"What about the house, Ellis's house," Tom said. "What can you see now?"

He heard Eric shuffling in his seat as he adjusted his position.

"No change... car's still there, lights are on," he said calmly. "All as it was when they got back."

"When you say the *lights are on*, which lights?" Tom asked. The question appeared to throw Eric. His reply was slow, uncertain.

"Erm... the lights... downstairs," he said. "Hang on." He moved again and Tom imagined the DC craning his neck to observe every angle of the house possible. "Yeah, looks like the front room, hallway... along with the kitchen, I reckon."

"Eric," Tom said, casting a concerned eye towards Cassie who cocked her head to one side when she registered it. He glanced at his watch. "It's nearly three in the morning."

"Yeah, I know."

"Have you seen an upstairs light go on since he got home?"

Eric thought about it. "No, no I haven't. Why?"

Tom didn't reply, he was too busy attempting to pull the threads together in his mind. Cassie came closer, slipping her radio into her coat pocket.

"What is it?" she asked, reading his expression.

He met her eye, lowering his mobile. "I think Catton was here earlier today... Tina saw him with Harry Oakes."

Cassie immediately understood his concern. "Does Ellis know?"

"Yes, she told him," Tom said.

"What was that?" Eric asked.

Tom lifted the mobile again. "Eric, I think they've clocked you."

"No way! I've been careful."

"I don't doubt it, Eric," Tom said. "Maybe it was earlier when you were in the pub... maybe they had their doubts and neither of us saw it but they've made you and they've played us. Get over to the house, find out whether Ellis is there. Hold off for five minutes and I'll have some uniform over to back you up. Kick his door in if he doesn't open it."

"Got it!" Eric said. He heard him opening the car door as he hung up.

Tom turned to Cassie. She inclined her head to one side. "Ellis implied he was ready to take matters into his own hands."

"Yes, and I reckon that's exactly what they're doing right now. I think Ellis has slipped out and he and Drew are looking to end this the only way they know how."

"What... going after Catton?"

Tom nodded. "Ellis thinks he's one step ahead the whole time. He's arrogant enough to think he'll outsmart a provincial like me."

"But you think Catton's responsible for all of this?" Cassie asked, looking to her left as if she could see through the house to the bomb-damaged hothouse behind it. "I mean, I know Tina's placed him at the scene and you've twigged I'm not Catton's biggest fan and all, but I don't see it."

He fixed her with a stare. "That doesn't matter. The point is, I think Ellis does. Round up some bodies from here, leave a few behind to maintain the crime scene and ensure Tina and the girls are safe and have that dog handler meet us at Catton's place."

JOHN CATTON AWOKE WITH A START, his T-shirt wet-through with perspiration. For a second he couldn't breathe, a lasting memory of his dream brought with him into his waking state. He gasped, sitting bolt upright and drawing a lungful of air. Man's Best

Friend lay alongside him as always. The little terrier lowered his head gently onto his lap, those large, brown eyes looking up at him. He was never sure if it was pity or concern but it didn't really matter, he cared. The little guy always had.

Catton reached forward with his right hand, stroking the crown of the dog's head affectionately.

"I know little man, I know," he said softly. The dog's ears lifted but his head remained where it was in his lap.

Sliding out from beneath the duvet, he suddenly felt the chill of the night air as it met the dampness of his clothing. The wind was up, he could hear it passing through the trees outside the caravan alongside a faint whistling as it was funnelled through the cracked window to his right.

It was still dark outside and he knew dawn was a long way off. Even so, there would be no more sleep tonight. The thought of closing his eyes scared him, knowing full well he'd most likely be pitched straight back there, the same as always. It was a cycle he had to endure; one with no end. Not that he felt tired, he never did after nights like this.

Scooping up a jumper from the floor, he pulled it over his head. The feeling of claustrophobia was still very much present, another legacy from his repetitive dream cycle. Pulling on his boots, he walked to the door. His dog whined softly, lifting his head from the bed and cocking his ears while watching him go. He looked back at the dog as he put his coat on by the door.

"It's all right little man. You stay there. I'll be back in a bit."

He opened the door and stepped out into the night. It wasn't as cold as it had been of late. The heavy cloud cover obscuring the moon and the rest of the night sky would keep the temperatures up, keeping the frost at bay. If the night air hadn't carried both the sounds of crashing waves and the taste of salt to him, he could be forgiven for thinking he was back there, staring out into the darkness longing for the security of the Forward Operating Base, seeing enemies in every shadows. But he wasn't there and never would be again.

Drawing his coat about him, he walked to the brazier at the back of the caravan, still glowing orange with the dying embers of the earlier fire. He gathered a handful of sticks he used for kindling and added them, gently teasing the fire back to life. Once the flames began to lick at the wood, he added a couple of larger pieces of branch from his stockpile, harvested from the nearby woods. Satisfied with the progress, he headed to his left through a break in the hedgerow and into the adjacent field. Relieving himself against one of the trees he shivered. The cold breeze drifting across his nether regions reminded him of his vulnerability.

Zipping up his fly and then his coat, he hurriedly walked back to the fire. Pleased to see the flames rising to the rim of the brazier, he felt the warmth as he approached. Sniffing hard, he rubbed at the end of his nose. It was still cold, just not as cold as it had been recently. A sound away to his right caused all thoughts to cease as he stared into the trees on the other side of the path. He focussed hard, narrowing his eyes as he searched for irregular patterns among the shadows. His eyes were adjusting to the dark, improving with each passing minute, but it would be a quarter of an hour before he would be able to pick out detail as he would like. For now, he listened for the sounds that shouldn't be there.

All he could hear was the wind whistling through the branches overhead, rustling the evergreen leaves of the hedgerows along with the distant waves breaking upon the shore. That was unusual, if the wind were lighter or if it were daytime, all ambient noise would choke that sound off. Out here, he was alone. Dismissing his paranoia, he moved back to the fire. The glow of which would damage his night vision but the primeval comfort offered by the orange glow was welcoming. Man's Best Friend arrived at the door of the caravan, settling himself down with his nose hanging over the lip, his eyes watching him intently.

"No need for you to miss out on some kip as well, you know," he said quietly, looking sideways at the dog and taking his seat in the camping chair by the brazier, holding his hands out to warm them.

A noise came from behind. He lurched forward but the reaction was too little and far too slow. Something was flung over his head and everything went dark as he was hauled back into his seat. The initial shock turned to panic as his head snapped back, he drew breath but no air was forthcoming. Reaching up, he frantically clawed at the plastic bag covering his face as claustrophobia returned triggering abject terror in its host. Grasping at the base of the plastic, he could feel it tight across his throat, he tried to force his fingers under the rim only to sense the presence of another figure in front of him who battled to knock his hands away. He tried to scream but no sound came, all that he could hear was a high-pitched ringing growing louder in his ears. Where it came from he didn't know.

Feeling the strength ebbing away from him, he managed one final burst of defiance. Leaning back towards his would-be assassin, he brought his legs up and struck out at the figure in front. His boots connected with something and he shoved away from them and felt the chair pitch backwards. There was no release of pressure on the bag though as he hit the ground, the frustrated grunts of his attackers beginning to drift away from him as if he was falling into a deep well, leaving them far above. The panic subsided as a sense of comfort returned only for all that to change in a fraction of a second.

The pressure around his head suddenly relaxed and instinctively he reached up, scrabbling at the plastic until he was able to rip it clear from his mouth. The sea air filled his lungs and for a brief moment the sweet smell of life calmed him as he realised he'd cheated death. His senses returned a moment later, feeling a burning sensation across his throat where the bag had almost penetrated the skin. Then came his hearing, replacing the ringing that had been present. Someone was shouting, the words coming clearer as he returned from the depths of the well. The shouts were more of a panic-stricken shriek than a command.

"Get this fucking dog off me!"

Man's Best Friend was snarling, swinging his head from right to left, his jaws clamped around one man's wrist as the two writhed on the floor. The other man was trying to pull the dog off him. The assailant turned, seeing him sitting up on his haunches staring at them. He was dressed in camouflage, both men were, their features hidden beneath black balaclavas. He ran forward, swinging a booted foot in his direction. Catton tried to move to his left and avoid the strike but he was still groggy and the blow caught him high in the right side of his chest. It was a glancing blow and he angled himself away from it as best he could, rolling on his shoulder and coming upright with his weight balanced equally on both feet, poised to respond to another attack. His vision swam momentarily but he blinked it away. His attacker took half a step towards him but now, recovering from the attempt at suffocation, he must have appeared to be a slightly tougher prospect. The man hesitated.

"Not so easy now when you can see them coming, eh?" Catton said, growling.

He weighed up his chances. The man in front of him was powerfully built, short and stocky. Glancing to his left, he saw the other still wrestling with his dog. There was no way he'd free those jaws, not while the canine had breath in his body. He remained crouched where he was. Glancing behind him towards the caravan, he considered making a run for it but knew he wouldn't get there in time. He turned his eye on the man in front of him, circling to his right, aiming to put his target between the two attackers. Once the other was free of Man's Best Friend, he'd be outflanked and at a significant disadvantage.

"What you wearing that mask for?" Catton asked, turning back to the man before him. "You dinnae need it, Greg. What is it, not man enough to show me yer face?"

His opponent raised himself upright reached up and pulled the balaclava off with his left hand, dropping his arm to his side. Greg Ellis took a deep breath, running his free hand through his hair seemingly relieved to feel fresh air on his skin. The dog shrieked in pain. Catton shot a look to his left just as his dog was flung into the hedgerow, yelping as he disappeared into the brush.

"Bloody animal!" Eddie Drew snapped from a kneeling position, clutching his forearm.

Catton glared at him. "If you've hurt ma dug I'll feckin' kill yer man."

"Sodding dog's given me bloody rabies!" Drew said, through gritted teeth as he first shook his arm before removing his own face covering.

"I hope you've not given him one of your STIs, Eddie," Greg Ellis said with a half-smile.

"So what's the plan, Greg?" Catton asked. "Choke me off and then make it look like a suicide?"

"More than you deserve," Drew said, inspecting his arm. The sleeve was torn to reveal bloodied skin beneath. He was clearly in some discomfort.

Catton smiled much to Drew's frustration, angering him further.

"Lost your touch when it comes to executing a successful operation, though," Catton said.

"We'll just have to improvise, adapt and overcome, Johnny. Usually turns out well."

"Aye, tell that to Lewis and Freddie," Catton retorted, spying Drew making ready to stand. He couldn't allow that to happen.

Catton launched himself to his left, side-stepping and kicking out at the brazier. The drum fell towards Drew showering him in flaming wood and glowing embers. Drew howled with rage, bringing his arms up to shield his face from the deluge of hot ash. Catton followed through, ducking as he passed to retrieve something stashed beneath the drum, and was upon Drew in a flash. He spun the man to put Drew between himself and the advancing form of Ellis, one arm around his neck and bringing the other up to reveal a blade which he held with the point an inch away from Drew's eye. He silently praised himself for the paranoia that fuelled his decision to hide weapons around his site. Ellis checked his advance, the dynamic shifting momentarily against the attackers.

Catton looked around, unsure of how he was going to press home his current advantage.

CHAPTER THIRTY-ONE

EDDIE DREW STRUGGLED under the grip of Catton, reluctant to give in, although he refrained from pushing too hard. The point of the blade hovering in front of his eye was enough to give him pause.

"What now, Greg?" Catton asked, watching his opponent closely. Ellis offered no sign of accepting defeat, staring intently at him poised to attack with his weight on the balls of his feet. It would be risky but Greg was always one to accept a challenge.

"You think you've found a way out of this?" Ellis asked. He shook his head. "You haven't. You've just staved off the inevitable."

"Which is?" Catton asked, hearing the tinge of fear in his voice.

Greg Ellis reached to the rear of his waistband and withdrew a pistol. Chambering a round, he raised it and pointed the weapon at Catton. Instinctively, Catton leaned in closer to Drew. If Ellis was prepared to shoot then the prospect of hitting Drew might see him hesitate… or not. Ellis side-stepped to his left, watching his footing and keeping the gun trained on him at all times. Catton forced a smile.

"New plan? It's going to be hard to make this one look like a clean suicide," he said. He was so close to Drew's face he could smell the man's breath as he exhaled; the stale smell of cigarettes and beer. The smile faded. "You shoot and I'll manage to stick Eddie with this blade on my way down."

As if to emphasise the point, he brought the knife closer still to Drew's face hearing him moan his displeasure at the prospect. No doubt his expression was one of abject terror. He only wished he could be nearby watching rather than staring at a loaded weapon. It wasn't the first time but it certainly felt different when he knew the man behind it.

"If that's the way it plays out then so be it," Ellis said flatly. "You stick him, Eddie drops you on the way down. Double tragedy."

"Hang on…" Drew whispered through Catton's choke hold.

"Shut up, Eddie," Ellis said, cocking his head. "Either way, I walk away from this and you don't."

"Must admit… decent enough plan," Catton said, smiling. Ellis was never one to make idle threats, he always carried through on whatever he said. Flicking his eyes to the side, he looked for help, something, anything to give him an edge. There was nothing. "I don't suppose we can cut a deal, like?"

"I'm always willing to listen, Johnny. Eddie and I both reckoned on taxing you a little. Perhaps," he said, narrowing his gaze, "we could relieve you of what you have left. Call it quits. What do you say to that?"

Catton knew Ellis well enough to know his words were hollow. Any agreement would immediately be reneged but he'd play along, all the while seeking another option.

"Sounds like a bargain," he said, "under the circumstances. So, how about you lower that weapon and we can behave a bit more like civilised men. I mean, you'd never get anything from a dead man, would you?"

Ellis held his gaze, the two men staring one another out before Ellis relented and lowered the barrel of the gun. He'd bought himself time. Not much, but maybe enough. That momentary relaxation coming after the truce was his undoing. So focussed was he on Greg that the realisation of the loosening of his grip on

Eddie came too late. Drew rotated his body in the headlock, reaching up with his left hand and pressing upwards and away at the base of his nose. The movement was a survival technique taught to them in hand-to-hand combat training. He was out of practice, Drew on the other hand was quite adept.

There was no opportunity to bring the knife to bear as he was upended and unceremoniously dumped head first into the ground. Catton was sure he felt something snap in his upper body as Drew used his own weight to pile drive him downward. Air exploded from his lungs and then his vision faded between momentary blackouts where all sound ceased and then he would hear the grunts and expletives thrown by his assailants.

Vaguely aware of being dragged along the floor, his body scraping against rock and branch, he tried to right himself only to receive a swift kick to the abdomen for his trouble. Snippets of conversation came to him in momentary lucid moments, barely making sense.

"... how are we going to find it if he's dead..."

"... no, like he did it himself..."

Lying on his front now, he felt a tightness constricting his throat muscles. A flash of panic tore through him, instantly alert now he sought to free himself, struggling for breath. It was no use and all of a sudden he was being hauled upright, what little light was available to him visible in blurred shapes and he felt all his strength abandoning him.

This was going to end, he knew it.

THE RESTRAINTS GONE... more light, only this time flashing... was this what death felt like? No. Pain... like nothing he'd ever felt before came rushing through his body. The rough, cold surface pressed against his face smelt like damp earth. It was... and he gasped for breath, relief surging as he was cut free. Rolling to his back he felt hands on his shoulder, straightening his head so he could see the sky. The hands were soft, the touch gentle. The clouds overhead parted revealing a glimpse of the heavens he was so familiar with.

"Can you hear me?" she asked. He focussed on the voice, turning his gaze on her. He nodded and thought he caught her smiling. He knew that face. He was still certain she didn't like him, even though she was smiling. A dog barked. Not his dog, this was louder, scarier. With the police officer's assistance, Catton levered himself up onto an elbow, taking in the scene.

Greg Ellis was kneeling a few metres away, his hands cuffed behind his back. Eddie Drew was face down on the floor with a uniformed police officer upon his back while another detective sought to disarm him. He was sure to lose this one but still he fought on.

"You okay?" the woman asked him and he nodded. She left his side and ran to assist her colleagues.

He didn't want to stay here, he felt unsafe. The caravan was fifteen feet away and he made to stand. His legs couldn't support his weight and he resorted to dragging himself towards it. Barely had he moved when out of the nearby bushes Man's Best Friend appeared, running to him and licking his face excitedly. He couldn't help but smile, but he continued on, the dog keeping to his side. Drew was running out of energy and the police patience. It would be over soon. All the more need for him to reach the safety of his home.

Part-way there, he felt more normal and managed to pull himself up into a crawling position and then tentatively onto his feet. Staggering forward like a Saturday night drunk, he stumbled into the caravan, tripping and falling to the floor. Feeling something run into his eye, he reached up. It was blood. Had he hit his head on the way down or was it from before... the fight with Eddie? He didn't know but it was superficial and he pushed on, reaching the seating area, he hauled himself up onto it. His dog leapt up alongside him, sitting bolt upright facing the door.

Catton drew a deep breath, reaching under the pillow he slept on and his fingers curled around a familiar grip.

This was all still going to end... tonight.

WITH THE SEEMINGLY INDESTRUCTIBLE Eddie Drew finally subdued, Tom Janssen passed him off to the two officers alongside him. Greg Ellis tracked his movements with a focussed gaze, unbroken by the German Shepherd barking at him barely two feet away. Tom would love to know what was going through his mind. Back at the station, he intended to find out. In the corner of his eye he saw Catton staggering back into his caravan, most likely seeking sanctuary after his harrowing brush with death. Cassie had the scene under control and now they were going to put an end to this saga.

The door to the caravan swung loose and he eased it aside, rapping his knuckles on the adjacent panel and announcing his entrance. Stepping up, he moved to the left finding John Catton sitting directly opposite him, the dog was by his side and a pistol lay beneath his hand on the table. Tom froze. Catton stared at him, unblinking. A trickle of blood ran from a gash to his forehead, partially smeared across his face and stretching down the cheek and into his beard.

The revolver lay on the table, Catton's hand resting gently over it. Seeing Tom's eyes lower to the weapon, Catton's fingers tightened around the grip and he hefted the gun upright. Tom felt his mouth go dry and he remained still, holding his hands out in a non-threatening gesture. Catton inclined his head to one side, his eyes narrowing.

"What's going on, John?" Tom asked softly.

"It's John now, is it?" Catton asked, his nose twitched but his eyes remained fixed on Tom. "Close the door."

Tom turned slowly, dramatising his movements so as not to induce any alarm. Coming to the door, he looked out. Cassie

Knight glanced in his direction. His expression must have triggered something in her because she stepped forward but he raised the flat of his hand and she stopped. A fleeting thought about stepping from the caravan came and went in an instant as Catton repeated his instruction.

"Close the door."

Tom reached out, grasped the handle and pulled the door to.

"Lock it."

He did as requested, turning back to face his captor.

"What's this all about, John?" he asked.

Catton gestured for him to return. Tom walked slowly back, casually eyeing his surroundings. They were cramped, dirty. There was only one door to the exterior and he'd just locked it. The windows were closed; from memory they were single glazed and would easily break, he was sure, but certainly not effective escape routes with a gun trained on him. Catton indicated the seat opposite and he eased himself into it, sitting upright and gently placing his hands, palms down, on the table before him.

Catton appeared to relax. He must be feeling secure now.

"You once asked me how I live out here," Catton said.

Tom nodded. "Something like that, yes." He ensured his tone was measured, calm.

"One day at a time," Catton replied, lifting the gun.

He angled it to the side in front of his face, still pointing it in Tom's direction, before releasing the cylinder from the frame. From his seat opposite, Tom could see five of the six chambers were empty with one cartridge visible in the sixth. Catton spun the cylinder with his left hand and snapped it back into the frame with a flick of his wrist. He cocked the hammer and met Tom's eye.

"Every night, I go through the same ritual. I ask myself what I did this day that makes it worth seeing the next." He held his gaze on Tom who kept silent. This wasn't his moment, this was John Catton's and he felt powerless to interrupt. Catton's eyes teared up. "I always come up with the same answer."

Tom rolled his lower lip under the upper, trying to find some moisture. His mouth was as dry as a desert. Catton watched him intently, waiting for a response.

"And what do you come up with?" he asked quietly.

"Nothing," Catton said, turning the gun on himself, raising it and placing the barrel against his temple. Tom tensed, he wanted to protest, to countermand the decision but words didn't come. His mouth fell open as Catton closed his eyes and squeezed the trigger.

Click. Nothing happened.

Tom realised he'd been holding his breath and released it in one short blast. Catton opened his eyes, laid the gun gently back down upon the table and withdrew his hand. Sitting back, he put both hands together in his lap, staring hard at Tom. The dog lay his head in his lap and whimpered softly.

"And then I stick around... for one more day," Catton said quietly, nodding towards the revolver as a tear escaped his eye and slowly ran the length of his cheek.

Tom eased his right hand across the table, half expecting the strange hermit to leap at him as soon as he touched the weapon but Catton remained where he was, completely passive. Tom slowly turned the gun on the table and brought it across towards him. The sense of relief he felt was palpable. Releasing the cylinder, he emptied out the solitary cartridge, slipping it into his pocket and setting the gun down. He glanced back at Catton who smiled ruefully.

"I'm not a monster, Inspector Janssen."

CHAPTER THIRTY-TWO

SOMEONE TRIED the handle on the caravan's door. Finding it locked, the person hammered a fist against it. Probably Cassie.

"It's all right," Tom shouted, keeping his eyes on Catton. "Just give us a few minutes, okay?"

Catton moved to the window, pushing aside the net curtain and observing the officers outside briefly before returning to sit where he'd been. The dog laid his head back on Catton's lap as soon as he was settled. Tom cast his eye around the interior of the caravan in more detail. The conditions were indeed cramped but he could see how one person could live here. Arguably there was only a little more space for him on his boat. Perhaps they had more in common than he realised.

"The peace and solitude that one finds in living away from others is something most don't appreciate," Tom said.

Catton eyed him warily, probably weighing up his sincerity.

"Aye, and what would you know about it?"

The question was asked in a non-confrontational tone, yet another way of assessing him no doubt.

"I live alone as well," Tom said, turning his gaze back on the dishevelled man. "Albeit on a boat but the point stands."

"Had you marked as a family man myself."

"And I didn't have you marked as a killer," Tom said.

"I'm not a killer."

"But you were at Harry Oakes's place tonight."

Catton sniffed, scratching absently at the end of his nose.

"Is that right?" he said.

Tom nodded, flicking a hand towards the boots set alongside the door. "Your boots are soaking wet, as are the base of those trousers you've tossed over there," Tom pointed to the wet clothes in a heap on the floor. "You've been out across the fields tonight."

"It's nae illegal to walk at night."

"Come on," Tom said, rolling his eyes. "Those two out there came here to kill you tonight. Nearly managed it too. Enough of the bullshit, John."

Catton sat forward, resting his elbows on the table. Running one hand across his throat, he grimaced as he rubbed at where the cord had been around his neck. Now it was red and sore, with several layers of skin having been scraped away. He fixed Tom with a stare.

"You know I was nineteen when I was first deployed to a combat zone."

"Helmand?" Tom asked.

Catton nodded, sitting back. "We'd been out on an extended reconnaissance patrol, a bastard run, but made it back to the FOB in one piece, you know."

"FOB?"

"Aye, the Forward Operating Base," Catton said, bobbing his head. "We were looking forward to getting some food and a bit of downtime. When you're out there you're always on it because if you're not someone gets killed, right. Anyway, the artillery boys are there and they're shitting bricks because they've lost one of their drones." Tom raised his eyebrows, Catton brushed off his concern with a flick of his hand. "Not one of the Reapers, no. This was back in 2007, like. They had these hand-held ones that you run with and launch with a big swing, you know. Sounds daft now but back in the day this was state-of-the-art kit." He waved away the detail as irrelevant. "The artillery had put six of these things up and only brought five back. Like I said, they were bricking it that this one was going to get into enemy hands and so, guess what... they needed a fast mech unit." Catton jabs a finger into his own chest. "We got the shout to go and retrieve this bloody drone. Proper pissed off we were with that, I can tell you. But off we go, twenty-six of us, half the group are Royal Marine Commandos and we made up the rest, with nothing but a six-point grid reference to go by."

"That takes us into a nearby village, folks are friendly enough like. I mean, we've been in and around the area for a while. No harm, no foul, yeah," Catton said, sniffing again. It was an irritating habit but Tom ignored it. Catton continued. "So there's me, nineteen years of age, wandering around some rocky scrub land looking for bits of this sodding drone. We were on a split call sign, half the troop were on one side of the village with us on the other, all spread out looking for this thing. I see this woman walking past me, head down, with a hand on her kid's shoulder... normal enough, you'd think, right?"

Tom nodded. Catton shook his head.

"Nah, I should've bloody known there and then. That's a bit of a giveaway, like... when the civilians are leaving an area it's a strong indication that the shit's about to hit the fan, ken."

"And presumably it did?"

Catton grinned. "Oh, right enough, aye. I wandered away from the vehicle a bit too far. Comms were playing up and I missed the initial shout. First I knew about it kicking off was seeing this puff of blue smoke and a black dot coming at me. Missed by a few feet, maybe more, I don't really know but when it struck the rocks behind me all hell broke loose."

"Someone shot at you?"

"Aye, with a bloody RPG... hell, how he missed a sitting target I'll never ken. Someone was looking out for me that day, I can tell you! I don't know if you've ever seen one of these things going off, I mean, it's not like in the movies or anything. If you hear it whistle past you, which I didn't by the way, the explosion goes off and it's raining rocks for the next few seconds and I'm running. I tell you, proper running like I hadn't done since I was five years old and the ice cream van was at the end of the street!"

Tom smiled. "As a child you think you can run so fast that you'll go until your feet fall off."

Catton laughed. "Aye, that feeling... but with a load of Taliban trying to shoot you in the arse while you're at it. We'd wandered into a village flooded with these bastards and they didn't feel like giving ground without putting up a fight. So like I said, it's going off like you wouldn't believe! We've got multiple contacts all over the place. It's gone from locating a downed drone to tearing up a local warlord or something. I was Greg's driver that day, we were operating in two or three man teams in each vehicle and I was damn pleased when I got back inside the Viking that day. Rounds are pinging off the armour like we're in a hailstorm but it's all good. Even an RPG just echoes when it hits one of those things. Bloody reassuring, I can tell you."

"So we get ourselves organised and start sweeping the village. Ellis is up top giving it socks on the fifty-cal and it's like something out of *Apocalypse Now*. Then we get this car coming at us, some mad suicide bomber in a car with sheet metal welded all over it in some half-arse, do-it-yourself, armoured cladding. It doesn't work obviously but the thing goes off. The street's narrow and we're blocked in. Now no one likes being a sitting target, even in a Viking, so Ellis has us out on foot going building to building aiming to link up with the other call sign who are kicking it on the other side of the village. And this is where things got interesting."

Tom didn't want to interrupt the flow but the thought occurred that, so far, this was sounding like his worst nightmare. To be facing it at nineteen... was it any wonder Catton appeared slightly off the wall?

"So we're passing through this compound, there's me and Greg, backed up by Eddie Drew, Woody and Harry Oakes. Andy Lewis and Freddie Mayes come into it later but at this point it's just the five of us. We're clearing this compound, going room by room and come across pallets of shrink-wrapped produce. I mean this shite is stacked to the ceiling and ready to be transported."

"What was it?"

"Drugs, man."

"Opium?"

"Aye, it's the warlord's currency over there. They farm this stuff, sell it and use the cash to buys weapons and shit. We were looking at four metric tonnes of the stuff. I don't know if you've any idea what four metric tonnes of opium looks like… but it's bales upon bales stacked on top of each other. There was enough there to equip them for three bloody years!"

Tom sat forward in his seat. "And that's why they were fighting so hard for the village?"

Catton laughed, a sound of genuine humour. "Aye, you'd think so, wouldn't you, but nah… I know we did at the time but it turns out they weren't too bothered about the opium. They had something far more valuable they were looking to protect."

"What could be more valuable to them than three years' worth of weaponry?" Tom asked.

"Occasionally over there we'd come up against some old Soviet equipment, stuff left over from the seventies or eighties, you know," Catton said, running both hands through his mop of unkempt hair. "You know, the odd tank they'd managed to keep running. Didn't have any shells for them usually, but every now and again they'd turn up with something handy. Think about it, you can always grow more opium… buy more guns but the stuff they couldn't get hold of is proper military kit. Turns out, they'd stashed an old Russian GMLRS in the village and that was what they were fighting so hard for."

"Sorry, what is that?" Tom asked, frowning.

"Oh, a transportable multi-grade rocket launcher. You don't come across those every day," Catton said, shaking his head and smiling ruefully. "They must have had it in their heads that we were in the village to recover that, not some downed bit of Airfix kit."

"What did you do about the opium?"

"Standard procedure was to rig up the bar mines and blow it, which is pretty much what we did." Catton grinned. "There must have been a cloud of opium smoke over the village that night that would have got everybody stoned!"

"You said it got interesting?"

"Aye, I did," Catton said. "I don't remember whose idea it was but we all got talking. I think it was a joke at first but then someone said *what if...* I mean... four metric tonnes... that's enough to buy our own private island, ken."

His gaze fell on Tom and the enthusiasm for his tale dissipated.

"You didn't?" Tom asked, his eyes narrowing. Catton chewed on his lower lip, avoiding Tom's eye. "How on earth could you pull that off?"

"Not all of it, obviously." Catton sighed, shaking his head. "That'd be proper mental. We detonated the mines and blew most of it up but... there was so much going on around the village. The marines were on top, the enemy falling back. It was all under control, ken. Bringing in Lewis and Freddie Mayes left us with three vehicles. We stripped out what we didn't need from one, doubled up in the other vehicles. It's not as hard as you think." He looked up, meeting Tom's eye. "We spent a lot of time out in the field, ahead of the forward lines. All we had to do was find somewhere to stash it out of sight. We ended up distributing as much as we could around several different locations."

"But you shipped it back to the UK... sold it over here? How?" Tom asked, not quite believing what he was hearing.

"There's always a way to route things past the MPs. Initially we were bringing it back in our MFO boxes," Catton said, splaying his palms wide. "Not hard to line it with a false bottom."

"I thought your kit was inspected by the military police before shipping," Tom said, confused.

Catton laughed. "Yeah, right. Don't get me wrong, it's not like they're incompetent or anything but as long as you're not trying to slip home with weapons or something, they're not too bothered. Whereas a single 9MM round sells for a tenner on the black market back home, I've come back from overseas with four grand's worth of cigarettes in two zip bags before now and no one batted an eyelid. Besides, the MPs are open to exchanges the same as the rest of us."

"Exchanges?" Tom queried. "You mean bribes, right?"

Catton shook his head emphatically, waving the question away. "Not in the way you're thinking, no. Over in Afghanistan the currency was in experiences, not money."

"What do you mean? I don't understand."

"Imagine yourself out there," Catton said, bubbling over with enthusiasm once more. "You're a military policeman. Back home everyone, family and friends, thinks you've got balls of solid rock for going to war. They watch the news, they hear the stories. What are you going to tell them when you get home? That you spent your tour handing out speeding tickets at Camp Bastion? Big hero you'll be then, eh?"

"So you trade... experiences," Tom said, still not comprehending but thinking hard.

"Aye... you offer to take them out in your vehicle the next time you're beyond the wire... maybe let him have a turn on the fifty-cal," Catton said, leaning forward, a gleam in his eye. "They get to go home and tell war stories, play the big man. I took a round in the plate out there, it didn't penetrate past the armour but the round lodged in the plate. Hurt like hell but that one piece of metal, with its massive ding in it, became a valuable souvenir. A sergeant in the RAF Regiment paid me a small fortune for it. He knew he'd be able to trade off that back home for years! Experiences, Inspector Janssen. They're worth a fortune."

"And what do you get for your efforts?"

"In exchange... maybe they turn a blind eye to you passing through one night, that type of thing," Catton said with a mock grimace. "There's an unsaid understanding that you'll no take the piss, mind you. It's not like back in the Balkans."

"Why, what went on back then?"

"Oh, you name it. We've all heard the stories. One of the best was when your deployment finished you shipped all your kit back home. That includes loading your tank... and I mean *your tank* on the transporter. You signed it on and you signed it off at the other end. The boys had to drain the oil, fuel, everything prior to transportation. They plastic wrapped AKs, mortar rounds and all sorts, stashed them in the sump and anywhere else they could find room to get them home. Not to sell on, I should say. Just souvenirs, you know." He chuckled. "They had a hell of a job to make sure they got them out at the other end, though, because you had to fill the vehicles up again before you could move them off the transporter. The MPs got wind of that one eventually and shut it all down."

"Go back a bit for me, if you would," Tom said, frowning. "You said initially."

"Yeah, you can't get much back in an MFO box... we had to do better. That's where Freddie Mayes came in. He was pretty pally with the quarter-master and that's how we stepped it up. Have you ever thought how the army deploys everything to somewhere as remote as Afghanistan and back again?"

Tom thought on it. "By air, I would guess."

"Aye, a lot of it but logistically that's not going to wash. It's shipped over land. We'd have shipping containers filled at Bastion, sealed by the quarter master and tagged by the MPs. Once that's done, they stay sealed. It's then routed over land through Pakistan and down to a friendly port in... say Saudi, before it's loaded on a boat and sent home via Southampton docks or wherever. You see, those sealed containers get back to your base in England, Scotland or wherever when they'll be signed for *and opened* by the same quarter-master who oversaw the loading."

"Experiences," Tom said quietly.

"Experiences," Catton repeated, gently pointing a finger in his direction. "I tell you, though, the Americans were the best. They loved us... or our kit at least. UK forces equipment is considered pretty cool stateside. I had a guy try and trade me a Desert Eagle for a hat one time when we were at Leatherneck." Catton shook his head. "I bet you think we were crazy." Tom inclined his head but didn't comment. "Aye, it's all right, Inspector. It was insane... and then we come back here and are supposed to go hang out at barbecues, walk the dugs or mow the lawn on the weekends. I'm amazed there aren't more of us who have gone to the wall."

Tom looked to his left and right, frowning. "Forgive me, but what you've described would be worth a small fortune on the street and you're living... well, here."

Catton chuckled, nodding his head vigorously. "I know! Mental, isn't it. The guys couldn't believe it either. By the time we managed to get home, we couldn't just rock up in Ferraris without people raising an eyebrow could we. Greg is from London, knew some people who knew people, that kind of thing. It took a while to set it all up. We had to build trust with them." He shook his head. "We had to bide our time, plan, invest and then to find ways to wash it before we could spend it. By the time we'd come up with various ways of doing so... something about it didn't sit right with me. After a while, it didn't sit well with Woody either." He looked at Tom, his expression darkening.

"What did Woody make of it?"

"At first he went along with it, right enough, same as me. The opportunity of a lifetime really. Then... Joe took a few wrong turns. Seeds were sown while Woody was away to be fair."

"Woody's brother, Joe?" Tom clarified.

"Yeah, Joe got in with a bad crowd, you know. Before anyone realised, he was too far gone and Woody got to see the other side of things. It wasn't new to me. Back home, I'd seen enough of it with mates getting strung out on smack and the like. That's one of the reasons I signed up in the first place... to get away from all that stuff. If I hadn't, maybe it would have been me."

"Tell me about what happened to Woody," Tom said, watching him closely.

Catton held Tom's gaze. "You'll know more about that than me."

Tom sat back, taking a deep breath. "You know everything you've told me will take some proving."

"It is what it is." Catton shrugged.

"Is there any way of corroborating this without getting a confession from the others?"

Catton sniffed once more, looking down and running the flat of his hand over his dog's head, still nestled happily in his lap. As soon as the tension drained from the situation, the dog had become incredibly placid. Catton looked back up at Tom.

"Promise me you'll find a good home for ma dug."

Tom looked at the dog who appeared to be eyeing him suspiciously. "Of course."

"Give me your word."

"You have it."

Catton pointed at the seat Tom was sitting on. He looked down, then shifted himself off it and pulled away the old rug thrown over it. The cushion beneath wasn't fixed and Tom picked it up to reveal the lid of a storage compartment. Lifting the lid revealed multiple packets neatly stacked on top of one another, each one roughly the same size as a kilo bag of sugar. They were wrapped in blue film. He looked at Catton.

"Is this what I think it is?"

Catton grinned. "That's what Ellis and Drew came here for tonight, besides taking me out. Helmand's finest."

Tom ran a hand through his hair, shaking his head. He fixed Catton with a stare. "This… is a good start."

"We were living in dark times, Inspector. Something incredible fell into our laps… one of those sliding-doors moments, you know? I regret it now but I'm not a killer, though, Inspector Janssen." He shook his head. "Not anymore."

CHAPTER THIRTY-THREE

"He was going to kill us!"

Tom Janssen maintained his composure as Eddie Drew rose from his chair. They were approaching the point of where they'd have to call time on the interview. It'd been a long night, dramatic, emotional. No one had managed to get any sleep and that was his call. Tension was evident and emotions were running high. Drew had the air of a man who was borderline ready to crack under the strain. He was the weak link in all of this and that was why Tom had chosen to interview him. The station wasn't large and seldom was there a need to keep multiple suspects in separate interview rooms. If there were three or more people who'd been arrested usually it was a fight in a pub car park late on a Saturday night. Even those were rare and they'd usually end up sleeping it off in the cells.

"Sit down, Eddie," Tom said calmly.

Drew stood with his fists clenched, knuckles pressed firmly against the table glaring at him.

"Sit down," Tom repeated, although this time more forcefully. Eddie Drew held his gaze for a moment longer, then he glanced at Eric sitting alongside Tom and acquiesced. Pulling his chair back to the table, it had slid back when he'd leapt to his feet, he sat down and sighed.

"He would have come for me next... or Greg," Drew said, sinking forward and dragging his palms up across his cheeks and continuing on until they met at the back of his head where he interlocked his fingers. Taking a deep breath, he righted himself and locked eyes with Tom once more. "I felt my life was at risk. That's a justifiable killing, isn't it? That's what you guys say..." His eyes flicked between both officers. "If your life is in danger then you have every right to defend yourself, right?"

"In the moment, yes," Tom said, nodding.

"He was going to kill us."

"So you say." Tom inclined his head to one side. "What took you to the caravan tonight?"

Drew averted his eye from Tom's gaze, shaking his head.

"You can keep silent if you want to, that is your right of course," Tom said. "But do you think Greg is sitting in the next room with his arms folded sitting it out or—"

"We look out for one another!" Drew snapped.

"Like you all looked out for Carl Woodly."

At the mention of the name, the lips of Drew's mouth parted slightly. His surprise was evident. Tom spared a thought for what was happening in the other interview rooms. They'd discussed the best approach. As expected, the DCI, Tamara Greave, was summoned back to join the investigation. A swift debrief saw her lay claim to Greg Ellis. Not because he was the apparent brains of the unit but because he was so sure of himself, so arrogant. A man who exuded such strength and apparent self-confidence would probably enjoy a battle of wits with someone he considered his equal, someone like Tom. Whether he'd react the same way facing not one senior female detective but two, Cassie Knight going in alongside her, was the chink in his armour they'd look to exploit.

Tom doubted it. Ellis was the only one clued up enough to insist on legal representation.

No. Eddie Drew was the weak link but Tom was well aware

that if he pushed it too far then the man's apparent distress might put a judge offside. Ellis would remain tight lipped until such time as he figured a way out, either for himself or for both of them. It's true, they were tight as a grouping. At what point would one throw the other under the bus in order to save themselves? Maybe never, choosing instead to take their chances with a jury. John Catton was unlikely to appeal to a jury of his peers, his military service aside. In his own experience, attacks on homeless people, drug addicts or those many considered beneath them often passed off with a lighter sentence than one might think and both Drew and Ellis were considered successful pillars of the community. John Catton, on the other hand, lived at the opposite end of the spectrum.

If a clever barrister managed to bring it down to a question of whose word could be considered the most reliable or trustworthy, then the accused had a chance. Eric opened a folder on the desk in front of him, calmly taking papers out and making a play of adjusting them so Drew could see. Drew attempted not to pay attention but his eyes didn't stray far from the folder. He was curious. Eric cleared his throat.

"We executed a search warrant on your business earlier," he said, absently looking through the paperwork. He laid it down, placing his palms above it, one hand on top of the other. "It made for interesting reading."

Drew's eyes flitted between the paper and Eric but he said nothing.

"Must be tough at the moment, selling cars, what with the cash position of your franchise being what it is."

"Been worse," Drew said, sneering.

"Has it?" Eric asked. "By the look of your bank statements you've pretty much maxed out your overdraft. How were you looking to recover the situation?"

"I'll manage."

"Perhaps you were going to pick up a little extra from somewhere else," Tom said, folding his arms across his chest.

Drew met his eye but said nothing. "How did you manage to set up the dealership in the first place? Takes quite a significant investment."

Drew matched Tom's stance, folding his arms defiantly.

"I managed."

"Yes, you did well," Tom said. "In fact, you succeeded in the same period as the others. Harry Oakes came into some money from an obscure relative he never knew he had. Enough of an inheritance to fund renovating and relaunching a business that'd become unviable years before. Then there's you and your dealership... Freddie Mayes and his successful bespoke building company which springs up out of nowhere."

"And not forgetting Greg's golf club," Eric added, tapping the collection of paper for effect.

Tom inclined his head towards Eric alongside him. "Yes, not forgetting. Solid investment portfolios across the board. Apart from Andrew Lewis."

"Yes, apart from Andrew Lewis," Eric repeated. "His portfolio was an MFO box in his garage stuffed with cash. A steady investment but with little by way of annual returns."

Drew shifted in his seat, looking directly at the table in front of him.

"Carl Woodly self-built a house," Tom said. "I'd love to get my hands on the invoices he received from Freddie Mayes for the construction. Inflating construction costs is a cracking way of laundering money... from illegal drug sales."

Drew's head snapped up. His attempt at maintaining his composure could be described as poor, at best.

"You know we have the power to seize any material goods that we believe have come from the proceeds of illegal activities: houses, cars... businesses? So, we're looking at drug smuggling, attempt to supply, attempted murder. That's a significant stretch. You'll be an old man by the time you breathe fresh air again, Eddie. Are you prepared for that?"

"You'll not make it stick," Drew said. "None of it."

"We have testimony."

"From that Scottish waster... Catton?" Drew scoffed, pointing at the wall as if he could see into the next room. "Leave it out. The man's a basket case, anyone can see it."

"There's always the murder charge as well," Eric said, looking at Tom.

"What?" Drew asked.

Tom's gaze narrowed as he sat forward. "Carl Woodly. He was the first, then came Mayes and Lewis... followed by Harry Oakes tonight."

"I never killed anyone. That was Catton, can't you bloody see that!" Drew said, slamming his hands down on the table. "Why the hell would I kill my friends? Ask yourself that. It was that lunatic, Catton."

"We found fingerprints on some of the fragments over at the nursery. We ran them through the system and they don't match Catton. Although, I dare say he was nearby, watching," Tom said. "We also checked, he has a rock-solid alibi for the night Carl Woodly's house went up along with the week either side of it. Can you tell us where you were?"

"You're mad, all of you!" Drew said. "You're clutching at straws if you think I did any of it. I wasn't even in the country when Woody died."

"We will check."

"Then check!" Drew folded his arms again.

"What about Freddie or Ellis for that matter?" Tom asked. "John Catton told us how Greg Ellis told him that if he stabbed you, Ellis would put him down, making it look like the two of you killed one another in the struggle. Think about that for a moment. Was Greg bluffing... or would he have sacrificed you to win?"

Drew looked at him, first rolling his eyes but then his expression changed taking on a distant look, his brow furrowing.

"Take some time and think it over," Tom said, sending a sideways glance at Eric and indicating for him to switch off the recorder.

Eric paused the interview and both detectives stood up. Drew appeared lost in thought. Tom opened the door and beckoned a uniformed constable over to keep watch over Drew after they left.

"Hey!" Drew called as Tom made to leave the room. He looked back at him. "Do you think he would have allowed him to do it; Catton, I mean?"

Tom shrugged. "If he had… you'd both be dead and Greg Ellis would be the last man standing. Seeing as we know the value of what Catton was sitting on in that caravan… how much do you think your life is worth to Greg Ellis?"

He turned and left the room, joining Eric in the corridor. At that moment the door to the interview room on the opposite side of the corridor opened and Tamara Greave stepped out. Behind her, Cassie Knight was visible sitting opposite Greg Ellis and his solicitor. Ellis's gaze followed the DCI out of the room, first meeting Tom's eye before passing to Eddie Drew behind him. Whatever passed unsaid between the two men, no one could know but Drew's pitiful appearance struck a chord as confidence visibly drained from Ellis as the doors were closed.

The three of them walked to the end of the corridor, ensuring they wouldn't be overheard from anyone in the interview rooms. Tom looked at Tamara, raising an inquisitive eyebrow.

"How did you get on with Ellis?"

She shook her head, admitting defeat. "He's solid. He won't break unless he has no other option. You?"

"Better," Tom said, leaning against the wall and running a hand through his hair. He felt tired now, the events of the day and the constant level of concentration taking their toll. "If we press him, I reckon he'll give it up. He thinks we have enough." Glancing at Eric, Tom smiled and gave the detective constable an appreciative nod. "Eric's theory on Drew's business issues looks spot on. Once we've actually had time to go through the accounts I reckon we'll be able to prove it too. There's a good chance he'll roll over on the others."

"How did you guess?" Tamara asked Eric.

Eric shrugged, clearly uncomfortable with the praise but enjoying it nonetheless. "My sister went to school with one of the admin staff at Drew's dealership. Staff talk... they reckon the business is in trouble. Drew isn't quite the businessman he likes to make out."

"What about the other murders?" Tamara asked. "Any movement there?"

Tom shook his head. "Claims he was out of the country when Carl Woodly died but didn't seem to argue the possibility he was murdered, which was interesting. Should be easy enough to check on his alibi. I reckon we've got him thinking about Ellis, though. I wonder if he's considering the same as us about him. As far as the death of Mayes, Lewis or tonight's killing of Harry Oakes goes, I don't see him being involved. The way they were murdered was too personal. Eddie Drew is so highly strung, he wouldn't have the composure necessary to set these things up let alone hold his nerve."

"Ellis would," Tamara said. "He's one cold, calculating individual who's had a grip on this group for some time now, but having reviewed your case notes, I don't see him killing his friends. Not like that."

Eric looked between the two senior detectives. "That only leaves Catton. And if we're right that Carl Woodly was the first, he couldn't have killed him."

"Why not?" Tamara asked.

"Catton was sectioned a week before Carl Woodly died in the explosion at his house," Tom said. "He wasn't released until the following week. He's got a history of PTSD since leaving the army."

"That's going to make the case against Ellis and Drew hard to carry in court with only his testimony to go on," Tamara said. Tom shot her a dark look and she dismissed his irritation with a shrug. "Don't look at me like that, Tom. It shouldn't be the case but you know how these things work. If it's Catton's word against theirs it'll fall apart. Are we sure John Catton isn't responsible for the recent deaths?"

"He says he's not a killer anymore," Tom said, chewing on his lower lip. "And I believe him."

"Well, I think the answer lies in one of these three rooms, Tom," Tamara said, indicating over her shoulder with a flick of her hand. "And as it stands, if it's not one of those men sitting in there, then we're running out of suspects."

Tom thought hard. There was something they'd missed but it was at the back of his mind and he desperately sought to tease it out.

"There's something Catton isn't telling us," he said, thinking aloud.

"You seem to have a connection with him," Tamara said. "Why not see if you can exploit that a bit further."

Tom shook his head. "No, he's vocal about what he's willing to share but pulls up when I get too close. He knows more than he's letting on. Tina Oakes placed him at the nursery speaking with Harry Oakes and I reckon he was there last night when it all went down."

"Isn't that enough to force the issue with," Eric said. "I mean, if he thinks he's going down for it he might speak up."

Tom doubted it. Maybe worth a try but he had the sense that with Catton it wouldn't work. What is Catton protecting with his silence? Then it came to him. He couldn't be certain and the Scot would never admit it. Something must have changed in his expression because he caught Tamara eyeing him expectantly.

"Tom, what is it?"

He took a deep breath, unsure if he should voice his thoughts; after all, it was just a theory and pretty short on evidence. He decided to keep it to himself for the time being.

"Can you give me an hour or two?" he asked. "Put those three in the cells for some cooling-off time."

"What for?" she said, her eyes narrowing. "Where are you going?"

"I need to check the registered firearms database and then pay someone a visit."

"Whatever it is, you're not going alone."

He looked at Eric. "I'll take this one with me."

Eric was confused. "What… where are we going?"

"One second," Tom said, stepping past the two of them and opening the door to the third interview room. Inside he found John Catton nursing a cup of vending-machine tea under the watchful eye of a constable. The officer looked in his direction and Tom indicated for him to step outside. Catton glanced up at him but his expression didn't change as Tom swapped places with the constable and closed the door leaving the two men alone.

"Are you taking care of ma dug like you promised?" Catton asked as Tom leaned against the wall.

"He's okay. I'm a man of my word."

"You'll not just take him to the pound, like?" Catton said. "I know I'll not be around."

Tom shook his head. The dog was currently being looked after by the custody sergeant, not that he was overly pleased about having it around.

"You're facing some time, sure enough," Tom said. Looking to his left, as if he could see into the other interview rooms, he flicked his head in their direction. "If they have their way, you'll be doing time for Mayes, Lewis and Oakes, too."

"Ah… man, I told yer," Catton said, shaking his head. "I'm not a killer."

"Talking to the team from the Royal Logistics Corps—"

"The blanket stackers, aye," Catton said, bobbing his head.

"The bomb disposal team," Tom said, ignoring the reference to the in-army joke. "They figure what did for Harry Oakes most likely came out of Yugoslavia. Have you ever served in the Balkans?"

Catton slowly moved his head from side to side with exaggerated movements.

"Nope," he said, smiling and revisiting his tea. "Check ma jacket, if you dinnae believe me."

"I do," Tom said. "I'm good at reading people, John, and you're right, I don't believe you're a killer. What happened to your former friends was premeditated and very, very personal. I don't doubt you think they deserved what each of them got but you didn't do it. I even think I know what lay behind the killer's motivation to do it, too."

"Is that right?" Catton said but the bravado was less evident in this reply, his eyes assessing what Tom might know. "Are you going to tell me, then? Show me how clever you are?"

Tom shook his head. "No, I don't need an audience. We can go over it later maybe, when I get back."

"Going somewhere nice?"

"If I'm right, then I'll not take pleasure in it, no. Tell me one thing though, if you don't mind."

"Aye, what's that then?"

"I've wanted to ask since we talked earlier. Back in the village when all this started. Did you manage to destroy that rocket launcher?"

Catton clicked his tongue against the roof of his mouth and smiled. "Never even saw the bloody thing. We got a proper kicking for it when we got back to the FOB. They'd put a Reaper overhead when it all kicked off, which was when they saw it. The first any of us heard about it was when we got back. Unbelievable..." he said, shaking his head.

Tom smiled, walking to the door and opening it, gesturing for the waiting constable to come back in. They exchanged places as Catton drained the remaining tea from his cup. Tom was leaving when Catton called after him. He glanced back over his shoulder, Catton sniffing hard.

"And we never did find the bloody drone either."

CHAPTER THIRTY-FOUR

ERIC PULLED the car up outside the property. The sun was threatening to crest the horizon at any moment, set to replace the overcast slate-grey of the predawn light. Tom Janssen moved to open the door and hesitated, glancing up at the house. The curtains remained closed, the lights off. It was the same for each house in the street. The only indication of movement came from the squat, brick structure adjacent to the house they were parked in front of. A sliver of artificial light crept under the main door and a shadow passed by inside signifying someone was present.

Tom looked across at Eric who sat in the driver's seat still with his hands on the steering wheel. Eric frowned.

"It's early but it looks like someone's up," Eric said.

"Yeah, I'm not surprised."

"Are you sure this is how you want to play it?"

"I think it will go more smoothly if we do," Tom said, pulling on the handle and cracking the door. "Just pay attention, come in if you feel the need."

"I will."

Tom got out of the car and walked up the drive. Ignoring the house, he approached the garage and found the up-and-over door was already partially open. He grasped the handle and pulled.

The mechanism shrieked its protest, more so as Tom gripped the bottom of the door and raised it fully. The man inside, standing at a work bench, looked up, directly at him but if he was surprised to see Tom then he didn't show it.

"Good morning, Inspector. It's a little early for you, isn't it?"

Tom took in his measure. He was dressed in casual clothes, jogging bottoms and a thick woollen jumper rather than the coveralls he'd been in on their last visit. His face was pale and drawn, a strong indication of a man who hadn't slept much the previous night. Having seen himself in the mirror before leaving the station, he could relate.

"Good morning, Paul," Tom said, glancing around the interior of the workshop. "I could say the same for you. Have you got a rush job on?"

Paul Woodly shrugged. If he had a reason to commence work so early, he chose not to offer it.

"Couldn't sleep."

"I imagine that's the after-effect of killing a man," Tom said, his eye drawn to several old jerry cans in a corner of the workshop partially obscured with an old Hessian dust sheet. "I expect it plays on your conscience… even if you've convinced yourself it was justifiable."

Paul Woodly looked up from his bench where he was adjusting a vice, clamping a piece of finely tooled wood that he was working on. Tom noted the file in his hand, roughly twenty centimetres long. Paul carried on with what he was doing, odd considering what Tom had just said to him. He finished adjusting the vice and lowered his face towards the wood. Reaching out, he ran his thumb along the length, then touched the end point with his right thumb, as if one would when removing a piece of fluff from a blazer. He brought the file to bear and gently swept it across the ragged edge with calm precision.

"Did you sleep after what you did to Andy Lewis… or Freddie Mayes for that matter? I somehow doubt it," Tom said. Still there was no reaction. "Or did their deaths just leave you feeling unsatisfied and hollow inside?"

Paul glanced towards him, his gaze lingering on him for a moment before he set the file down alongside the vice. With both palms pressed against the bench, Paul Woodly lowered his head. Tom could see his lips pursed, considering his response. Tom allowed the moment of silence to carry. He wasn't in a hurry. Besides, he was more likely to get answers now than if he dragged the man back to the station in handcuffs.

"It's the damnedest thing, Inspector... wrath," Paul said, staring straight ahead. "If you allow it all out at a given moment you will no doubt damage everything around you... your property, relationships... let yourself down, embarrass yourself in front of your loved ones." He looked at Tom now. "Do you know what I mean?"

Tom nodded he did. After all, almost everyone loses their temper from time to time.

"And yet, if you don't release it..." Paul said, standing upright and taking a deep breath, "you allow it space in your head to grow... to fester. You build a narrative in your mind putting people in situations, contemplating their actions and motivations. When coming at something from a dark place, you tend not to see the best in those people." He laughed. It was a bitter sound. "Perhaps asking yourself if their best ever existed."

"It's more than that, though, isn't it?" Tom asked. Paul looked at him quizzically. "You did see the best in them, they helped you, helped your son... and then betrayed you—"

"They *helped* as a way to protect themselves," Paul snapped. "To keep Joe in their circle. To keep us from seeing the truth."

"What is the truth?"

Paul Woodly stared hard at him. Tom shrugged.

"The remaining two, Greg Ellis and Eddie Drew are in custody," Tom said. "They attempted to kill John Catton last night."

"Is he all right?" Paul asked, taken aback, his mask of

controlled anger slipping to be momentarily replaced with concern.

"Catton's just fine," Tom said. "We got to him in time. He was useful. Filled in many of the blanks for me, so to speak. Not all of them. I was confused for a while."

"What with?"

"The way the troop was targeted. I had the sense that what befell Freddie Mayes, setting him alight and watching him fall, or jump, to his death was a very personal act. The thing is, once I started to look into it somehow I didn't think he could have come first. Andy Lewis being shot dead soon after only confirmed my unease. Those two came so close to one another, it was obvious someone was going after them but I couldn't understand why."

"But then I learned of Carl's death. And that struck me as too coincidental. Freddie Mayes builds the house your son dies in and then Freddie meets such a grisly end, also dying in flames."

Paul held Tom's gaze but didn't speak. The pain at the mention of Carl's death visible in his face.

"And I wondered if Carl was the catalyst for all of this somehow. The first… even. For a time I was considering whether Carl was even present in the house when it went up," Tom said, taking a half step to his right and leaning his back against the work bench that extended the length of that wall. "But he was, wasn't he, Paul? You knew that."

Paul Woodly nodded, his eyes tearing.

"And when was it that John Catton came to you with his theory? Because he did come to you, didn't he?"

Paul took another deep breath, bracing himself against the bench with both hands. "It's true, John came to me… told me what he thought happened."

"Which was?"

"That they killed my boy," Paul said quietly. Then he glanced down to his right before turning his head in order to meet Tom's eye. "They feared him… and so they killed him."

"Catton told us what they did, bringing the drugs back to the

UK, selling it on via Greg's connections in London," Tom said. "But he never gave me you. I knew he was there to see Harry's death, or at least there that night but I didn't think he'd done it himself, so it had me puzzled." Tom smiled ruefully. "Really stumped me as to who he was protecting. I mean, it could have been John easily enough, he has the ability, experience and let's face it he's disturbed but... I've come across plenty of killers in my time and John Catton just wasn't up to it."

Paul shook his head. "No. He wasn't. He desperately wanted to be, wanted to be that man who stood up for his mate, to stand side by side... but it just isn't in him anymore. That's what war does to you, Inspector Janssen. It forces the best and the worst of us to the fore... strips everything back to the absolute basics. You kill those in front of you and protect those by your side." He raised a pointed finger, aiming it at Tom, his hand shaking almost imperceptibly as he spoke. "They chose to put that bond aside. They broke the covenant... *and had to pay.* "

"And you saw to it, " Tom said grimly.

"What put you on to me? Not that I guess it matters much," Paul grumbled.

"The way they died told me their killer cared, more so than just from a perverse pleasure in pain," Tom said. "It was personal. They had to suffer, you had to make them suffer if you could."

Paul nodded slowly, seemingly grinding his teeth, perhaps recollecting his methods.

"And then finally it was Harry Oakes."

Paul cocked his head, his eyes narrowing. "What about it?"

"I guessed John Catton was there to admire your handiwork. He wasn't prepared to kill but he held no truck with how you went about it. The fragmentation mine is thought to be Yugoslavian-made by the bomb disposal team," Tom said, absently scratching an itch on his neck as he spoke. "By all accounts, smuggling souvenirs was well practised by our troops serving in the Balkans, even the more obscure collectibles besides guns. How else might such a device find its way to Norfolk?"

Paul Woodly slowly bobbed his head in understanding.

"And I checked. None of these guys served in the Balkans, they were too young... but you did. A tour as part of the peacekeeping force, right? You told me as much yourself."

"Well remembered, Inspector," Paul said, with a resigned smile.

"And before coming out today, I checked the firearms register. Do you still have your shotgun?"

"No," Paul said bluntly. "I got rid of it."

Tom looked at the vice and the array of saws hanging from the wall.

"Easy enough for you to saw the barrels off, make it more transportable. That I can understand but what I don't, is where you get the idea that it was your right?" Tom asked.

"They took my boy!" Paul snarled, lifting his hands and slamming them back down on the bench. "I have every damn right. Every right!"

"And how much of the anger driving your revenge stems from what they did, and how much from Carl's actions?"

"I don't know what you're talk—"

"Yes you do," Tom said, fixing him with a stare. "I can see it in your face, Paul, clear as day. You see the damage heroin does to people, you see it every day when you look at Joe... and then you had to accept Carl's role in putting it on the street. Because he did, and he's as guilty as the rest of them."

"Yes," Paul shot back before his anger dissipated. His head sagged as he all but whispered, "Yes, he did."

"And you set yourself up as judge, jury and executioner."

Paul looked down to his right, Tom following the path eyeing an old, blue metal toolbox, the kind that opens at the top and spreads out to either side. It was in front of him on the bench. It was the second time Paul had done so.

"And who was going to deliver justice for my son, Inspector? You?"

"You should have come to us—"

"They investigated the fire and ruled it accidental..." Paul said accusingly. "So what would we have after so long... an allegation from some mental case living alone in the woods..." He waved a hand dismissively in the air. "Catton? Alongside the accusations of a grieving father lined up against established pillars of our community... successful businessmen? Hell, Greg Ellis sponsors the town's charity fun run for disabled kids every bloody summer. Eddie Drew sponsors a kid's football team. Who would believe us over them?" He almost spat the last words. "No, they deserved what they had coming to them. They *earned it*."

"And did you think about anyone else apart from yourself?" Tom asked. "About Tina Oakes who's left to explain to two young children how their father died or—"

"I don't care about them!" Paul said, interrupting him. "They're not my responsibility."

"More lives ruined because you wanted to settle a score," Tom said. "Including yours."

"Paul..."

They both turned to see Sheila Woodly standing in the doorway to the garage in her dressing gown and slippers, hugging herself tightly. How long she'd been there, Tom didn't know. By the look on her face it was long enough for her to realise what was being discussed. Paul averted his eyes from her gaze. Tears streamed down her face.

"Say it isn't true, Paul, please..." she said but he didn't reply. Instead, his gaze drifted back to the toolbox. Tom took a step closer. Paul glanced up at him.

"Don't," Tom said, shaking his head. "It's over."

Paul held the eye contact for a moment before nodding slowly.

"I miss my son every day, Inspector Janssen. I miss him so very much."

With that, Paul Woodly stepped away from the bench, crossed the garage and sat down on an old wooden stool, a broken and dejected figure. He looked up at his wife who came alongside him.

"I'm sorry, love," he said. Sheila drew her hand across his face. Paul Woodly stared hard at her but he didn't flinch, remaining silent. She stalked from the garage almost colliding with Eric Collet as he appeared in the doorway. Eric watched her retreat back into the house and then braced his hands against either side of the doorframe and flicked his eyes between the two men inside. Paul Woodly's shoulders dropped and he turned his eye to the floor in front of him.

"Everything all right?" Eric asked.

Tom nodded, indicating for him to keep an eye on Paul as he opened the blue toolbox. The mechanism lifted the compartments out and at the bottom he found an old pistol. He lifted it out, surprised by the weight, judging it to weigh over a kilo. There was a five-point star on the pistol grip with the country of origin stamped on the barrel. It, too, had been manufactured in the former Yugoslavia. He shot a glance towards Paul Woodly who merely shrugged.

"Seemed sensible to have around… just in case," Paul said apologetically. "I should have guessed they would be more likely to go for John rather than me. Maybe I credited them with too much intelligence. I'm pleased he's okay. Johnny, I mean. Really, I am."

Tom released the magazine from the gun with some difficulty. It didn't appear to be particularly well maintained and he wondered how useful it would actually be if called upon.

"What will happen to him, to John?" Paul asked.

Tom shook his head. "I'm sorry, I don't know. No doubt his mental state and his service record will be taken into consideration… but," he said, looking directly at Paul, "he knew what you were doing. He'll probably have a charge of aiding and abetting levied against him. You must have told him what was going to happen last night, even if not the details." Paul looked away, clearly not wishing to confirm it. "It won't go well for him either, the things you've done."

Tom gestured for Eric to detain Paul Woodly and the constable helped the man to his feet, drawing his arms behind his back and placing him in handcuffs before ushering him outside and towards the car. Paul Woodly made no effort to resist.

Happy that he'd made the gun safe, Tom placed the pistol down on the bench, taking out his mobile with the intention of calling Tamara. No one involved in this case was going to walk away from it unscathed and his thoughts inevitably turned to the innocents, the family members, who not only had to endure seeing their loved ones give so much of themselves for a cause that wasn't their choice but, having survived that, would now be facing an altogether different challenge. How they would navigate that path, he had no idea.

His mobile beeped, receiving a text message. Opening it, he found it was a photo selfie of Alice and Saffy. He recognised the breakfast table in Alice's kitchen. They were both in their pyjamas, smiling stupidly for the camera. The accompanying message simply read *Missed you this morning. Hope all's well. We love you x x.*

He was already looking forward to seeing the two of them later, pleased to be thinking of something positive ahead. The climax of this case left him feeling hollow rather than euphoric. By all accounts the team had had a significant result but the human cost in this case was high. These events only reinforced the notion that life was fragile. It could change in an instant.

The message to him was clear; to make the most of the time you have. Alice and Saffy were his future, and he was sure of that now.

FREE BOOK GIVEAWAY

Visit the author's website at **www.jmdalgliesh.com** and sign up to the VIP Club and be first to receive news and previews of forthcoming works.

Here you can download a FREE eBook novella exclusive to club members;

Life & Death - A Hidden Norfolk novella

———————

Never miss a new release.

No spam, ever, guaranteed. You can unsubscribe at any time.

Enjoy this book? You could make a real difference.

Because reviews are critical to the success of an author's career, if you have enjoyed this novel, please do me a massive favour by entering one onto Amazon.

———

Type the following link into your internet search bar to go to the Amazon page and leave a review;

http://mybook.to/Hear_No_Evil

———

If you prefer not to follow the link please visit the Amazon sales page where you purchased the title in order to leave a review.

Reviews increase visibility. Your help in leaving one would make a massive difference to this author.
Thank you for taking the time to read my work.

THE DEAD CALL - PREVIEW
HIDDEN NORFOLK - BOOK 6

TAKING CARE ON THE BOARDWALK, still wet and slippery from the morning's storm sheltered as it was under the canopy of pine, she gingerly made her way towards the wetlands. This close to the sea the dunes were often reshaped by strong winds and tidal surges. The path was heaven sent both to help visitors traverse the coastal trail as well as to keep the damage to the Nature Reserve's fragile ecosystem at a minimum.

The cold breeze tore through her that very morning, a day starting dull and overcast with a chill to the damp and foggy air, so much so that she'd not bothered to check the afternoon forecast. As it turned out the storm front skirted by them, sparing The Wash and the north coast making landfall further south. The grey and threatening skies were then replaced by blazing sun, not unheard of so early in June but nonetheless a pleasant surprise. She'd dressed for the cold again, though, and as the twilight faded with the setting sun she felt uncomfortable having spent much of the afternoon sweating in her waxed jacket and boots.

Clear of the pine trees, she entered the dunes now. Here the boardwalk was dry underfoot which came as a relief. There were areas needing to be replaced where a process of make-do and mend was no longer sufficient. She would need to press hard to ensure this happened before footfall massively increased as it always did when the summer season properly got underway. For now, at least, she knew where to take care and where she need not concern herself.

She was alone now, the few birders she'd come across in the hides having already packed up for the day. There had been a larger turnout than she'd anticipated, possibly resulting from the expected storm. There was always the chance to catch the last waves of spring's migratory birds stopping off to take shelter on the coast but that was perhaps a little optimistic at this point in the season. When conditions were right you could catch sight of scarce migrants, possibly in numbers, but judging by the aura of anti-climax shrouding them as they left, today wasn't one of those days. Unsurprising. Hopefully they weren't too disappointed with having to settle for the nesting Avocets instead, far from endangered but no less wonderful to see.

Maybe they'd been drawn out by the talk of the Stone Curlews? Facing a steep decline in numbers, and seldom seen this far north, they were largely limited to the marshland and lakes of the Brecks spanning Norfolk and Suffolk. If it was true, however, that they had been seen then she needed to be out here. It was possible. The short vegetation, open space and sandy soil was suitable for their ground nests meaning it was plausible, if unlikely, that they were here. Word spread fast amongst the community and the temptation would nag at the usual suspects who would undoubtedly fail to resist their urges.

Pitiful fines and a harsh telling off. Pathetic.

Passing the next hide, she found it empty. The boardwalk rose from here to one of the high points where she could scan the dunes in either direction for as far as she could see. Raising her binoculars, hanging from the strap around her neck, she muttered a curse as a familiar pain stabbed at her right shoulder causing her to take pause and draw breath. These moments were becoming more frequent now, lingering for some time rather than passing quickly as they once did. She'd learned to cope, to manage, but the vigour she brought to the battle was waning as time passed.

Lifting the binoculars again, she slowly scanned the dunes in a sweeping motion from the beach towards the wetland marshes. No one was visible, not even a solitary dog walker. The car parks around the visitor centre were empty but they would be cleverer than that. They knew she regularly noted down vehicle number plates. She knew who owned which car anyway, so they would never park where they could be easily spotted. It would give them away. No, they would park in the nearby town and walk out as if rambling like any other. It was the lingerers who needed watching, those waiting for a moment to slip off the path and beat the bushes in the hope of putting up whatever was nesting.

Not this night. Not if I have anything to do with it.

Another surge of pain, this time in her chest which was an alarming development. Reaching out with her left hand, she braced herself against a fence post, doubling over. Allowing the binoculars to swing free, she clutched her chest with her right hand and sought to catch her breath. It didn't come easily. Each inhalation was forced and came with a rasping exhale. It was no use. She was done for the day.

The moment passed and despite feeling dizzy, she began the walk back towards the centre where the car was parked. By the time she reached the pine trees separating the dunes from the centre she felt much better. Within the shadow of the trees it was dark now. The waves crashed nearby, the taste of salt carrying to her on the breeze. Approaching the gate she stopped. A number of shadows moved in the gloom in front of her, barring her way. Something unnatural, unexpected. Taking the head torch from her pocket, she turned it on and angled the white light along the path ahead of her. They weren't here when she passed before. Anger flared within, tinged with fear but she quelled it, ensuring the watcher wouldn't see. She couldn't allow them the pleasure.

Turning the beam to either side of the path, she scanned the trees and brush, seeking who or what she didn't know and silently praying she wouldn't see anyone. The beam was cut out by the birds, all five of them decapitated and hanging by their feet from wire tied to branches overhead, swaying gently back and forth in the breeze.

"Do you think this frightens me?"

Only the breakers on the shoreline and the breeze passing through the canopy overhead broke the silence. She raised her voice, shouting now.

"This doesn't scare me!" she called, hearing the edge of panic in her tone, angering her further. "I'll not stop!"

Movement above saw her start, glancing up to see something pass through the beam of the torch. It was probably an Owl. On another night she'd be delighted.

Not this night.

Taking a half-step backwards she almost stumbled on a fallen branch, rattled by this experience. She felt the need to leave as quickly as possible. Sidestepping the display left for her, she found her gaze lingering on it as she hurried past. The white light cast by the torch in her hands gave the scene an ethereal glow, fuelling her growing anxiety as she eyed the birds side by side, noting they'd also been crudely gutted. Both the heads and entrails lay on the path at her feet. Turning her back she hurried to the gate, struggling to open it despite the latch being unsecured. The path down to the centre, itself locked up and in darkness, was well laid and the safety of her car was only a few steps away. Reaching it, she fumbled with her keys, dropping them on the floor. Kneeling, she rummaged around blindly for them with one hand whilst casting the beam of light back towards the path in case anyone should appear. Not that she would know what to do if they did. Her fingers curled around the fob and she unlocked the car, clambering in and slamming the door shut before pressing the button to deadlock the doors. Only now did she feel safe.

With difficulty, her fingers trembling, she slotted the key into the ignition and started the car. Casting aside the torch, she turned on the headlights which illuminated where she'd just come from.

The beams penetrated deep into the gloom of the pine trees. The silhouette of a figure appeared, its features masked by a hood and a thick overcoat. The dead birds providing a macabre backdrop.

She thrust the car into gear, forgetting to depress the clutch. An awful grinding sound followed and the car lurched forward as the engine stalled. She turned the key again, pressing the accelerator repeatedly but the engine merely turned over and over, failing to start. Casting an eye back to the gate, the figure was gone. Somehow that fuelled her borderline panic even more. The engine burst into life and she pulled away. Her phone rang, connected through the car speakers, and she accepted the call, relieved to hear another voice.

"Hello," she said, looking behind her through her mirrors as she left the visitor's centre. Nothing moved.

"I see you, Mary."

"Who is this?" she asked, glancing at the display registering an unknown caller.

"Wherever you go, Mary... I see you," the voice repeated. It sounded throaty, brusque and terrifying.

"Leave me alone!"

The caller laughed. A slow, soft melodic sound.

"*I see you.*"

The next book in the series;

The Dead Call

Hidden Norfolk - Book 6

BOOKS BY J M DALGLIESH

In the Hidden Norfolk Series

One Lost Soul

Bury Your Past

Kill Our Sins

Tell No Tales

Hear No Evil

The Dead Call

Kill Them Cold

Life and Death*

*FREE eBook - visit jmdalgliesh.com

In the Dark Yorkshire Series

Divided House

Blacklight

The Dogs in the Street

Blood Money

Fear the Past

The Sixth Precept

Box Sets

Dark Yorkshire Books 1-3

Dark Yorkshire Books 4-6

Audiobooks

In the Hidden Norfolk Series

One Lost Soul
Bury Your Past
Kill Our Sins
Tell No Tales

In the Dark Yorkshire Series

Divided House
Blacklight
The Dogs in the Street
Blood Money
Fear the Past
The Sixth Precept

Audiobook Box Sets

Dark Yorkshire Books 1-3
Dark Yorkshire Books 4-6

A NOTE FROM THE AUTHOR

At the time of writing, to put it mildly, 2020 has been a curious year. The livelihoods of many people have been dramatically affected, none more so than those who live and work in the hospitality sector.

The Viking Festival of Scira featured in this story is held annually in Sheringham, around February school half-term, and the re-enactment day takes place as the culmination of a week-long series of events.

Sheringham does a wonderful job of welcoming thousands of people across the week, organised by multiple groups and managed safely and efficiently, and is a wonderful experience for the whole family. Our children enjoy it immensely. Many other events are organised in and around the town throughout the course of the year.

I am hopeful that the future is bright and that we will be able to return to some form of normality in the coming months. Whenever the festival is next held, be it in 2021 or later, I would encourage you to consider supporting the community by visiting the town. I'm sure the local economy will need us all more than ever.

Best wishes & please stay safe.
Jason

Made in the USA
Monee, IL
19 June 2021